The Messengers
Will
Come
No More

BY LESLIE A. FIEDLER

NONFICTION

An End to Innocence
No! in Thunder
Love and Death in the American Novel
Waiting for the End
The Return of the Vanishing American
The Stranger in Shakespeare
Being Busted
Collected Essays

FICTION

The Second Stone
Back to China
The Last Jew in America
Nude Croquet

The Messengers
Will
Come
No More

LESLIE A. FIEDLER

The atoms of Democritus
And Newton's particles of light
Are sands upon the Red Sea shores,
Where Israel's tents do shine so bright
— WILLIAM BLAKE

𝔰𝔡

STEIN AND DAY/*Publishers*/New York

First published in the United States of America
Copyright © 1974 by Leslie Fiedler
Library of Congress Catalog Card No. 74-78540
All rights reserved
Designed by David Miller
Printed in the United States of America
Stein and Day/*Publishers*/Scarborough House, Briarcliff Manor, N.Y. 10510
ISBN 0-8128-1732-X

To Sally
who broke the block,
with love

To Phil
who showed the way,
with thanks

ONE

Writing this in the shadow of the *tel,* the mound or grassy
midden heap which is all that remains of the last great City of the
earth, I feel myself oddly dislocated in time; transported back out
of our dying twenty-fifth century to the world of my remotest
ancestors. Indeed, I feel myself such an ancestor. My own ancestor.
I am by profession an archaeologist, which is to say, a time traveler, though in one direction only: toward a past, which my actual
ancestors sought to flee, dreaming themselves into a future, which
is, of course, our present. That present is with me, too, interrupting
my attempt to set down what has happened to me and what is
about to occur: the not very special events that have made me, and
the unprecedented quest that lies ahead.

I keep this record not with any of the more recent projective
techniques, like the much-advertised Metagraph, which stores
information potentially rather than actually. Since its protodata
become available only in the future and under preset conditions, it
is ideal for keeping secrets. And there are those from whom my
quest must, at all costs, be kept secret. If it is not already too late.
But even if the Authorities were to make a Metagraph available to
me, I would not know how to set it; because I do not know for
whom I write.

Not for my son certainly, who, if he is still alive, is a slave in a
land to which I am forbidden to return by the Eternal Decrees and
the will of Megan, his mother. It is of them I must have been
dreaming last night. Indeed, of what else could I have been
dreaming, since they are my only past and I have no future? But I
could remember nothing when the grinding of my own teeth
awakened me just before sunrise. For a long time I did not even

open my eyes, much less try to stand. Only shivered as always in the predawn chill, the ground through my thin blanket colder than my sleep-warmed flesh. And forcing my lids apart at last, I saw the empty sky, not blue, not gray in the half-light, but color-less—a hole opening into nothing.

"Alone," I said, before I knew I was speaking. "Alone, alone, alone." The whole thing has become by now a ritual, my aching jaws, my shuddering flesh, the nightmare that eludes me on wak-ing, and my meaningless complaint. To complete it, therefore, I lifted my hands up before my eyes, surprising myself once more with the knotted veins which patterned them, the liver spots, the fuzz of hair long since faded from auburn to gray.

"I am old," I cried then, "old, old, old." But the sound of my voice repeating that melancholy word somehow cheered me, as it always does; perhaps because hearing myself speak it, I know that at least I am not dead.

And anyhow the rising sun was turning the colorless heavens to gold between my outspread fingers. "It is a new day," I told myself. "A really new day and anything is possible." That I had spoken the same formula daily for five years made no difference. At least not to my heart, which I could feel banging against the cage of my calcifying ribs as if to demonstrate that *it* could never grow old.

But of course it has not turned out to be a really new day at all; just another day, indistinguishable from the fifteen hundred which preceded it. I have washed in the brackish trickle of the stream beside which I sleep, combed my hair with my fingers, pissed into the sand, gnawed on a dry Syntho-Bagel and returned to my endless job: digging, sifting, refilling. Pausing only to write such notes as these when I can no longer stand the tedium.

And now I am interrupted by the screaming of kids: a party of schoolchildren, naked, brown, with long, tangled hair and strident voices that cry:

"Hey, you!"

"Hey, you!"

"Hey, you up there!"

"We're here again," one of them yells, "the 'goddam pests' are here. Try to catch us." He is quoting my own words back at me; and the whole batch of them giggles and breaks for the horizon, east, west, north and south. One boy even pauses long enough to throw a stone in my direction.

But the harried and panting teacher, who has theoretically brought them to see the Diggings, arrives at last; bowing and touching his forehead, lips and navel, as is the custom of his Sect. He and the children are Ancestor Worshipers from the nearby state of Liberated Palestine, who come to this unlovely tomb of an unlovely city to be lied to piously. Therefore, when they are duly assembled and the formalities over, I lie to them.

"Wish peace to the Master, boys," their teacher tells them; and in chorus they cry, "Peace to you, Master, and to all your sons." The one who has thrown the stone at me grins and winks. Unlike his teacher, he has seen through my sham, knowing I am not in their sense of the word a "man" at all, much less a true Master and father of sons.

But I answer, as I have learned to do, "Peace to you, little ones, and to your fathers blessed by Male children."

I do not permit myself, until the pieties are over and they have all gone, to try to imagine what my own son is doing. He must be fifteen or sixteen by now, his head shaven and his body hair removed like mine before him and my father's before me. Perhaps he has already been inducted into the Service of Women and the Codes of Courtesy, which forbid his running naked in public like these demianimals. Nor would he, like them, be permitted to mock a stranger. Not even another Male.

"Jacob," I say in the silence of my head, "Jacob, Jacob, Jacob." But I am not sure whom I am evoking: my son, my father or me, all called by the same name. "Jacob," I say again, "Jacob," letting the echoes blur into the other names which haunt me: Mindy, my mother; Marcia, my first Mistress; Megan, my second.

Only in dreams do I allow myself the luxury of such personal memories. Waking, I prefer to think of the vastness of time before I was born. And so I return to my pen, my paper and Tel Aviv, that dead city to which I came some five years ago, after Megan had sent me away.

I rejoiced in the midst of sorrow when I first found myself before the pile of rubble it has become. Much explored by my fellow specialists in the culture of the twentieth and twenty-first centuries, it still poses unique problems, about which I cannot resist writing—perhaps out of sheer pedantry, perhaps in order to avoid more personal griefs. Created after environmentalists had decided that the City had outlived its usefulness, Tel Aviv has survived older urban clusters like Paris or New York or Tokyo, which have been converted into picnic areas, amusement parks, museums: occasions for time-tourism. Such tourism has kept my profession alive, while others, most notably law and medicine, have been abolished by Eternal Decree.

No one, however, could think of anything to do with poor, vestigial Tel Aviv—referred to in one debate in the World Council as "the vermiform appendix of our body politic." It was, therefore, ignored, as insoluble problems tend to be among us. Small boys hurled rocks at its remaining windows (in its time, glass was still used to let light into interiors without exposing the inhabitants to extreme changes in temperature); while its elevator shafts and subway tunnels were occupied by Bedouins, Maoris, Amerindians, and Hypsies. Those nomadic populations still exist in interstices of our stable world; though their final extinction has been promised for generations, even centuries, by politicians seeking seats on the World Council.

There were no real tears shed, therefore, though many pious speeches made, when Tel Aviv was first totally pillaged, then burned to the ground in one of those tribal wars so characteristic of our era. Some falling-out between (or among) two (or more) of the seven quasi-sovereign states which divide the tiny territory controlled in the late twentieth century by the single nation of Israel. Only an expert on such matters any longer recalls, or could ever have understood, the precise nature of that conflict, of which most of us have remained blissfully unaware, since we are no longer exposed to daily doses of what was once called "News." These accounts, always, one gathers, inaccurate, purported to record in detail all calamities, small or large, private or public. And they were "printed" in conventional signs called "alphabets" on thinly rolled sheets of the pulp of trees.

But I will deny myself the pleasure of instructing you further, unknown reader, beyond telling you that the world in which my account is being written is, however immune to News, not immune to certain old-fashioned calamities—in particular, wars. We continue in fact to endure ever smaller wars between ever smaller nations, whose constant creation is one of the hallmarks of our time.

Excuse, please, the break in my narrative. The schoolmaster stood over me again, clearing his throat to gain my attention; so that I did not even have time to hide my manuscript.

He had returned, he explained, because he had forgotten his "pipe"—tobacco being, he informed me for perhaps the tenth time, the Privileged Drug of his Sect. But he had obviously left it on purpose; lingering after I had found it in the dirt at my feet, and had handed it to him.

"Well?" I asked, trying to make clear that I looked forward only to his leaving.

He had really come to apologize for the rude behavior of his boys, he began; he could not understand why they— Then he dropped that tack, got to the real point. "I see you are 'writing,' Master," he said. "That is the proper word, is it not, Master? 'Writing'?"

"Yes," I answered, "writing." But I would go no further, though he waited patiently, his head bowed as is considered proper in his Cult, in the presence of an Elder. To me, he seemed still a boy, barely twenty, perhaps, scarcely older than the kids he presumably instructed about the past.

"Among our people," he continued, convinced, I suppose, that I would say no more without further prompting, "it is an activity practiced only by certain Priests."

Silence on my part.

"I have never seen anyone do it before."

More silence.

"I am told that in the rest of the world it is entirely unknown."

Still silence.

"Even to Priests. If such exist in other places."

"True," I responded at last. "Even to Priests." For a moment, touched by his awe, I was tempted to give him a piece of my precious paper, or a ball-point pen I could no longer repair. But it would only have got him into trouble with those Priests whose name he spoke so reverently.

"Go in peace," I said instead. "And have Male children." I

must confess I found it hard to say the last words of the formula; but I could trust nothing short of the full formal farewell to send him packing.

"Stay in peace," he responded, bowing thrice, each time lower. "And rejoice in your sons." I settled for rejoicing in his going, and for the chance to return to my manuscript at the point where I had abandoned it.

Some five centuries ago, I was about to say, it became clear that the thousand-year-old dream of a transnational community was no longer viable in a world moved by the aspirations of ever more atomized groups. Whether defined by class, race, sex or generation, such groups came to believe that their continuing existence depended on a militant self-consciousness, which in turn depended on conflict with all others. Twentieth-century prophets had been vexed by nightmare fears of a world nuclear war, which they dreamed could only be averted by the creation of a world state. But, of course, neither that conflict nor that state ever came into existence, since men turned out to need occasions for violence more parochial and humane.

In short, man's insatiable need for continuing war made it impossible for the Last War to begin. The realization of this caused the Great Trauma of which our historians speak: the so-called Psychic Wound which paralyzed the final decades of the twentieth century, as men came to realize that all politics based on sponsoring or preventing Atomic Warfare was obsolete. But I am simply rehashing for you the theories of the late, great Valerian Digby-Lapidus, available at any Information Retrieval Center as Vidspool AG 4N3377, or by directly dialing your— What am I saying? When you read this, whoever, whenever you are, the IRC and all its satellites will have been razed or have crumbled to dust; and its very existence will be remembered only in footnotes or graffiti or idle gossip.

Once men were willing to grant that nations and wars would last forever, it became possible to create out of the wreckage of the old United Nations the World Council—or, as some mockingly call it, the WC. Saying that obsolete abbreviation, they make the motions of pulling a chain, though no living human has seen a gravity toilet outside of a museum. Like its predecessor, the UN,

12

the WC is an intolerably muddling, stuffy, corrupt and inefficient body. Yet it no longer has to contend with the old problem of the Great Powers, at least. The former Soviet Union, for instance, has split into thirty-four nation-states, and the former United States of North America more modestly into thirteen.

It is from one of the latter, the Free Republic of Upper Columbia, that I come: a state which only recently granted suffrage to White Males; and in which the Established Cult, the Religion of the ruling classes, is Transcendental Meditation. I am a member of three so-called Protected Minorities within that state, being not only White and Male, but also a member of the least numerous of the non-Established Cults. About that much maligned group, the Old Scientists, I promise you I will have more to say later. For now I want only to state that neither I nor my fellow communicants, despite the indignities we endure, are advocates —as it is rumored—of yet another Secession. Enough is enough, I say, having in my relatively short lifetime (I will be fifty next month) lived through two such traumatic splits.

I look rather to the World Council, which, inefficient as it is, has learned that most of what was once called politics is irrelevant in an advanced technological society, and can therefore be safely left for ever-multiplying ministates to play at. The Council has insisted on keeping in its own hands only what they refer to, in their highfalutin way, as the "parameters of conflict," meaning, in plain English, the limits of war. Consequently, the Eternal Decrees forbid organized combat among nations or other small groups with nuclear weapons. There are no lower limits, of course; spears can be used, bows and arrows, stone axes or wooden clubs. But *fire* seems to remain always and everywhere the favorite; as if it, rather than some superbomb, were the ultimate weapon.

In the place of politics, the WC has come to concern itself with technology: a pure technology, be it understood, separated from metaphysical-political theorizing, as well as the sort of free, i.e., irresponsible, research once referred to as "Science." Such Science survives among us only as the Cult to which I belong: one among many comprehensive metaphor systems or cosmic fictions. It had a hard time getting itself accepted on an equal footing with traditional creeds like Divine Light, Yoga, Reformed Jungo-Freudianism, Macrobiotics, Neo-Marxism, Hedonism, Analytic Buddhism or the Native American Church. But this was due to a confusion in the popular mind between Old Science proper and three border-line Cults, the first two of which have recently been banned: Christian Science, Scientology and Science Fiction. Even after that confusion was resolved, however, Old Science had to face charges of being covertly theist. And in our world any Cult teaching or implying (by speaking, for instance, of his, her or their death) the real existence of a god or goddess or gods is forbidden by Eternal Decree.

That ban was instituted only after long experience had demonstrated that belief in actual divine creatures, especially a single divine being, leads to exclusivism and intolerance; i.e., the rejection of the principle of Viable Alternatives. The so-called Terrible Three, Judaism, Christianity and Islam, in their last desperate bid for survival, sought to deny the real existence of their traditional God, but it was too late. Not only were their cult practices banned, but their Scriptures, Instructional Manuals and other exegetical materials were forever removed from the Information Retrieval Centers, both on earth and in the Terran Colonies of the other planets. And what the IRCs do not remember, none of us remembers. To be sure, the Bibles, as they were once called, of the Christians, Muslims and Jews are preserved, but solely in the archaic form of inscribed paper leaves bound between boards. They are thus available only to scholars: trusted students of the past, preselected by computer, like the author of this record.

Again an interruption, as responding to a faint noise overhead, I rise to stare up at the First Secretary of Federated Canaan and his entourage. They pass over me so low that I think for a moment I could, rising to my full five feet six inches, touch the underbellies of their Double Bubbles: those wholly transparent shells so suitable for reconnaissance in this territory of gullies and scrubby vegetation. The First Secretary, however, is not interested in seeing but in being seen, or rather in displaying his entourage, which consists of twenty-eight young women, completely nude except for their golden helmets and goggles.

"His wives?" I ask myself, though I have watched them many times before. "His concubines? His daughters? His daughter-concubines?" He is, after all, very ancient, this Old Man of the

Mountains, as the local fellahin call him. "And why twenty-eight?"

The fellahin are willing enough to answer such questions, even before they are asked. But who can trust them, to whom lying is a way of life. And anyhow he is surrounded by secrecy, concealment of its own practice being the Perpetual Privilege of the Canaanite Cult. Though I know something of its origins from my researches into the past, its later developments are shrouded in mystery even for me. The Yitts from the neighboring Kingdom of Nitgedaiget have much to say on the subject, too, all of it slanderous. And no wonder, since the first Canaanites were renegade Jews who, in the late twentieth century, withdrew into the mountain fastnesses to revive the aboriginal religion their ancestors had destroyed five millennia before.

To be sure, the names inscribed on the Bubbles provide a kind of clue; the one in which the First Secretary rides being labeled "Marduk-Mordecai" and those which bear the twenty-eight girls "Ishtar-Esther." They return, moreoever, every twenty-eight days on the morning after the dark of the moon. And as they swoop by at less than five hundred feet from Beersheba to Dan and back again, every Male head in the Seven Nations gazes upward in admiration and a kind of longing from which, oddly, ordinary desire is entirely absent. How dusky brown their bare bodies, how gold their long, loose hair!

They have not aged and altered in the time I have watched, the Ishtar-Esthers, indistinguishable not only each from each in any given year, but each in this year's form from last year's, or the year's before, or the year's before that. Perhaps they are only, as some say, induced hallucinations, mirages projected by the Canaanite Priests; or, as others assert, robots. True, cybernetic devices in human form have long been forbidden by Eternal Decree. But Canaan exists, as it were, out of time—a place more dreamed than known.

Even now, as I gaze directly into their golden crotches, the twenty-eight blurred into one by the speed of their flight, I feel as dazzled as if I had been looking into the heart of the sun. And a moment afterward, I am unsure whether I have seen or imagined them; whether I wake or sleep. Can it be that I have dreamed this identical dream sixty-five times—and always just after the dark of the moon? Or do I only dream now that I have dreamed it before? Perhaps I am just waking from my troubled night's sleep, my earlier awakening too a part of the dream. But why, then, am I staring up at an empty sky and repeating like an invocation, *"Ishtar-Esther. Ishtar-Esther. Ishtar-Esther"*? Why do my hands tremble when I raise them to wipe the sweat that runs down still into my eyes?

And why is there a fresh excavation beside me, flanked by the Muslim schoolteacher's pipe (forgotten a second time), and my journal open to a page on which the last sentence ends, ". . . like the author of this record"?

Let me begin again, then, with the obsolete skills I practice. How tedious they seemed to me when I had just been chosen by the Great Computer we call Mother, and was experiencing for the first time the rigors of a nonerotic school. Those were unhappy days not merely because I found my studies uncongenial, but also because I was mateless. Marcia, the first woman at whose feet I knelt and whom I serviced exclusively for two years, ejected me summarily on the day of my matriculation, "for cause," meaning that I had been selected to become an archaeologist.

She could not abide a student husband, much less a working one, she screamed at me by way of announcing our separation. She didn't care *what* Mother said, or rather what they said Mother said; since her enemies, rivals for promotion at the end of the quadrennium, had fixed the whole thing, etc., etc. It is, of course, difficult for a woman of her class to share a mate with some remote bureau, while most of her friends are reveling in the total possession of their chosen servant-companions. Moreover, she was an overpassionate woman, and I fear (I hope it does not sound like boasting) that I had accustomed her to a life of almost unremitting orgasmic release.

In any case, she cast me out, plunging me into a depression from which I did not recover until, to my astonishment and the envy of my classmates, I was taken on graduation into the household of Megan—dear, sweet, rigorous Megan with whom I lived for nearly twenty years. Then she, too, as is her right, sent me away, even arranging, as I have already suggested, my transfer to this remote spot. It is clear to me now, though I did not suspect it then,

16

that the whole matter was arranged with the connivance of a certain Errand Boy in the Population Control Office, whom she had already decided was to be her next mate. If only I had suspected sooner, I might have— Foolishness! There was nothing I could have done; and, in any case, the Errand Boy was not the real reason for my second dismissal.

Besides, it serves no useful purpose to look backward; though it .s an activity characteristic of Males, especially if they be White, in the society from which I come: a role, if I may say so, to which we are trained from birth. But I am, after all, a Scholar as well as a Male; at this point, whether I like it or not, a Scholar *first*. This I dare not forget. That I have paper at all is a minor miracle, the result of a fortunate dig in the Desert. And I must not, therefore, waste that precious material writing about trivial domestic crises, when a decision of immense importance looms up before me. All important decisions have been made for me for more than twenty years; yet on the action I *must* take within a few days not my destiny alone but that of all mankind depends. "All mankind depends," I have written, developing a grandiloquence which I have been taught all my life to consider unseemly. How totally a few short years of (unwilled) independence and (secretly lusted-for) power can corrupt even the best of us Males. Megan was right.

Back to other matters, then; and first of all, to the business of reading and writing. It is already the year 2500 for those of us who begin our computations with the Winter Solstice or the Vernal Equinox, and here I am holding a "pen" and writing on "paper." Yet by the middle of the twenty-third century, the "book," which is to say, a bound volume containing information in a printed phonetic code, had already become obsolete. Subverted first by miniaturized film scanners, in whose unbroken flow its "pages" lost their autonomy, it was soon replaced by a series of postprint transmitters climaxing in the Omni-Sensory Information Storage and Retrieval Bank.

Even our beloved OSISARB is at this moment about to be superseded by a device as yet unnamed, which, it is reported, can transmit information from the electronic circuits of one brain to those of another without the detour of words. I must confess that I do not really understand what I have just put down. But a delegation of those who purport to do so, three Master Meta-Technicians from the Para-Space Program, have just arrived; and they intend—I gather from the Bedouin boy who even now stands impatiently before me—to visit me tomorrow morning.

It is the third interruption in what has turned out to be, after all, the truly new day I have been promising myself for so long. But at first I take it as just another trick on the part of one of the youngsters who come when school is out to torment me. And so I cry, "Go away! Don't bother me! Eat shit!"

I have learned to use with children the only language they seem to understand. But this boy stands his ground, even when I pretend to aim a blow at his head. "Master, I am not fooling you. They have really sent me, the other Masters from out of the sky, the Masked Ones." And sensing he has my attention, he goes on to repeat as nearly as he can the message he has learned by rote.

He garbles all the key words, but I recognize "Meta-Technicians" and "Para-Space," manage even to understand that they have sought me out because I can "read" and "write," because I know "Old Testament Hebrew." But why should they be interested in the dead language of the accursed Jews, if they are who they pretend to be?

Useless to ask the boy—who is gone after his last word anyhow, without even waiting for *baksheesh.* Useless even to speculate, though I cannot help doing so, anticipating the restless night ahead. Equally restless for the Meta-Technicians, too, perhaps, since if they spend the night in this desolate spot they will have to lie on animal skins in shelters quite as archaic as my own: more animal skins draped over poles. And insects everywhere, biting, crawling, stinging vermin, to whom this archaic environment still belongs.

Well, it will help pass the time to continue writing this journal in a form more secure than any code, should it fall into the hands of the Secret Police from the Seven Israeli nation-states who surround my *tel.* They are disguised, they all fondly believe, beyond recognition. But they fool no one—not me, not each other, not even the Bedouin, or the Hypsies who inhabit a tent colony less than three or four miles south of here.

I have come only recently to understand why the existence of such parasites is winked at by the police. What better source of

18

information than these drifters, who prefer begging and stealing to all other forms of survival, but can be persuaded to bestir themselves, if the end in view seems sufficiently subversive of settled ways of life. Yet what do the police expect to discover in this wasteland? Never mind. I, too, have access to the camp they consider their own preserve; since it is the home of my poor Melissa-Melinda, of whom I have grown fond, despite the fish-belly whiteness of her skin and her extreme youth.

She is, she tells me, "somewhere around eighteen," though, like most of her kind, she does not know exactly when she was born. And, in any case, I have learned to tolerate her immaturity, as I have the strange accoutrements she wears, the traditional garb of the Female Hypsie. During the centuries which have produced a hundred revolutions in fashion for the rest of the world, their costume has remained unchanged. And there is, consequently, something ghostlike about this frail creature in the gold-rimmed, round spectacles, the baggy, tie-dyed robe which trails in the dust fore and aft, the wooden-soled clogs which make her filthy feet look deformed. Yet I have come to feel affection toward her, which I must believe she shares, since she no longer asks me for Credits when I spend the night in her tent, nor does she steal small items when she comes to mine. And she keeps me informed of the plans of the police, several of whom she must doubtless be screwing with that indiscrimination which is for me not the least of her charms.

Why else, indeed, would she ever have come into the arms of an outcast like me, with no favors to grant—especially since in her community youthful Males are prized more than mature ones? Yet I shall feel no guilt when, meeting her tomorrow night at our customary rendezvous, I pump her once more to discover the local gossip. Guilt is not a word in her vocabulary, and it has almost disappeared from mine. Besides, I am especially eager to know what the police imagine I am up to, holding in my hand what they have no way of knowing used to be called a ball-point or a Bic.

It was as antiques that I had these items officially jump-teleported five thousand miles, once Megan—who understood them as little as any Bedouin—had given permission. And indeed for a long time I considered them only memorabilia, since I had been collecting them for years before I realized they had been originally intended as writing implements, and learned to refurbish them. As memorabilia, however, I never prized them as highly as my cigarette filters, of which I own some thirty varieties, all perfectly preserved, or my beer cans, recovered intact from ancient sites. Yet for my present purposes, it is these humbler ball-points which have proved especially valuable, along with the supply of legal foolscap which I came upon only a few months ago.

On that foolscap, and with my Bics, at any rate, I continue to write what there may never be anyone to read, not anywhere ever in a Universe which, the Meta-Technicians like to assure us, will someday run down. And yet I cannot help hoping that some odd turn of fashion, some nostalgic urge to recapture what is lost merely because it has been lost, will make reading and writing chic again. Almost everything is revived by the whirligig of taste. Is there not, for instance, a fad at this very moment in the Terran Colonies on Mercury and Venus for the obsolete dishes of the twentieth century; so that two of the largest food-synthesizing plants in the world are presently counterfeiting Hamburgers, Pizza and Kentucky Fried Chicken?

Meanwhile, I find more and more pleasure in the mere recording of events real or fancied, over or yet to come. I believe that if I had been born, say, three hundred years ago of the appropriate sex for the place and time, I would have turned into what was once called a writer. No, I will say more. Despite the inopportune era into which I was actually born and my unfortunate sex, I *am* a writer. And you, therefore, even if you do not exist, are my audience.

TWO

So they have come and gone, the Meta-Technicians of the Para-Space Program, leaving me committed but troubled. And now I have Melissa-Melinda to contend with before I can begin to think it over. Hard enough to come to terms in loneliness with the promises I have made, the quest I have engaged to undertake. But with her endless chatter in my ears, her restless hands all over me—impossible. Yet there she is still, clearly visible behind the bushes where she was crouched since midway through our interview. Why the Meta-Technicians did not spot her I do not know. Or care.

"Beat it," I shout in her direction. "Go home, Melissa-Melinda. You're not fooling anyone."

Silence from the clump of gray vegetation she thinks conceals her.

"Don't be a fool," I yell. "I know you're there."

More silence, broken by the giggles she can no longer repress.

"And don't ask me any questions," I add to make sure she understands I am dismissing, not welcoming, her. "Whatever you heard, OK, but no questions. I don't want to talk. Because I've got nothing to say. Not to you."

"When do you *ever* talk, man?" she answers, rising slowly to dust herself off, and letting her hands linger briefly as they touch her breasts. "Hey, who were those creeps anyway?"

"Go home, Melissa-Melinda," I repeat, stretching out my arms to repel her as I see she is charging full speed toward me. But she has flung herself between them before I can stop her, snuggling up against me so that her head fits into the hollow at the base of my neck. Close up like this, her dwarfish stature, like her pallor and her animal stench, offends me. The other women I have known were all taller than I: their skins deliciously dark, and redolent of expensive scents called Stardust or Nebula or Outer Space, so that she seems to me not quite human: a monster, a freak. Yet she excites me, too. And she knows it.

"Hey, man," she says, "let's not wait for tomorrow night. Let's do it right here, right now. I'm ready."

"You're always ready," I respond, falling into the trap.

"And you're never ready, right?"

"Right," I say. "So go home. *Go home.* GO HOME!"

"I'm going," she answers. "I'm on my way, man. But like I heard everything anyhow. Every fuckin' thing. How do you like that?" Turning to slip out of my arms, which had closed—involuntarily, I swear—around her, she bumps her full buttocks against me, to check, I suppose, whether I am hard or not. I am. And to make sure I know she knows, she continues, "I take it back, man. You're always ready."

But for what, I think wearily, *always ready for what?* I look again at my hands, trembling in the air before me, and I ask myself why they have aged so much faster than my stupid cock. Why don't we grow old at the same rate all over, head and heart, limbs and loins, waking self and sleeping self? In my dreams I am forever young, so that the shock of waking increases as the disparity in age between the self I am and the self I dream increases.

Meanwhile, I no longer hear Melissa-Melinda, though she continues to talk as she backs away from me. But her voice grows louder with distance, loud enough finally so that I can no longer block her out. "Remember," she is screaming, her dwarfish figure dwarfed even more as she continues to retreat, her unpleasantly high, thin voice growing ever shriller. "Tomorrow night. Remember."

I remember tomorrow night and nod assent, not sure she can see my gesture. But it doesn't matter. I will be there as agreed, I know, there, as always, on cue. The head may dream of the eternal Stars, but the body responds only to other bodies as mortal as itself. No, I tell myself, we will not make it beyond the solar system this time either, whatever the Meta-Technicians say, unless we manage to go in spirit only, leaving the flesh behind. And why then have I pledged myself to the search for a useless secret?

But Melissa-Melinda is screaming at the top of her voice now. "Shit, man, *answer* me. Tomorrow night, right?"

"Tits alive," I yell back this time, "I hear you. I *hear* you. Tomorrow night." Suddenly I am aware that I am saying "Tits alive," like my father before me, and I almost blush.

"What kind of example are you setting for little Jacob?" my mother would hush him when he cussed like that in my presence, using epithets of his caste and generation. "Tits alive," he said mostly, though sometimes "Bloody Quiff" as well, and other phrases I can no longer remember.

It was not me my mother was worried about really, as much as the unconcealed Winkie in the ceiling of our single isochamber—turned on, we all believed, for irregular spot-checks of our behavior. But of course, the Guardians had greater problems to worry about than the foul mouth of some hopeless Sex-Role Reject like my father.

I know why he is on my mind, that poor slob I have always feared becoming; for the Meta-Technicians had improbably reminded me of him as I had known him, and as my mother had described him to me in love and contempt. He died when I was eight or nine, that man inscribed on the birth rolls as Jacob, like me and his father and my son. Among us, all Males in the same family are called by the same name, I suppose to remind us that we are identical, replaceable units in a world we have never made and will never control. My father's friends, however, usually called him "Jakey-boy" or "Joker," while my mother referred to him invariably as "poor Jake." Shaking her head from side to side in her slow, bewildered way, she used to tell me tales of his failed life and mysterious death.

"They wouldn't even let me see the body," she would invariably conclude. "Not Them. What did They care? A White Male Without a Rating. And killed, nine chances out of ten, by some other WMWR. They wouldn't even feed it into Their Computer." By "They" she meant, of course, the Guardians: Black women with Ratings of CW 20 and above, whose pawns we all are. My mother, being White herself, and poor to boot, had by law to mate with a White man, unlike Black women who can choose Black or White.

Quite like their White sisters, however, they are obliged at some point between their fortieth and forty-fifth birthdays to mate with one or the other—celibacy being a crime against the state. For obvious reasons, however, reasons finally disquieting to any White

Male, it is from among us that our Black women rulers usually select their mates. They get, naturally enough, the pick of the crop, the strongest and most beautiful, leaving for Females like my mother the rejects and losers.

"Slim pickins," was the way my mother liked to put it, alluding specifically, of course, to my father and his pals, none of whom we ever saw after his death. I suppose one or another of them actually did kill him for the customary reason: because he had a few Credits on him, or they thought so. But it is also possible that he was murdered by mistake, in the midst of one of those roughhouses men like him seem to need periodically. In any case, his friends all disappeared right after his death, shipping out on unlicensed flights to the moon, or signing on to work in the whorehouses of the remoter satellite stations.

Anyhow, it was just such "slim pickins" that the Meta-Technicians seemed to me, partly, I suppose, because they were, like my poor dad, White—and of the same age he had been when he died. This I could tell immediately, though all three wore full space garb: helmets, pressurized jumpsuits with feet and hands, like a child's pajamas, the works. I had never seen a real space suit before outside of the Smellie-Feelies; since people like me are not likely to tug themselves loose from earth's gravity, or to socialize with those who do. No, that kind of escape is for the very rich, with their weekend business trips to the moon and all-expense-paid summer vacations on Mars; or the very poor, willing to accept a one-way ticket which means permanent resettlement on some desert planetoid.

I had no more trouble recognizing those outfits for what they were, however, than I did recognizing the men who wore them for what they were. But I could not figure out why anyone would wear a space suit for the short hop from New New-York to the Palestinian no-man's land I inhabited; and especially why he would not take it off after landing. Maybe, I told myself, they were hypochondriacs of some sort, afraid of sudden changes of air. Or maybe in the totally weather-conditioned center from which they came, they had heard horror stories about the climate of undomed territories like this. In any case, their gait, stance, gestures, the inflection of the first words they spoke gave them away immediately as aging White Males. Nor could their sheaths of inflated Syntho-Rubber hide their potbellies and bandy legs; while the sun glinting off the tops of their Fullerium helmets made them, whether they were really bald or not, seem as hairless as my ill-fated father.

They did not talk the way he did, however. Or the way my mother did till the day she died—worn out with suckling rich women's babies after carrying them, as a paid host mother, for six to eight months in her sagging belly. No, these men talked with the kind of assurance I looked for in Blacks or Females, accustomed to attention and obedience from those they addressed.

"You will forgive me," the apparent leader of the group began, after a brief exchange of formalities, "if I do not waste your time and ours with politeness. Or evasion, which is only another name for the same thing." He glanced down at the topochronometer which he wore on a chain about his neck, checking his precise location in space and time. "We have come far to see you. And we have even farther to go before we sleep."

He waited, as if for a response. But I wake slowly, and they had come to my campsite at first light, kicking the dust into my face with their leaded boot soles. So I settled for sneezing a couple of times, and said nothing.

"Good health," the second of them responded, the one who stood just behind their leader; and "Long life," the third, stationed just behind *him*, added. But the leader continued without acknowledging my sneezing fit at all. "Much farther to go before we sleep. To the Stars." He swung his topochronometer back and forth between his gloved fingers, watching me from behind the thick Permoplastic of his helmet. It was clear that he inhabited another weather; the controls of his suit preserving always the mean average temperature and barometric pressure of his native place for the time of day and stage of the year indicated by the device he held. "Do you understand me, archaeologist? To the *Stars!*"

He dangled the swaying topochronometer before me, as if he were trying to hypnotize me; and his voice, electronically magnified, boomed against my unprotected ears.

"No one goes to the Stars," I answered. "It is forbidden not only by the Eternal Decrees but by the Laws of Nature. After the fiasco of the Planets, the Council decided—"

"Fuck the Council," he interrupted me, turning up his zoom mike to full. "They are the tools of women—being women themselves in their deepest hearts. But we are about to leave the world of women. Forever. We will go to the Stars, archaeologist. And talk with the Masters of Life who inhabit them."

"No one inhabits the Stars," I answered, repeating what I had been taught ever since I could remember, at home and in school. Taught, it occurred to me for the first time, by women. But I persisted, not only because I suspected we were being monitored by the police, and wanted at all costs to avoid saying anything subversive. I *believed* what I said. "There is no life anywhere in the Universe, except on the Third Planet of our own solar system. Mankind is a Unique Accident. This is our glory and terror. We are alone. Forever alone."

"Why are you repeating to me the words of an old song, archaeologist," the chief Meta-Technician bellowed. And it was true, of course, that I had been echoing certain verses of the Transnational Anthem, "Forever Alone." It was a song, however, which, like everyone else, I despised; preferring our National Hymn, "Selene, Shine on," of which I could usually recall only the obscene parody I had learned as a schoolboy. How could I say any of this, however, with the monitors going behind every bush and tree. "You are speaking treason," I said instead.

"You are a fool, archaeologist," the leader responded. "A slave. A lickspittle of women. Your brains have been sucked down into your balls. Besides—*no one can hear us,* so stop looking over your shoulder. I speak to you on a frequency which would disable the equipment of any police force in the world."

"But I hear you without difficulty," I protested, "or discomfort."

"That is because you listen with your ears. But the police everywhere have become the slaves of their electronic equipment. They have forgotten how to listen directly, being able only to record and replay. But I cannot be recorded, nor can you, as long as you stand behind the communication shield my words create."

I could not help laughing at the thought of the local cops, twiddling their dials and screaming at each other in frustrated rage, when they could have heard whatever they wanted with the naked ear. And the three Meta-Technicians laughed with me, so that suddenly we were in cahoots. Like my father and his buddies exchanging jokes or quick snorts of Meta-Methanane out of a concealed flask, when my mother had stepped out of the room for a moment.

"That is why," the leader went on, "we can speak candidly and without fear. There are those who *can* overhear us, intelligent beings as superior to us as we to the idiot robots who serve us in the city-state to which I owe allegiance. But they are not our enemies. Indeed, it is possible that they made us, that we are *their* stupid robots."

"I do not believe it," I said. "And I will not believe it. Not now. Not ever."

"Your belief or disbelief does not matter, archaeologist. All that matters is that there is intelligent life everywhere in our Universe. Not only here on earth, archaeologist, but on those colonized planets we have declared uninhabited, on the sun about which they orbit, and on the remotest Stars. That our senses do not record such beings is irrelevant. We are not a Unique Accident. We are not alone."

"But how do you know this?" I cried, hope surging in my heart, in spite of my skeptical head. "How do you know what cannot be seen or heard or smelled or tasted?"

"It is Science which tells us so," the Meta-Technician answered, "that Old Science travestied in your Religion, whose wisdom has never died, merely gone underground in a world ruled by the Eternal Decrees. No decree is eternal for us, archaeologist, we who have passed on from one to another, father to son, mouth to mouth, the secret which we dare no longer keep from our brothers. Because they have guessed it. Those Others, the Mothers. And close in to kill us." It was he who glanced over his shoulder now, clumsily, nervously. "Which is why we have come."

"To me?" I asked incredulously.

"To you, archaeologist."

"But how could I help you who know the secret tradition? I with my slave mentality, my brains drained down into my balls?"

"It is *only* you who can help, archaeologist. This is the irony; that you hold in your hands the keys to the Other Kingdom, the World of the Undying Masters. The World we perceive but cannot enter without you. Help us, we beseech you."

He went down on one knee, the two others following suit, and seeming in their fulsome appeal more like my father than ever. My father, in fact, at his worst, drunk and declaring his love to my mother; or preparing to touch her for a hundred Credits to invest in a strontium mine on Pluto, a scheme for extracting edible protein from spatial debris, or simply more booze to get even drunker. But I found the Meta-Technician convincing all the same (as my mother perhaps had found my father, because she could scarcely afford not to) when he went on to explain the developments in their underground Science which had brought things to a climax: the leap in communication technology only recently achieved.

"Image to image," he said, touching me for the first time. "Or rather, meta-image to meta-image. Like flesh to flesh, archaeologist." But it was not flesh I felt when he laid a hand on my shoulder, only a Plasto-Gauntlet of simulated flesh. "It is more like making love than talking; for we do not use words. No words. Yet I have to use words to explain it. Do you understand, archaeologist?"

"No," I said; though a glimmering sense of what he must mean stirred in me as he spoke and set me dreaming of the possibility of a real escape from the limitations to which I had been born, and inside of which I had been taught I would die. "No, I don't understand. And what's more, I don't care. So leave me alone."

But he knew I was lying, perhaps, or was too caught up in his own excitement even to register my response. "It was there all the time," he continued, "right there in front of us. Tantalizing." And went on to tell me of the signal which for centuries technicians like himself had been hearing, recording. It was a sound pattern not random or mechanical, like that of some pulsing quasar on the edge of space; but repeated and regular, like that of an SOS, or an alien voice calling over and over from the alien dark, *"Is there anyone there? Is there anyone there? Is there anyone there?"*

"But until only yesterday, literally last month, we could not crack it—or, of course, respond. Only dream and surmise, archaeologist. We whose predecessors had, with equipment incredibly archaic, solved ages ago the speech codes of dolphins and whales. Then bees and ants. Finally, even the wild kestrel and the household cat—all of whom, it turned out, had nothing to tell us, nothing we did not already know. We could not decipher the signal of what we suspected must be the Ultimate Strangers, recorded dimly in myth and fable, the Masters of Space."

He clutched me by my long, graying red hair, in a sudden spasm of an enthusiasm scarcely distinguishable from rage; pulling my head toward him until the tip of my nose almost touched the tinted window of his helmet. His eyes seemed to be swimming in the space inside, growing larger and smaller as they approached and retreated from that transparent shield. Large or small, however, they looked at me mad. Quite mad. "And do you know why, archaeologist?" he asked.

"Why *what?*" I answered, pulling myself out of his grasp.

"Why we could not decipher their words." This time he did not wait for me to respond. "Because they were not words. Not words at all. Only images, or rather meta-images, naked impulses of perception, unmediated currents of ideation. It is not a verbal code, do you follow, archaeologist, but a meta-verbal one. Precisely the code which we ourselves are on the verge of inventing." Moving toward me once more, he prodded me with the swollen forefinger of his right glove. "*Re*inventing, I should say. Inventing for the second time. Or the hundredth. Or the millionth."

"Please," I said. "Never mind the theory. Just tell me what you want me to do. *Me.*"

"Or the millionth," he repeated, obviously having forgotten that I stood before him, that he had come in the first place to convince me, win me to his side. "Who knows how many times it has been invented in the time-space continuum we inhabit? Or by how many groups of intelligent beings, living in worlds impossibly remote from our own, or invisibly tangent to it? Beings with all of whom we will be able now to exchange information, pool knowledge and perception."

He paused, out of breath, giving me a chance to reenter the field of his attention by asking, "But what will they be able to give us, even if they do exist, these others who speak your new language?"

"Science," he answered. "They will give us back the Science of which the Mothers robbed us, leaving us only fragments and scraps."

"Science," I cried, remembering the ancient history I had studied for so long, and forgotten for a little while under the spell of his rhetoric. "But that Science in its pride brought us once to the edge of disaster. And where can it take us when it is revived? Over that edge?"

"You talk like a fool again, archaeologist. And a slave. It will all be different this time. Something new, not under the sun, but beyond it."

"How can that be?" I asked, feeling the hope that had blossomed in me wither. "We will be the same old men, will we not? Or will we become immune to pain? to age? to death? to rejection by those we love?"

"Yes," he answered. "Yes. Yes. Yes."

THREE

It was at this point that I first caught a glimpse of something moving behind the bushes on the crest of the nearest hill, then the glint of sunlight on metal. It is the Palestinian Police, I thought, the Hoggie-Woggies with their Scanners; but an instant later the topmost branches of the scrubby juniper parted to reveal the face of Melissa-Melinda, winking, grimacing, sticking out her tongue.

I did not dare make a sound or a gesture in return, since the three Meta-Technicians stood between us, their backs to Melissa-Melinda. But I thought interdictions as hard as I could, *"Don't move. Don't talk. Don't. Don't."*

She was laughing now, soundlessly, her head rolled back, her hands raised above her head in bewilderment or mockery. Somehow, though, she seemed to get my message, disappearing again behind the gray vegetation as abruptly as she had appeared.

And not a moment too soon, for the leader of the group turned slowly about, as if to see what I was seeing. "What are you looking for, archaeologist? We are unobserved. And if we were, it wouldn't matter. How many times must I tell you?"

"Once more," I answered. "At least once more." They were fools, I knew then, oafish clowns who could be spied at by a girl with dirty feet and not know it. And so I was not surprised when they went on to explain that there was a catch in the whole thing, just as in some dazzling scheme of my father to synthesize living cells from the dung of the mutated donkeys of Jupiter. The Meta-Technicians could, it appeared, only transmit and receive ("at this point," their spokesman assured me, "but everything else is around the corner") unmediated wave perceptions of sensory experiences: sights, sounds, smells, textures. Feelings still eluded them, as did all abstractions, while syntactical connections might well remain forever outside their grasp. This meant that they were not able really to decode the ancient signal from Outer Space which had baffled them for so long; though they had succeeded in "answering" it, by projecting the visual images of their several selves in a matching code. And they had managed to record, once more without comprehending it, most of a long message they had received in return.

"Never mind, archaeologist," the chief Meta-Technician responded, when I snickered a little at this. "It is a beginning, a real start. Only imagine how they must have felt, Out There, when after long silence our stuttering answer reached them. Why should we be any less hopeful?"

"Furthermore," the second of the group added, "it was not just our own inadequacy which got in the way. We had to contend with interference throughout. Deliberate interference. Jamming, I tell you, and I should know, being the Signalman of the outfit." He held up a finger portentously. "There are those who do not want us to get through. Ever."

"Women," their chief explained, that being, I gathered, his explanation for everything. *"Cherchez la femme."*

But they have spotted her after all, I told myself, starting to sweat even as a chill set my teeth chattering. And I turned in my tracks to see if Melissa-Melinda had broken cover again, or had decided in typical fashion to join the party.

"There's no point in looking over your shoulder, archaeologist," he continued, however. "If they are here, you cannot see them. Nor we either."

"I'm not interested in women," I lied to conceal my fear and relief, "visible or invisible. What interests me is what you got out of the return message. If anything."

What they had got, it turned out, was a single visual image: not fixed, but moving in, through time—its own time rather than theirs; as if, somehow, over a period of days or weeks, though ou their chronometers its duration was only a few microseconds. "It was in color," the Signalman said proudly. "Full color in sharp focus. And only ten days ago we would have had to be satisfied with blurry black-and-white."

"The image of an old man, very, very old, moving across a

Desert terrain very much like that just south of here," the chief of the delegation continued.

"Not 'very like.' It was that Desert itself. The Negev, beyond any shadow of doubt. I can plot the coordinates of the exact spot."

Quite clearly, the Signalman had been touched on a tender point of professional pride; and the leader hastened to placate him. "The Desert itself. The Negev. That is what I was trying to say. But it is the old man who will interest you, archaeologist, since he seemed to come out of the time which is your special province. A figure bent with age, wearing a skullcap and draped in a shawllike garment of vegetable fiber. It was blue and white, with golden fringes. And when the wind blew it aside, we could see on his breast a sort of shield of silver. With two stones or jewels set in a pair of metal knobs which rose from that cuirass just where his nipples would be. Or perhaps they were not jewels at all, but spots of light, strange and shimmery."

"As if they were never quite in focus," the Signalman added, "though everything around them was."

"A Priest," I mused, more to myself than to them, finding my conjecture absurd even as I formulated it. "An ancient Israeli Priest, wearing a *tallith* and *tzitsith* and *Urim* and *Tumim*. That is what it sounds like. But it makes no sense. Why should such an image be projected from outer space in the year twenty-five hundred? Unless . . ."

I do not know how I could have continued, if the Meta-Technician had not interrupted me, saying, "He held in his hand—or rather in both arms—a thing I did not recognize. An arrangement of two wooden rollers attached to either end of the treated skin of some beast, shaved very thin and inscribed with symbols repeated in a series that would not compute. At least in the scant time we had."

"And with the imperfect picture we managed to receive through the 'snow' of the interference," the Signalman finished for him.

"It is a parchment Scroll you describe," I explained. "In ancient times, it was the standard way of recording, transmitting, preserving information. Before the invention of even those medieval books bound in boards of which you may have seen examples in museums. If you report accurately, your image comes not from beyond our galaxy, but from the patch of earth on which we stand as it existed twice two thousand years ago."

"Wait," the head of the delegation interrupted me, "did you say 'preserve' information?" It was as if he had listened to nothing else I had been telling him.

"To record, transmit and preserve information," I repeated.

"But 'preserve' is the clue," he said. "He was burying the Scroll in the sand. On the slope of a dune. Before the mouth of a cave."

"Of which I can indicate the coordinates," the Signalman assured me once more.

"And the marks on the Scroll are—" the chief Meta-Technician paused for an answer.

"Writing. What used to be called writing. In Aramaic or Hebrew, no doubt, perhaps both."

"And you can, how do you say—?"

"Read."

"Read both languages? Read it?"

"Yes," I answered. "Not easily, perhaps, but I can read them. In this part of the world, language has changed slowly, being for a long time artificially protected, fixed. For political reasons."

"But now you know," the chief said, his voice lowered almost to a whisper. "It must be there in the Scroll. The secret we seek. Inscribed and buried in the sands of the Desert, where nothing decays. This is what the Undying Ones were trying to tell us, and I have been trying to tell you."

"But why *me?*" I knew, of course, but felt obliged to stall a little while longer.

"Because only you will be able to read it, archaeologist. And, as always, a talent is an obligation. You must find the Scroll, translate it, and keep it intact until we can come to claim it. No matter how long the time. Or what the perils. But have no fear, our skills will protect you."

"And if"—I paused—"just *if* I do what you say—and, mind you, I am promising nothing—what then?"

"Then, my dear archaeologist"—he paused in turn, an absurd little man in his outlandish garb, moving slightly in place, seeming almost to dance—"then—to the *Stars!*"

He drew the others to his side, one under each inflated arm, and together they recited: *"When will we discover that only without spaceships can we reach the galaxies; only without cyclotrons know the interior of atoms; only without circuitry speak to other life, past, present, and to come."* As they chanted, they tilted their encapsulated heads backward as if to see the heavens, laying their gauntleted hands on their pressurized suits, beneath which it was hard to believe human hearts beat.

"An old saying attributed to a mythological flyer," their leader explained, noting my bewilderment. "A part of the Unwritten Tradition."

For a moment I was moved by their grotesque nobility— thinking that, after all, even the pioneering Astronauts, those first men in space, had been equally comic and equally glorious. Had they not begun by broadcasting vapid pieties to the listening world; and ended running for absurd offices, embracing ridiculous religions, enduring anticlimactic deaths in bed or at seedy bars? Perhaps even Charles Lindbergh had been no better and no worse: that ambiguous hero out of the century of my expertise, from whom their garbled quotation had really come. He had been no mythological figure at all, but the first human to have flown the Atlantic Ocean; a piddling puddle to us, perhaps, but measureless space to the 1920s, which he survived to become the tool of corrupt politicians.

Then my mood changed abruptly, as the leader of the group returned again to his obsessive theme, his paranoiac fantasies about women—in response, I must confess, to my own foolish protests. I did not believe anything they said, I objected; and even if it were all true, I would still be unwilling to set off alone into the Desert. I was too old, I insisted, to think I would live forever, and not old enough not to care.

"What do you think I am," I cried to them, "some kind of a hero?" And I went on to explain why I had never ventured more than a day's journey from the local Teleportation Center. As they themselves knew, supplies could be shipped by such showy but inefficient means in hops no longer than a hundred miles. Moreover, the trip they proposed would take me even farther from the single Thermal Dome in my vicinity. And such domes were for me necessities rather than luxuries, especially in the hot season which lay just ahead, since I had spent the first forty-five years of my life in a controlled environment quite as benign as their own.

"You are soft," the leader bellowed at me through his speaker; ignoring the fact that he stood there in his pressurized, air-conditioned Omni-Suit, while I endured the morning sun in nothing but a short, mail-order tunic. "Soft, soft, *soft*. You *deserve* to be taken over, with your talk about supplies and domes. But why should the rest of us suffer for you, we who are willing to fight the dominance of women, whatever the weather?" He was, like all fanatics, immune to irony, unconscious of the ambiguities of his own position. "It is not a question of what will happen someday. They are taking over now. And only with Science, the renewed Science of the Masters, can we drive them back. On the level of politics and technology, they are unbeatable."

"You forget that I was brought up in Upper Columbia," I started to argue, "that I have always—" But he would not hear me out.

"Of the seven thousand four hundred member states of the WC," he began portentously; but this time I interrupted him.

"Seven thousand three hundred and fifty," I said. "It is more like seven thousand three hundred and fifty."

"What difference does it make? Of the seven thousand three hundred and fifty states, more than three thousand eight hundred are, at this very moment, gynocracies of one kind or another. But this represents a shift in the direction of Female Power of nearly twenty-five percent over the past half century. Meanwhile, on all legislative bodies of the Council, the percentage of Female representation is even higher. The result, needless to say, of gerrymandering, pettifogging and falsification of the electoral rolls."

It was a canned political speech I was getting, the speech of one brainwashed by what I had been taught were the obsolete defenders of dying Male Supremacy. And I answered as my teachers had prepared me to. "Look," I said, "it is easy enough to say 'gynocracy,' but one such state is quite different from another. Besides, everything everywhere is changing with time. And the tide has set against the domination of one sex by another, whichever sex that may be." Saying the words, I felt them quite as standard and false as his had been on the other side: the speech of some Male fellow traveler trying to make it into the Chamber of Deputies of my own homeland. "Why, even in Upper Columbia—" I tried to continue; but the name itself was too much for him.

"Upper Columbia," he repeated, as if it were an obscenity; and the window plate of his helmet fogged over, as if—forgetting that he wore it—he had tried to spit.

I kept right on, however. "Even in Upper Columbia, men—not excluding White men—have been given the vote. Marriage has been restored as a Viable Alternative. And beginning in twenty-five ten, Bilateral Divorce will be gradually substituted for Unilateral Ejection."

"Tokenism," he answered, "the most vicious form of oppression. But tell me the truth"—once more his arm lifted ponderously in my direction, as he worked whatever gadget controlled it from somewhere deep inside his cumbersome gear—"did you never dream in the forty-four years, seven months and eleven days of your servitude to women"—he hesitated just long enough to let me register how accurate his intelligence sources were—"did you never, even for one moment dream—I won't say of rebelling against the regime, or murdering your Mistress—but of running away to some place where your life would be freer, your opportunities more varied and open? To the Beta Moon of Mars, for instance, where, in the Earth Colony, there is no sexual exploitation. Because there all sexuality is forbidden, and the population must be renewed every twenty years or so by immigration from earth. Or to our own city-state, where a man is allowed to have as many wives as he can feed and satisfy. All of them duty-bound to obey him in anything not contrary to the laws of the land. Did you not ever grow weary to the point of suicide at having to crawl and snivel and beg your bread? Not to mention fucking on command, like a barnyard animal. Well, archaeologist, did you or did you not?"

How could I have answered him? With his final words his right arm had fallen. Or, I suppose, had been released, cranked down, so that its gloved hand could be pressed palm to palm against his other, already waiting at the blank juncture of his padded legs. Blank.

His two comrades stood behind him in identical positions; the sun shining directly into their helmets now, making their faces seem as featureless as their bodies. Featureless.

The three of them looked at me exactly like those newfangled dolls which had been on display in the Lydda-Beirut Space Port when I first arrived. Naked, hairless, featureless and blank as the

Meta-Technicians before me, each doll had gripped in its plastic fist a kitbag full of adhesive noses, eyes, cocks, cunts and ears. There had been a sign above them reading: MIXEM AND MATCHEM! ANDROGYNY BEGINS AT HOME! And dangling from that sign was a sample doll with a penis in place of a nose, an eye in the center of its crotch and a red-haired vulva on the top of its head.

It came to me all at once, then, that the Meta-Technicians must be, under their space suits, just such scrambled monsters of indeterminate sex; and that, like all such monsters, they were impotent, null, incapable of reproducing themselves or providing pleasure to another in bed. What could they know, therefore, of women and servitude? To them the encounter of Male and Female was a word only, or a meta-image they might someday learn to transmit; rather than a smell, a sensation, an assault on the senses beyond pleasure and pain. Consequently, they could imagine sexual relations only in political terms, like the relations of Haves and Have-nots, Ins and Outs.

But the delicate, the momentarily shifting balance of a power, never quite understood by either, between a man and a woman at the moment of blind rut, could not be captured by computers programmed to deal with *coups d'état,* campaign strategies and electoral returns. Much less, deballed men programmed by those Computers. Surely none of the Meta-Technicians had ever, as I had more than once, felt the tongue of his Mistress—his owner and exploiter whom he had just screwed out of her mind—thrust up into his asshole. Or had looked down at her sprawled on the floor, her black skin glistening with sweat, her mouth open and dribbling saliva, as she cried, "Beat me. Shit on me. Tear me apart! Make me your slave!" Where the hell were politics then? Or tokenism? Or servitude to women?

Yet when the spasms which had racked her were done, and our mingled juices dried to a crust on her inner thigh, Megan's bullying would begin all over again; along with the complaints, the orders intended only to assert authority, the slaps across the face, the cries of "Here, boy, *here!* On the double." And, of course, the mindless routine of tidying up and stowing away, which would last until the next access of passion blew apart the balance of power once more.

What woman had not finally betrayed me? Not Megan, certainly, nor Marcia. Not even my mother, who had loved me more tenderly than either, it is true, but had in the end surrendered me to the Guardians from the School—smiling ambiguously down at my tears, as I had left her house for the last time. Yet what had I expected; since, as the boys in the School taught me with the almost ritual formula, "No Male can be betrayed by a Female, no White by a Black, no Prole by a Boss." It is, therefore, foolish to call betrayal indignities perpetrated by a natural enemy. Only a natural ally can become a traitor.

"Never mind whether I ever wanted to run away," I found myself saying, startled to discover myself talking at all, and dismayed to hear my own words. "I'll go where you send me. I'll do what you say. Just tell me where, when, how."

"We will do better than tell you," the leader answered, "we will show you." He gestured toward the Signalman, who lifted to eye level a microminiaturized laser projector I had not noticed until that moment, and beamed into the air above my tent a kind of three-dimensional map: a scale model of the entire Negev, one hundred-thousandth its actual size, but in perfect scale.

Slowly, slowly, the image shrank in scope, enlarged in detail (the effect was of a camera zooming in for a close shot), until it consisted of nothing but the Desert valley revealed to the Meta-Technicians in their communication from Outer Space; then only of the cave mouth and the pile of sand blocking it: the hiding place of the Scroll. For one instant, I imagined I was actually there—seeing the surface of the sand ruffled by the wind, the quick spurt of a frightened lizard; the movement of shadow as the sun declined in the simulated sky, faster than any real sun had ever moved.

And all the while I watched, I could hear—not in my ear, but, as it were, inside my head, a voice calling out directions, map coordinates, landmarks, wind velocities, all of which I knew somehow I would not forget.

"You will not forget," the voice of the chief Meta-Technician said, as if by way of confirmation. "You will find the Scroll and do what has to be done. We do not thank you now, since it was for this quest that you were born. Nor will we thank you when we return to claim what you have discovered, though for this you shall probably die."

Each of the three then touched the living flesh of my right hand with the nonflesh of his: the Signalman first, then the one who had scarcely spoken, last of all their leader, who said, "It is you who should thank us, you who will be remembered until the Stars burn out. As a hero. The last hero."

At the sound of that ridiculous word, I could feel my stomach heave over in revulsion. But "Thank you," I responded, like the true son of my foolish father, "thank you, thank you." Three times I repeated the polite formula, with an almost-bow in the direction of each, though they had blasted off before I was quite finished.

And finding myself bowing to empty space, I remembered Melissa-Melinda, imagined how she would mock me. "Thanks for what, you creep?" I fancied I heard her saying, a id I answered her imaginary words aloud, "Thanks for nothing, of course. As usual."

But I could discern no sign of her when I looked out toward the patch of furze (if that is the proper name) where she had revealed herself earlier. And so I turned away in relief, looking first down at my feet, then up into the sky. It was hard for me to believe that the Meta-Technicians had come and gone, leaving me trembling between the antiheroic conditioning of a lifetime and the open possibilities of a future which kept my heart pounding. Yet there was the evidence of the grass seared black by the blasts from their jet backpacks; and the vapor of their jet trails still hung in the otherwise unblemished blue of the sky over my head.

Only when the last trace of their silvery wake had vanished did I look toward the horizon again, and this time I caught the glint of sunlight reflected from Melissa-Melinda's spectacles. It was then I hollered until she showed herself, as I have already told you. And when at last I persuaded her to leave, I sat down to write this. In part, I suppose, for the record; in part to try to make sense of what began immediately to seem to me as meaningless as a half-remembered dream.

But if you believe, as I did then, that Melissa-Melinda was gone for good, gone until tomorrow evening anyhow, you are as wrong as I was. For when I had reached just this point in my account, there she was once more, breathing against the back of my neck and saying, "Jeez, there you go writing again. Why don't you beat your meat at least?"

Before she spoke, however, I had already started to my feet, thinking that the Alien Forces of whom the Meta-Technicians had warned me had crept up on me unawares. But after one glance in her direction, my fear turned first to relief, then anger. "Don't do that," I yelled. "Don't ever do that. Not ever."

"Hey, man, I'm sorry," she said.

"Hey, man, you're sorry," I repeated. "You *should* be sorry. Look, I'm not here. I'm dead. I went away. I'm somebody else. You're in the wrong dream."

"Everybody's in the wrong dream," she answered, surprising me. "So what's new? Hey, I don't want to hassle you, it's just—"

"Just *what?*"

"I mean, like if you're in trouble, man, I just wanted to say—"

"Say *what?*"

"Say I got friends, see? I mean, no shit. So if those dudes came to bust you or anything, I thought—"

"Thought *what?*" It was, I guess, a kind of astonished gratitude that made me keep shouting "what" like a fool.

"Thought maybe I could help. I mean, like—"

"I told you a thousand times I hate it when you say 'like' and nothing is like anything." I thought I was approaching her to shove her away, but found myself touching her shoulder, the top of her head, tenderly.

It must have surprised her as much as it did me, that uncustomary tenderness, for she ducked away, saying, "Like I mean those dudes looked like some kind of cops, so I thought—"

"Melissa-Melinda," I said, laying my hand this time across her mouth to hush her, "you're an idiot. Those 'dudes,' as you call them, came to me for help. They need *me.*"

"Don't put me on, man," she answered, backing away. "You never helped no one. Same as me. When the fuzz talk about help to somebody like us, they're just trying to get the goods on somebody. Most likely you. If you don't watch out, man, you're gonna end up in some Wog-slammer, and you better believe it."

"Bloody Quiff," I cried, thinking, *Tits alive, now I said that, too. It's a crazy day.* "They wanted help, real help. From me. And you better believe *that.* To get to the Stars." I regretted my last words, saying them, and even more the gesture I made to underline them, my arm lifted straight up, my index finger pointing to the heavens. Paranoia is catching, and for one moment I found myself suspecting that poor M-M might be an agent of the Enemy, one of Them.

"The Stars? You mean, like the *Stars?*" She imitated my preposterous pose, and for a little while we stood there together like a double statue pointing toward a region we both knew no men would ever reach.

"The Stars," I repeated, figuring I might as well brazen it out. "That's what I said."

"Far fuckin' *out*," she said, and was gone, like a weasel, a stoat, a scared bush hare. Gone before I could even say the next word that trembled on my lips, and which was once more—believe it or not—"Thank you."

By then I was unendurably weary, but I forced myself to write again until the pen fell from my hand. Only then did I permit myself to laugh and to cry. And, at last, to sleep.

FOUR

J ust before dawn, I woke to wonder about the way in which the Meta-Technicians had left and presumably come. I had assumed all along that they must have traveled on some super-speedy official flight, or one of the slower, more crowded ones open to anybody with the price of a ticket. So conditioned am I by the life I have lived that at first I took their mini-backjets for the purses used by Males in Upper Columbia to store eye makeup, lubricants, mechanical devices for increasing sexual pleasure, and the accumulated junk of daily living. I have grown up, I am trying to say, carrying on my back only what weights me down, not what can release me from the tug of gravity. And for a moment, therefore, I let myself envy them. What a thrill it must have been for those ordinarily deskbound bureaucrats to move through the upper air, their bodies vibrating to a rhythm not their own, yet as intimately synchronized with the beating of their hearts as another human heart in the act of copulation.

I have never soloed myself, though I wished it those few times I strapped myself into place in one of the five-thousand-passenger transports which people who have never seen a cow still call cattle cars. My last flight, which was, in fact, only my third, I found especially irksome, as I might have expected, since it took off from New New-Haven and landed at Lydda-Beirut. Both of these provincial terminals call themselves, grandly, Space Ports, but they ordinarily serve places no more remote or romantic than Biro-Bidjan and Big Timber, Montana. Occasionally, it is true, they offer nonscheduled "cheapies" to Venus or Mars, which are always oversubscribed, though more often than not they break down just into the stratosphere. And the rescue operations which follow are likely to end in wrangles (one of them erupted into a seven weeks' war) over the question of whose national aerospace was the locus of the accident, and who, therefore, should foot the bill. The passengers have always got back to land, except in the one instance that ended in hostilities. But the abandoned equipment floats forever with all the other junk that has cluttered Near Space since Home Degravitation Units became generally available and all of us learned to dispose of rubbish by throwing it upward.

Whoever you are, you will understand the special difficulty of the quest proposed to me by the Meta-Technicians only if you understand the nature of my world as well as my place in it. Like others of my skin color and sex, I have been taught from birth I can never be a hero; and like everyone, regardless of race or gender, I was cut off from the Stars by a belt of orbiting garbage. Perhaps in your time the substratosphere will have been cleaned up. Even now there is much talk about it in the streets, and many resolutions passed in the legislative assemblies. But many of us have grown accustomed to seeing trash in the sky, and some, who cannot dream higher than the reach of sight, have come to like it, particularly at sunrise and sunset. I, for instance. But I was writing about what I *dis*liked, was I not, about my intolerable flight from New New-Haven to Lydda-Beirut.

It began, as usual, with a minor disaster, two misfirings of what the crew called familiarly "Big Bertha": the mechanism which propels such short-distance Non-Powered Projectile Flights into a precalculated Parabola, from whose acme they fall into the electromagnetic field of their Destined Port of Arrival. The theory behind it is, of course, unimpeachable, as are all the theories of the Meta-Technicians. No fuel is expended, except at the moment of initial thrust. And we are living through yet another of those fuel shortages which plague us from time to time. Moreover, there is no possibility of a foul-up on the part of crews less and less well trained as air traffic increases and they are rushed through Flight School more and more quickly. Having no other duties, they are left free, therefore, to drink and dope with the passengers—drink and dope and hope that there is no need for the emergency procedures which, it is safe to assume, none of them remembers.

Nothing is absolutely foolproof, however; and the weak point of NPP Flights is thrust-off, when almost invariably something goes wrong or breaks down. Yet until that flight, I had remained blissfully unaware (and here in semiretirement I could not care less) of the *inefficiency* of everyone and everything apparently endemic in advanced technocracies—certainly common enough in ours. But my indifference, I discover, is equally common, perhaps also a function of such societies. Certainly everyone I have encountered in a world community so badly administered by the Council seems to have adapted to inadequacy and uncertainty: the radical imperfection of those very techniques which are our proudest boast.

In any case, the 4,999 other passengers on my flight seemed to accept the delays of blast-off with a kind of good-humored cynicism: applauding in mockery each failed effort, turning up their individual music and Thermo-Vibrator Seat dials to full; but chiefly crying out in chorus, "When the hell does the FPS begin?" Motion sickness is a special problem on the NPPs, particularly in the Free-Fall phase after Acme-Attainment. For this reason, I presume, in-flight entertainment is lavishly laid on: not just ordinary bone-conduction music and thermo-vibrating, but "fully participatory sex." The latter phrase, or rather the initials FPS, are used on all posters and advertising brochures to remind potential passengers that the pleasures provided by NPP Flights go far beyond the possibilities for voyeurism afforded on autopowered planes. Their Stewards and Stewardesses fuck, suck and blow each other on a strictly hands-off, look-but-don't-touch basis.

On the NPPs, sexual activity also is carried on by the Crew, who might otherwise perish of boredom; but it serves chiefly as a preliminary, a come-on, a tease. When, in the opinion of the Captain, sufficient time has passed for the passengers to be adequately aroused, he orders an end to exclusive crew copulation; and taking personal charge of the music tapes, starts and stops them at irregular intervals. It is generally understood (and there are frequent announcements to explain it to the uninitiated) that each pause is a signal for the passengers to grab the nearest attendant and do with him or her what he feels most inclined to do at the moment. When the music is cut off, however, everyone is supposed to freeze in whatever attitude he has assumed; and anyone too carried away to notice or too excited to stop not only becomes the butt of general hilarity, but is excluded from the next round.

Abstinence is, of course, also possible, since it, too, has long been recognized as a Viable Alternative. And I must confess that I myself chose it, or rather endured it; since I was horrified to the point of temporary impotence at the sight of Males taking the sexual initiative in a kind of orgy which began with rather than climaxed in the blurring of all hierarchal distinctions. Moreover, I was aesthetically displeased to note that Stewardesses as well as Stewards, both naked from the start of the flight, were totally hairless, depilated everywhere: head, armpit, crotch, chest, belly and legs. In my own country only men are required to remove all their hair, while women glory in its luxuriant growth, especially on their bodies; so that I felt faintly ill at the sight of all those unadorned Female pubes.

Finally, however, I think it was the *smell* which most offended me; for after a while the whole plane was redolent not of the natural odor of sweat and those bittersweet juices swapped in erotic play, but of strawberry, orange, lemon and lime. We still have in my own country Botanical Reservations in which the real fruits which originally produced these flavors grow out of the real earth on real plants or trees; though, of course, they are now chiefly synthesized in great automated plants immune to the weather or the vagaries of temperamental workers. Perhaps in your unforeseeable future, dear reader, the very names of those fruits and their savory tang will have been forgotten completely. But at the moment I write, you must understand, they are especially prized for their sexual potential, being combined with balancing alkalines and an unguent base in the manufacture of Cupid's Quiver, Mark IV. It is a very ancient product, recently reintroduced in improved form, and, I gather, the rage everywhere on earth except in our benighted Upper Columbia. Both the Stewards and Stewardesses on our flight had, at any rate, anointed their once private parts with their own favorite flavors, or what they hoped would be the favorites of their customers. And the mingled smells hung so heavy —despite the ventilators—that one felt he could *taste* them. Which was, I guess, the point.

I therefore resisted the repeated appeals of the attendants, and ignored the mocking hoots of the passengers closest to me, double-strapping myself into my seat as a declared nonparticipant. But even that was not enough; for I had to watch the consummation of pleasure I did not share, to hear grunts and moans that appalled me, and especially to endure the fruit-flavored smell of someone else's rut. So I touched the button just over my head which released about me a force field that cut all my senses off from the stimuli which assaulted them; plunging myself, in short, into a state of Total Sensory Deprivation, from which I knew I would emerge on landing shattered and terrified, disoriented and unstrung. It is the most brutal of all hangovers, following the weirdest of all forms of intoxication. But it did not seem inappropriate to the totally new way of life I was contemplating: a way of life I have been pursuing for five years now without regret.

I find myself, however, on the verge of changing it once more; though for what I do not really know. For death, it would seem, if the valedictory rhetoric of the Meta-Technicians can be believed. But this time, I am sure, I will rue the change, even if I survive; since I have grown used to working in the weather and following, like the small beasts and birds around me, the pattern of the natural year. And I have even come to love the terrain which at first so appalled me: this pseudo hill, not heaved up by volcanic forces out of the earth's burning core; but piled up, like a child's sand castle, by whimsical winds mingling a topsoil ground down by glaciers a half-million years ago with the rubble of a city not yet five hundred years dead. It is through this *tel* that I work each day from sunrise to sunset, digging, discovering, classifying, layer after layer, stratum after stratum. An endless task, which, beginning in duty, has climaxed in love.

Yet how different this place is from that to which I was born, the great conglomerate which is the nerve center of my native land. How shall I describe it: an ever-changing, never-finished sculpture made by countless human hands in collaboration with the single Great Computer we call Mother. A versatile environment, whose open spaces have been composed as cannily and casually as its enclosed ones, the two together covering some thousand square miles of water and land surface, none of it open to the weather. Over all arches the Great Dome, here high, there low, here opaque, there transparent, in response to the total will of the community—the resultant force created by the fantasies of two hundred thousand separate hearts and heads—which also controls the alternation of dark and light, heat and cold, wet and dry. And where everybody does something about the weather, nobody talks about it, as every casual passerby does here in Israel, where all live at its mercy. What a thrill to curse the storm in whose making one has not collaborated and is therefore free to flee or confront in quest of supplies or out of simple bravado.

But the Desert is quite another matter: not the product of human will or even folly, but the final residue of exhausted possibility. A place not for living but for dying. And I find I do not want to die, not even in the long run, as I know I must; and certainly not now, as I hope it is in my power to avoid. But I have pledged my word, and there is apparently no way out. Cry as I will, "I was not born to be a hero," I am somehow *locked* into my decision, at a level beyond the reach of will. The coordinates of the place I must seek keep ringing in my head, along with the inner voice which repeats over and over, "I will go. Send me. I will go. Send me," until my spoken protests are drowned out.

And when I close my eyes I see the Old Priest, the Scroll, the cave; see the wind ruffling the sand, the quick spurt of a lizard and the uncanny westering of the sun falling faster toward darkness than I have ever known.

So I shall sleep tonight perhaps for the last time in this place at once so strange and so familiar. But not alone. I will go to the camp of the Hypsies as Melissa-Melinda and I have agreed. There we will couple on the ground in the outlandish fashion she has taught me: I on top, pumping, pumping; she almost inert beneath me. Then, at first light, I will rise and look down at her sleeping. She will seem this time, perhaps, young and pallid as she is, almost beautiful to me. Then, turning from her in regret, I shall . . .

FIVE

It was the insistent whine common to all communication devices which brought me to my feet so abruptly that my papers fell to the ground. For a long time I stared at them stupidly, while the wind lifted and dropped them, each time a little farther from where I stood. I knew that I ought to chase them, lest hours of painful work be lost. But, as always, that rising and falling sound terrified and paralyzed me—seeming to come from all directions at once, seeming as if it had never begun and would never end.

"Why doesn't someone pick up the receiver?" I said to myself; but no one was there except me, and no receiver except the unique grid of my Electro-Neural System, on which someone was homing in. Someone who knew me well, or had access to Central Archives, where all such grids are recorded.

"Just wait a minute," I yelled, to no one in particular, and went galloping off in pursuit of my papers, which skipped maliciously a step or two ahead of me, until a chance gust deposited them all in a hollow. Jumping with feet first to trap them, I cried, "Got you, you little bastards." In my triumph, I did not notice that the continuing whine had stopped, meaning final contact had been established.

I nearly dropped my manuscript again, therefore, when a voice answered, "Got *who?*"

It was a voice out of nowhere, but oddly, heartbreakingly familiar; so that even before looking up, I knew it belonged to Megan, my second Mistress, on whom I had not laid eyes for nearly—for exactly (I had counted, I confess it) fifty-eight months. "Megan?" I said twice, "Megan." The first was a question, the second a sigh, almost an endearment; though endearments had not been permitted between us, except in the act. "You're here."

She laughed then a little mockingly, seemingly from right behind me. And I turned to confront her, making sure first to set my papers securely on the ground and to weight them down with a rock. She had changed very little since she had cast me out. She was in full-dress uniform, however, which is to say, in a tight-fitting sheath of lusterless black leather, except for the single face hole, through which her skin showed shinier and blacker than the leather about it, and the three hair holes, one under each arm and one at the crotch, through which three great shocks of crinkled white hair splayed forth like fireworks.

How proud she had always been of her hair, which razor scissors or depilatory had never touched. To be sure, her upper lip, her navel, the cleft of her breasts, her nipples, even her legs remained almost bare of fuzz, despite the so-called growth inciters in which she was always investing, in the vain hope of equaling some of her furrier friends. But the luxuriance of her pubic bush and armpit tufts awed the most supercilious of them. I could not touch that luxuriant growth with my fingertips or lips in so public a place, but I kneeled formally before her to kiss her foot. And tasted cold stone.

Once more her laugh, more tender than mocking this time; or so it seemed to me. "Jacob, you are a fool. As always. I am not really 'here' at all."

And, of course, she was not—as the communication beeps should have warned me—present in the flesh, but only "in touch" or "on the line," as we continue to say, using terminology based on technological devices long since defunct. What I had taken for Megan was a three-dimensional laser-beam projection, exactly like the "map" which the Meta-Technicians had shown me earlier. And like it, she, or rather her phantasm, was immune to that tug toward the earth's center for which we have still found no better name than gravity. Even when she seemed to touch the ground, she did not bend the grass beneath her feet. And sometimes she would disappear into it as deep as her ankles, appearing to wade in earth as if it were water. But how magnificent she looked. How lush and unwithered despite her seventy-odd years. How starkly black and white, except for the unpredictable blue of her eyes.

What had she made of my encounter with Melissa-Melinda, I

found myself wondering, as if she were really there, could really see me. And how did I look to her with my hair grown out? Surely she must be repelled by the color my skin had turned, unshielded as it was from the sun, morning, noon and evening. I was brown everywhere that my scant tunic did not cover, except for the liver-spotted backs of my hands, and my cheeks and nose, which were nearly purple. But she had kept me always smooth and hairless and pearl-pale, forbidding even the artificial ultraviolet exposure recommended by some for health and sexual vigor.

Then I remembered that having made the contact, she could not see me from her end, only hear me. The technicians had been promising us two-way visual Lasercom for as long as I could remember; but even the experimental models had been junked at the time of the Great Budget Squeeze. Fortunately, however, two-way audio had been perfected before then, so that my voice at least was in that beloved ear. Had it changed, I wondered, did I speak my own tongue with an accent?

In my befuddlement I had apparently forgotten to speak at all; for the next thing I heard was, "Well, say something. Something charming and intelligent. I've come a long way. So to speak."

"Tits alive," I said, by way of an answer, the old habit so strong now that I forgot whom I was addressing. "A long Lasercom like this can't be cheap. It must be costing you an arm and a leg. Why did you do it?" I should have known why, even at that point, but I did not. "You shouldn't have," I concluded, sounding like an idiot, as I always do talking to her.

"That's charming? That's intelligent? Jacob, boy, you haven't changed a bit. You were, I'm afraid, never a very witty fellow. But beautiful. If I make it to a hundred and twenty, I'll never forget the first day I saw you. You were still short of nineteen and not even properly depilated yet. Fuzzed like a peach. A tender, delicious, small peach."

"You should see me now," I responded mournfully.

"I *can* see you now. In my mind's eye. Though 'mind' is not what I mean at all."

She went on then, talking nervously, almost chattering, as is not her style. And why was I not able to understand that she was both approaching and evading the real point? But I was not understanding anything, to tell you the truth, merely letting the stream of gossip flow over and around me: the names I had forgotten or never knew, the events important still in a world no longer important to me. And the whole time, I was remembering, remembering.

In my country a boy-child is inducted into sex early, at first by his own mother, who is encouraged to diddle and suck him. But especially to diddle him, since success for the Male depends largely on the size of his penis, and—among us Poor Whites at least—it is firmly believed that "everything over six inches is handmade." Mothers, however, are likely to think more of giving pleasure than of receiving it; and so at age four or five a boy is put into the hands (and mouths) of twenty-year-old girls. From puberty until that age, such girls have been allowed only to masturbate, manually or with the aid of machines, and to play with each other erotically; and even at that point they are not permitted full genital sex with a male. That does not occur until at age forty they are mated, typically with an eighteen- or twenty-year-old partner; at which point they are taken off the chemical regime which has until then inhibited not just ovulation but menstruation itself.

This means that for the middle two decades of their lives they find what satisfaction they can with small boys, abiding always by the Eternal Decree which provides for "unlimited osculation and manipulation"—but nothing more. No wonder I found them nervous and demanding, these girls in whose charge I was required to remain until my First Come. And sometimes, as I do not ordinarily permit myself to remember, cruel in ways that mere "nerves" cannot justify. But enough of that.

At age eleven or twelve I was turned over, like all other Puberts, to what we call "the Dames": women, usually Lesbians or female eunuchs, who do not respond easily to men. From them I received my final instruction in sex; the only kind of instruction permitted to Males in our society, unless like me they are lucky enough to be selected by Mother for special assignment. I must confess I do not remember the clichés about the proper roles of men and women which we were forced to memorize and recite; but I do recall vividly the first time I was ridden by two of those women at once: one straddling my crotch, the other my head.

They were an incredible pair of dark-brown hefties, totaling nearly 600 pounds between them; while at that point I could have weighed no more than 140, not yet having attained my full height of five feet six—nearly four inches less than Megan's. They set to work at either end of me, at any rate, grinding away as if they intended to make mincemeat of my poor, Male flesh. How proud I was when they fell from me simultaneously, exhausted and breathless and wet to the knees; and looking down to see what was left of me, I found my cock still erect, ready for more. I must have crowed with childish delight; for I was beaten unmercifully, right then and there, by the same thick-armed pair, having committed Offense One: that of regarding my own pleasure rather than that of my mate. Looking back on the incident now, it occurs to me that they may have enjoyed the punishment for its own sake; but then I remember only vowing that I would never boast of my sexual prowess again. Not that my narcissism was driven out of me, you understand, only that it retreated underground, to be kept secret with all else the women in my life could not endure.

Especially during the first continuing relationship of my life, my two years with Marcia, it was myself I admired, my athletic prowess, and the satisfaction I visibly gave her. Marcia was a Sex Therapist by profession, though on a very junior level—a CN 11 or 12, no more—and therefore more skilled than I at first in the simple mechanics of the act. But it was clear from the start that she was incapable of the erotic detachment affected by women of her class; and being the slave of passion, she could never become, in the full sense of the word, the Mistress of my body, never make me love or think I loved the status to which as a Male I had been born. That she proved jealous of my job and resentful of the Computer which assigned me to it was, though not unexpected, the last straw. She may have been a Female, and therefore intended by nature to command; but I came—I confess it—to regard her with contempt. And so I was glad when she took from my neck the great Golden Chain she had fastened about it on the day of our mating; and slapped both my cheeks—first right, then left—in the ritual gesture of ejection.

Only with Megan was I able to achieve and sustain for twenty years, despite the strains attendant on growing old together, real happiness: what the Omni-Sensory Cineromances we were shown Monday nights at School called "enduring bliss." I do not mean that Megan was a reasonable woman, or even one who tried to adapt to the changing mores of a time which was beginning to call into question everything, including Man's Place in the Home. Far from it. True, she did not cavil about the hours which my archaeological studies took from my time for household chores. Moreover, she permitted me twice to go off on a three-week Summer Dig; and even allowed me to vote, in accordance with the Reform Bill of 2497, which provided for Male Suffrage in parochial, provincial and national elections. "Just don't tell me about it," she said. "I can't abide men talking politics. Not in my own house." But she remained resolutely traditional in one respect.

What I mean is that I was forbidden to wear any clothes inside our private quarters; though the more advanced even among Megan's own women friends spoke of the required in-house nakedness of Males, which their mothers had taken for granted, as "antediluvian nonsense." Still, they did not seem displeased when I would come nude into their midst—more often than not erect, since I have been conditioned to respond in that way to all women, especially Black ones over the age of forty. And Megan, who had, to begin with, summoned me to her on some contrived errand, would call attention to the size and rigidity of my penis with what purported to be a snide remark about the mindless sexuality of "those men." But she was proud really, knowing—from, I can only presume, considerable extradomestic experience—how seldom the legendary bigness and hardness of White Males proved to be so in fact. Indeed, I am inclined to believe that it is not for our superior sexual endowment that our Black Mistresses prefer us to our Black Brethren, but for our greater docility.

Especially during the earlier years of our connection, I was embarrassed on such occasions, actually blushing, since I was still scarcely more than a boy, but by the same token growing longer and stiffer. Nor did it help when one of the assembled women commented in turn, sometimes in mock deprecation, more often in frank admiration, on what Megan insensitively referred to as my "equipment." "They don't make them like that anymore," was a standard quip; more often than not the prelude to a friendly caress or squeeze of my extended organ. It is a privilege not often exercised in polite society, though custom permits and law does not forbid it. And I suppose that the temptation must have been great as I bent over their shoulders to replace a used tape or remove a dirty plate.

Very rarely, one or another of Megan's guests would excite herself, by such playful caresses, to the point where she would feel herself too distracted to make a full contribution to whatever committee meeting or discussion group was in session. At such moments my Mistress would signal me discreetly to take her off and pleasure her somewhere out of sight and, if possible, out of hearing; for, you understand, our upper classes prefer privacy for the act. She had made it clear to me, however, from early on, that I was never to spend more than ten or fifteen minutes with such exigent colleagues of hers. "Time is Credits," she had explained to me, "and Credits life." But I could not help flattering myself that she wanted me to save my energy for her.

Yet after the first year or two of our mating, she would often let weeks pass, even months, without calling me to her bed; too annoyed for sex, perhaps, by the bureaucratic problems which plagued her as Director of Food Synthesis and Supply. Or simply too *distrait*, as she was accustomed to say, too vexed by a metaphysical anguish which she never condescended to explain to me, though I am sure I would have understood and helped her. Understandably, I endured paranoid fantasies at such times about her having found other men to pleasure her; but, she assured me, under certain conditions she could live for as long as a year without sexual release or any desire for it. I, on the other hand, should feel perfectly free to masturbate as often as I liked during such intervals, and she would not resent it; since, as she typically put it, she knew "how it is with you men."

What made things difficult was that I never knew when the impulse would move her again. And woe to me if I was not ready on demand. Or if, after long lack of practice, I proved unable to sustain an erection for the optimum fifty-minute hour recommended by the Sex Therapists, to whom, like all members of her caste, she went once a month for inspection, advice and a workout with the Vibrators. Her rage was terrifying when I failed her thus, ending more than than not in her screaming, cursing and hurling any movable object she could lift (and she was a well-muscled woman, you may be sure) at the walls, floor, ceiling—and especially me; though even at her most rabid she never aimed below the navel.

It was at such moments that I dreamed, in fact, though I had refused to confess it to the Meta-Technicians, of running off to some not too distant place where Males still held power in the state and family, or where sex was totally forbidden. But after our first couple of months together, during which I would weep myself to sleep night after night and wake to contemplate in horror her unchosen body next to mine, I found I had slipped almost imperceptibly into happiness. It was not merely that I had grown habituated to, hooked on, Megan, I was also fond of her; in love with her, it sometimes seemed to me, though "love" is an expression ordinarily used among us only by the poorest of Poor Whites, creatures even more shameless and *lumpen* than my own outcast mother and father.

That Megan could reciprocate in kind had never occurred to me; but why else would she have taken the trouble, after all these years, to contact me in just this way? To make a public Lasercom call is by no means simple, requiring not only a large deposit and an extended interview with the Tele-Authority, but—normally, at least—a waiting period of two or three months. And why was she saying now, shocking me out of my reverie, "Jacob, did you never suspect that I loved you? Though I could not tell you, of course."

"No," I said. "I never suspected. It would have seemed too . . . too . . ." I let it go at that, not knowing quite how to express what I felt even to myself. Basically ashamed, I guess, ashamed both for myself and her; but especially for her. I could only assume that she was high on Syntho-Hash, the Privileged Drug of the Established Church of Transcendental Meditation, whose services I suspected she attended chiefly for the sake of the S-H. Yet I had seen her before when she had been as high as she seemed now, even higher; and she had never said to me anything more tender than, "Service, boy. On the double."

"I could not tell you because, as you are aware, that is not a permitted word in the circles into which I was born. Love." She paused for a moment, as if savoring the sound of it. I could hear the sharp intake of her breath, see her breasts rise inside the restraining sheath of leather. "I had never even heard it spoken until I heard you say it in your sleep. Only seen it on the walls of school privies, where naughty girls had written it."

"I said it in my sleep?" I asked more of myself than her.

"Yes, more than once, Jacob. And remembering that, I realize that in some sense you must love me still, will always love me. As I do you—I, a woman beginning the eighth decade of her life, who wakes at dawn in the arms of a youth not you, for you are no longer young, Jacob. A youth who would sleep to twelve if I let him. But whose name I do not find on my lips waking thus, do not hear in my ears spoken by my own voice. Do you know what name I find on my lips, Jacob?"

I did not answer. How could I have presumed?

"It is your name, Jacob. And with it that tabooed word: love, love, love, *love*. You see, I have grown accustomed to it, speak it as shamelessly as any girl of the people."

"But what do you want? Why have you come, appeared to me, called—I do not even know how to say it. What do I have that you who have everything could possibly desire?" Was it some idiot hope that rose in me as I spoke, setting my heart to thumping, my limbs to trembling; yes, making my cock rise?

"Because I have always loved you, Jacob, I have kept track of you always. Pleased at your good fortune. Saddened by your every setback. Despite your betrayal of me, Jacob." She had not called me by name in all of our twenty years together as often as she had in the few minutes of our present encounter.

"I never betrayed you," I protested, wanting to say her name in return, but not daring to, even at that point. "Never. I only—"

"Sh!" Laying a finger to her lips, she hushed me like a child. "I know that you did not *mean* to betray me then. Any more than you mean to now. But you are on the verge of an even grosser betrayal—an action on behalf of those who hate everything for which I stand. Everything by which you and I lived, Jacob, during those twenty years of shared"—she hesitated for an instant, as if held back by some last scruple, then said it—"shared bliss."

It was that last word which did it, I think, gave her game away. She was trying to use me, I suddenly realized, and not out of passion or political commitment, either one of which I would have understood and forgiven. But only to protect a system of privilege whose beneficiary she had been for more than seventy years: a way of life for which she was willing to do or say anything.

One does not necessarily expect morality from those who rule over him, but good taste at least. "I will not be used by anyone," I howled. "Not even by you. Not now. Not anymore."

"Jacob, you are always more foolish than seems possible. Do you not realize that you *are* being used by those who are themselves mere pawns of the Para-Space Authority? And that the Para-Space Authority is being used in turn by— But never mind, you would not understand if I told you. And in any case, it is those demimen who háve just left you that I have come to talk about. Those bunglers who avoided interception only by the skin of their teeth. Not through wit or cunning, you understand, but sheer dumb luck. They are the ones who are using you."

"And why should they not?" I cried. "They owe me nothing."

"Nor do I, Jacob. It is you who owe me everything, which is why—"

"You are full of shit," I shouted her down. "You were always full of shit." And I pressed the Interference Button on my belt, which, like all the rest of humanity, I wear in accordance with the Eternal Decree promulgated after the Privacy Riots of 2399.

Neither electronic intrusion nor electronic surveillance was abated after those riots; and they continue to harass us even now. But from that time forth, every citizen has at least had it in his power to jam any bug or tap imposed on him by no matter what Authority. And to blank out at will any public broadcast he finds annoying, as well as any private threats or obscenities beamed at him on his own personal wavelength. So long as he remembers his rights, and acts in time.

I am not sure whether or not I acted on time on this occasion. But using that button, I obliterated her, blotted her out: my dear, lost Megan, whom I am doomed to recall thus for the rest of my life—her image blurring from focus. Her voice fading and swelling, fading and swelling, as I pressed and released, pressed and released the automatic wave-eraser. It was like committing murder; and the last thing I heard before she disappeared forever was her failing voice saying, "Don't ... don't ... don't ..."; then, "I ... I ... I ..."; then, nothing.

Or perhaps divorce is a better, a more terrible and accurate word for what occurred between us; though it is a word long unused in our world, since, in theory, the calamity to which it refers no longer exists. But murder leaves only one victim, one survivor; and we, Megan and I, were two victims, two survivors, quite as in the old-fashioned case of divorce; she left alone with thoughts I could not surmise, and I thrown back to memories of our first separation.

The Circumcision of my son Jacob had been its immediate occasion: the last and littlest Jacob of us all, about whom I had forgotten to ask during our brief interview. Forgotten. My poor son. Imagine it. But even if I had asked, what would, could she have told me, knowing nothing, I am sure, and caring nothing. From his birth, he had been the cause of pain and contention between us; first of all, simply for having been born a boy. For a long time she had refused to have any children, speaking sometimes of her career as the reason, but more often of not wanting to share me with anyone. Then one day she had come to me, saying, "I want a girl, Jacob. Right away. Now. We must give up all contraception, psychic as well as physical. We must will it together."

She was only sixty at the time, and even then the period of fertility for women had been lengthened by the new technology: menarche having been pushed back to eight or nine, menopause advanced to nearly seventy. But the chances of a female birth were considerably better at an earlier age. Or at least so she had been convinced by her more knowledgeable friends—almost certain, in fact, they told her, if her will and mine remained unwavering, and she faithfully followed a prescribed regimen of diet, exercise and meditation. Nine times out of ten, maybe even ninety-nine out of a hundred, the Genetic Technicians can thus control the sex of a child; but this proved to be a tenth time, a hundredth. Yet Megan, to make doubly sure, had carried the fetus in her own womb for twice twenty-eight days, before surrendering it to a host mother. And morning and evening on each of these days, she had followed the prescribed psychic exercises—stealing time from her duties and eschewing Syntho-Hash lest it diffuse her concentration.

Her grief had been extreme, verging on hysteria; and I, who, I must confess, had wavered a little in my will, felt obligated to pretend to share it. Indeed, in a society like ours, only a fool like me, given the choice, would wish to be born a boy or desire his child to be so cursed. Yet secretly I rejoiced, for reasons I dared explain to no one, *traitorously* rejoiced. I had, of course, been terrified, too; afraid that I would lose my son before he was two days old to the Program for Selective Infanticide, which shortly before had been voted into effect by our National Assembly as a replacement for old-style Open Abortion.

The arguments on behalf of what the Population Controllers called the New Expedient were convincing enough on a rational basis. Abortion, particularly when left to the whim of the individual expectant mother, is unselective to the point of total blindness: losing Females, for instance, and permitting the birth of Males when the former are needed for demographic balance; as well as putting pressure on our already overcrowded Sequestration Facilities by producing congenitally maimed, ailing or feeble-minded babies. Moreover, once the proposition has been accepted that an unwilling prospective mother can destroy a six-, or seven-, or eight-month embryo, it seems a mere quibble to treat the elimination of a one-day-old child as something morally different in kind—murder as opposed to sub- or quasi-murder.

But, as usual, the matter was not settled by rational argument; PSI having been attached as a Rider by the Radical Left to a Bill sponsored by the Radical Right making marriage once more a Viable Alternative. Afterward, there was an expression of general discontent with both the original Bill and the Rider on the part of the leaders of the Responsible Center, who included my own Megan. "What can you expect," she shouted at me one day, apropos of nothing at all, "once the vote is given to you honkey Males?" I did not trouble to tell her that only ten out of the fifty Males in an Assembly of five hundred had even voted on the issue; and that their ballots had been split right down the middle. What would have been the use?

Fortunately for me and my Jacob, in any case, the Three-Year Demoplan in operation when he was born called for a 7 percent rise in the Male population; and his penis was found by the Sexual Technicians, charged with such measurements, of adequate potential to justify survival. And why not, considering his heredity? Having escaped one danger, however, I was supercautious ever after; waiting until my son was nearly ten before permitting the Arch-Surgeon, as he was called in our Church, to cut away his foreskin. Ordinarily, we Old Scientists have the Circumcision performed on the Monday closest to the child's first birthday, for reasons which no one any longer remembers. But it has been permissible, ever since the Persecution of the late twenty-third century, which made all observance difficult, to perform the Rite at any time before the child's First Ejaculation.

You must understand, dear reader, that Circumcision, though in contravention of the ordinary laws of our land, is a Privilege granted to our Church, along with the right to consume Acetylsalicylic Acid for ritual purposes. Such exceptions are, in fact, protected by an Eternal Decree granting to every recognized Cult the practice of one Forbidden Act and the use of one Tabooed

Drug. The polyandrous sect, for instance, known as the Revised Temple of Kali, has been allowed, following an acrimonious debate of some ten years' duration at all governmental levels, the Privilege of "sacrificing annually not more than three postpubescent humans of either sex." And Megan, therefore, was not justified in standing between me and the "discharge of all legally recognized commandments and injunctions of a legally recognized Church." This is, in fact, one of the inalienable rights guaranteed by the Constitution of Upper Columbia to "all residents of this nation, not excluding White Males with no other perquisites of citizenship."

How absurd of her, then, to contend later that what was at issue between us was not a matter of religious freedom, but the status of our child, who was, of course, hers to do with as she pleased *within the limits of the law.* This limitation was in no way contravened by any court decision, or even the famous Bill of Privilege of Human Females: a series of amendments attached to our Constitution at the moment when a total gynocracy already existed *de facto* in the realm of economics and social control. Megan, however, is an expert at the sort of logic-chopping and legal quibbling which has tended to grow more common rather than less ever since the abolition of the legal profession and the establishment of the principle, "Every Woman her own Councilor."

In any case, I have never doubted for one moment that what motivated Megan in this matter was not a concern even for the letter, much less the spirit, of the law, but her deep-seated prejudice against Circumcision in any form. More than once she has screamed at me (a moment after declaring all discussion of religion forever forbidden between us) that the ritual trimming of foreskins is an insidious vestige of the banned theistic Cult of Judaism. And Judaism is a Cult reprehensible not only for its belief in the real existence of God, but also for its patriarchal bias; which, she liked to argue, had been the source of a tyranny of men over women that lasted in the Western world for two thousand years.

How could I say to her, I who was her subject, her chattel, that she knew nothing of Judaism but gossip and idle rumor; since everyone except us archaeologists was forbidden to read its texts? I did not even dare to remind her that I myself was circumcised, and that possibly some of the pleasure I provided her could be attributed to the increased sensitivity of an organ without a prepuce. It is true, of course, that Circumcision was central to that quite properly banned Jewish Rite. Yet our own tradition descends, as revealed by its accoutrements, its very terminology, not from the Commandments of their long-discredited tribal deity, Jehovah, but from the practice of Medicine: the sole formerly revered Science which has survived in religious form, though it has been forced long since, of course, to abandon its claim to have achieved "miracle cures."

In retrospect, I wish I had invited Megan to attend the Circumcision of our son. She could not, I think, have failed to be impressed by its solemnity, its symbolic truth, particularly if she had partaken, along with the rest of us, of the Acetylsalicylic Acid which so mysteriously relieves tension and pain. I do not regret that moment despite the anguish it has caused me ever since; for it seemed then the high point of my hitherto eventless life. I can see it all again as I write: the Arch-Surgeon in his long white coat (soon to be spotted with blood), occasionally swinging open to reveal *his* circumcised cock. His ceremonial headdress, consisting of a black band which circled his shaven skull, and a reflecting mirror in which we could watch our own distorted faces as he swung his head slowly from side to side, observing our responses to his words and acts. A flexible black rubber tube hung about his neck, terminating in a hard cone of the same color which dangled just below his heart. And he placed on the white table beside him a leather bag, blacker, it seemed, than headband or tube cone, from which he drew forth, at the climactic moment, the Knife of the Circumcision.

But what most moved us was the actual cutting of flesh: the short, deft stroke almost too swift to follow, the trickle of blood and the ritual cry, first intoned by the Arch-Surgeon, then repeated by us all: *"May you never give Cancer to one whom you pleasure. May you never bring Death in the act of Love."* Cancer, dear reader of the future, was a fatal disease which especially terrified the twentieth, twenty-first and twenty-second centuries, because it seemed an inseparable concomitant of increased longevity; and men in those days still dreamed of immortality. But the disease is gone along with the dream; and, in any case, it does not matter. The point of the prayer remains universally and immitigably valid.

And this Megan herself would have perceived if she had been

there to see how our son rose from the table on wheels which had been the place of his Circumcision, to confront the congregation. Blood continued to dribble down onto his still tiny scrotum; but he smiled and stood erect without trembling, though at this point three of the adult communicants lay on the floor to which they had fallen, one after another. For a moment or two there was consternation, since on rare occasions the Permitted Drug proves fatal for reasons no one quite understands. But it soon became clear that they had only fainted; so that stepping over them, the rest of us came one by one, as is customary, to embrace the bleeding boy and to bless him.

In fact, however, Megan could not have been present, for only Males are allowed to attend the Ceremonies. And at the time my strategy was purely and simply to keep her from finding out. Ever.

I had deliberately picked a peak period in the food-planning cycle, assuming that, even if she were not too indifferent to her Male child to take notice, she would be too busy to discover my crime. And a crime it was, as such things are defined among us; since the morning before, she had issued to me a specific command, making my act mutiny. "I know what you are thinking, boy," she said, "so that there is no need to spell it out. But I am warning you, don't. Just *don't.* " Yet for some reason I had not taken her seriously; or perhaps in my vanity I had hoped to deceive her. Vain hope. Before the night of the Circumcision was over, she had found out, shaking me awake before dawn to vent her rage.

Maybe the child himself had roused her, crying out in pain or fear when sleep had eroded his defenses; and going to comfort him, she had found his coverlet spotted with blood. Or maybe she had been reached via Deep-Sleep Audio by some anonymous aspirant to my place. Or is it possible that despite her declared principles and long conditioning, she was accustomed—like my own shameless and ignorant mother—to sneak every night to the child's bedside, while the rest of the household slumbered. It comforted me somehow to think of her laying a hand on his head, his cheek, even taking his small prick in her mouth to soothe him, if he groaned or tossed restlessly. But in any event, she had discovered my "crime," my "betrayal." And before the sun rose, she ejected me formally, waking two witnesses and saying, as she removed the chain from my neck: *"Henceforth you are banned from my bed and board. Go and do not return."*

"But the child," I protested, when I could speak. "What will become of the boy?" It was useless. I spoke only to her back, or rather the space she no longer occupied.

Moreover, I had scarcely unpacked the few items I managed to take with me, and laid myself down among the other losers and outcasts in the Bachelor Male Quarters, when I learned that my transfer had already been arranged. The messenger who brought the news, a hanger-on accustomed to suck up to me in the days of my prosperity, said not a word. Shuffling and shamefaced, he merely handed me my ticket for a one-way projection to Israel, along with a note reading: "Because I never want to see you again. Never have to think that you occupy the same national space. M."

The initial was perfectly, and, I presume, intentionally anonymous; since all women in Upper Columbia, whatever their rank and ethnic origin, are called by names beginning with that letter. It might have been my mother, therefore, who bade me so abrupt a farewell. Or my first Mistress. Or any of the casual visitors to our house whom I had pleasured once and never met again.

Consulting my ticket, I found I had a scant two hours to assemble my gear, clear Customs, board my plane and strap myself into place. Certainly there was no chance ever for me to find out via a friendly house servant (if, indeed, any of them dared still to be friendly) what Megan had done with my son. I knew very well that the Eternal Decrees forbade her having him executed or exposed or exiled. But I found small comfort in this; since she remained perfectly free to send him off to the kind of school in which I had been so painfully initiated, rather than keep him at home, as her rank made possible. There he would be inducted into sex by her own maids and cooks, rather than being deflowered by those to whom he would seem nothing more than a number on a list.

No Upper Columbian father can afford to mourn long in such circumstances, however, especially if he has, like me, wished his poor child a boy. It is ourselves we mourn for really, mourning thus; and self-pity is a luxury inappropriate to Males. If he is lucky, my poor Jacob will find a Mistress, powerful and kind, no matter where and how his first erotic experience comes. If not . . .

SIX

How long ago it all seems as I sit here now on the hard-packed sand floor of my cave, cross-legged like a scribe in an ancient wall painting, writing, writing. Outside, a light rain is beginning to fall, each drop hitting the ground with a separate and distinct *plop*. The water sizzles as it touches the hot earth, and the steamy smell of it moves me deeply somehow, stirring in me old memories I cannot quite bring to focus.

Imagine it, real rain in the Desert! It is an event which happens maybe once every two or three years. And it is beginning to come down in earnest now, the drops not only larger and heavier, but closer and closer together, so that their individual sounds blur into one indistinct murmur. Perhaps it will cool things off a little, which wou'd help; for it has been unendurably hot all along—and in the last couple of days, unbelievably, it has grown even hotter. I sit stark naked in the cave entrance, in hope of a breeze that does not come; the sweat running down my face, my chest, my back, though I pause occasionally to fan myself with the page on which I am working.

And now a wind has risen, not strong, but strong enough to dash the rain into my face, which is welcome, and to wet my manuscript, which is a problem. I shall have to move farther back into the interior, where the sunlight does not reach. But it grows darker and darker outside, anyhow, though it is scarcely past noon; and in any event, I have in the poison ring which I wear on the little finger of my left hand a miniature solid-state power source, good for light, and heat, too, if ever I should improbably need it. It was, as I shall explain shortly, a kind of farewell present from Melissa-Melinda.

Meanwhile, I must get it all down—not just the story of what happened to me in the camp of the Hypsies, but the whole thing: the crossing of the Desert, the earthquake which has trapped me here. But first I shall rise and look out to see if anyone is approaching. It has become my habit, during my two weeks in this cave, to do so as regularly as I can: during the day, every hour on the hour; and at night, more fitfully, since I doze and wake, doze and wake—incapable of sleeping soundly. In the beginning, it was the police I watched for, afraid they would apprehend me before my task was finished. But now it is the Meta-Technicians; since my translation is complete, and my supplies begin to run low, along with my patience. Moreover, I have admitted to myself, at last, that I cannot get out, that I will not *ever* be able to get out. Not without aid.

No longer worried about the law, I even use my feeble transmitter in the vain hope of reaching them, guiding them in. But the atmosphere is full of static electricity, the worst form of interference. Indeed, for a whole week before the rain began to fall, the sky rumbled incessantly with dry thunder. Besides, they know the coordinates of this place, do they not? So why the hell don't they come, these experts in communications and travel? If they have already discovered the secrets of the Stars, and are on the very verge of leaping faster than light through trackless space, how can they remain unaware of my distress, or be cut off from coming? After all, I am less than a hundred miles from the nearest Space Port, served by commercial flights from everywhere in the world. Why do they wait?

It is stupid, however, to complain to myself, to a piece of paper, to a future reader who may never exist. Stupid and vain. So let me return, if not to the beginning of it all, at least to what I have come to think of as the beginning of the end, the beginning of *my* end: my setting off to see Melissa-Melinda. Or rather, my not setting off as I had planned, because there was so much to do just to get ready. First of all, there were the official arrangements, beginning with a quick videogram to the Regional Headquarters for Archaeological Research to report that I was about to leave on an urgent field trip. Then came the logistics, involving chiefly a visit to the Lydda-Beirut PX. Such short hops are no problem really, since I am provided with a Puddle Jumper: a kind of jet-powered pogo stick also used by the local police.

But I find I am incapable of remembering the need for such arrangements early enough, or of carrying them through with any kind of efficiency; because, I suppose, for so many years I had been accustomed to have everything arranged for me by the women in my life. But even as an ex-well-tended slave, I realized in time that without formal leave I risked serious embarrassment, perhaps even a short spell in jail; since the RHQ automatically dispatches a search posse in pursuit of any employee who does not check in at regular fourteen-day intervals. And without a trip to the PX, I would be in even worse trouble, i.e., in danger of death by starvation.

I told HQ, at any rate, that certain reliable Bedouin informants had tipped me off to the discovery of a lost twentieth-century city some fifty miles to the north of me. Uncovered by a recent sandstorm, it was already being looted by nomads. And what little they would leave was in danger of falling into the hands of rival archaeologists: a party from remote Lower Szechuan traveling in a territory which really belonged to us, on invalid visas granted by the Trucial Kingdom (last remaining monarchy in the world) of Nitgedaiget. I was therefore taking off, I begged to inform them, without waiting for permission, hoping to be back within two weeks or three—a month on the outside.

Having thus bought myself time, I set out in quest of food. Lydda-Beirut, you should understand, was then a Free Port. But its governors had been forced, after a particularly nasty series of small wars, to grant extraterritorial rights to the armed forces of seven countries, including Schleswig-Lichtenstein, which sells by mail Captaincies in a nonexistent Navy: commissions carrying with them the right to use their Lydda-Beirut PX. Our own RHQ, I am pleased to say, has bought such Captaincies for all of its employees of sufficient rank. Therefore, I was able to load up on the newest encapsulated, reduced, compressed and dehydrated delicacies of the world—including my favorite Upper Columbian breakfast treat, Filboid Studge. Moreover, I was lucky enough to find still in stock a Perdurium Shrinko Sack to hold them. It is a carrying device not only impervious to heat, cold, mold and blight, but capable as well of further reducing even the most drastically preshrunk products by half again.

I lost a whole day and a night in such battening down and tidying up; and, having slept through the entire next day, was finally ready to slip out at sunset. The habit of caution had taken over by then, however, so that, more as a matter of course than of fear, I did a twenty-mile infrared scan of the territory between my camp and Melissa-Melinda's. And it was fortunate that I did, because there were cops, it turned out, everywhere: one behind every cactus bush and rock, and three in the palm grove which was our usual place of rendezvous. At this my heart sank, though I knew really that both the Yitt police and the Palestinians of various brands and persuasions (whom M-M insists on calling the Wogs in her archaic dialect) could stick to a job for no more than three or four days at a time. At the end of that period they would be drunk or stoned, or in bed with some Hypsie girl, or playing three-dimensional Chester with each other: a game they use chiefly as an excuse for starting the fistfights they so enjoy. Certainly they would be in no shape to spot, much less stop, me.

So I sat tight, packing and repacking, rereading what I had already written, adding a clarifying detail here and there. Then, on the third night, sure enough, they were gone—the prickly pears merely prickly pears again, and the rocks just rocks; while the palm grove was empty of everything but the small rodents who waited for dark to gnaw the coconuts.

I was not surprised when M-M turned up right on cue, and even less surprised by what she had to tell me. "The fuzz are everywhere," she whispered behind her hand, enjoying the sense of conspiracy. "Like you can't even take a shit without finding some pig looking up your asshole. I mean, let's get out of here, man."

She called everyone "man," you understand, not just adult Males, but Females old and young, children, creatures of indeterminate sex. It was a habit of her people; or rather, I guess I should say, a standard term in the jargon based on English spoken by Hypsies all over the world, a jargon I particularly abhor. I could not pay much attention to what she was saying, however, remembering that this might well be my last night with a woman for a long, long time. So I grabbed her from behind as she emerged from the trees, not yet seeing me but talking already. Wordlessly, I cupped her breasts in the palms of my hands, pressing my urgent hardness into the softness of her buttocks. They were extraordinarily large, both breasts and buttocks; a little astonishing in a bone-thin girl shorter even than I.

But she pulled away impatiently. "Cool it, man. You crazy or something? I mean, what the hell, where's the fire? Because, like I say, we got to split or you're gonna be sorry. Real sorry."

"And where do you suggest we go?" I asked, as always finding my own language stiff and formal in contrast with hers. "I'll give you five to one there are more police in your camp than in the whole area between here and mine. What am I saying? There are *no* cops here at all. I know." I tapped the Scanner on my belt, to show her how I knew, but she didn't seem a bit impressed; so I decided to try another tack. "Look," I said, "I haven't got much time."

"So why are you wasting it rapping? What I mean is—" Backing toward me as she answered, she reached a hand behind her to touch my erection. "Like why don't we go back to my pad? Here in the dark, man, I get uptight. But on my own turf, it's different."

"Sure, it's different," I answered. "All the cops are there." But what could I do? I wanted her, she wanted to go home; so we went, neither one letting go of the other.

Once we were inside, however, I pulled her down with me onto the floor, rolling her over and over, until we came to rest on the pile of filthy rags she called her sack. It was one of her words which I especially hated. "Let's sack out, baby," she would say, and I would feel my passion cool; but tonight was different. The only issue between us was position: I trying to get under her, she maneuvering me so that I would end up on top. Meanwhile, her skirt had hiked itself up to her chin, and her bare legs held me clamped tight against her naked crotch. But it was no go; for just as I could feel the head of my penis parting her pubic hair, the soft lips of her pussy, there was a great thundering at the door flap, sending clouds of dust into the interior of the tent.

I clapped a hand over my nose and mouth, but I sneezed anyhow, as M-M tried vainly to hush me. "Jeez, what kind of creep are you? Do you want to get both of us busted, or what?"

"And what makes you think it's a cop?" I asked, superciliously. But it was a cop all right, a cop's thump at the door followed by a cop's voice in our ear. He was yelling in the French-English pidgin of the Wog police what cops always yell.

"Hey, whatsamatta, you dead? You smoking dope in there, *hein?*" Then, more gently, *"Hey, bébé, c'est moi, tu sais. C'est moi, ton Dodo, et j'ai besoin d'un fix."*

"Get lost, you dumb *flic,*" Melissa-Melinda answered, waving me to the farthest spot from the fire that smoldered in the center of the tent; then she poured over it the contents of a glass at the foot of her bed, sending up a small cloud of smoke. "Like I said, pig, beat it, get lost, split. 'Cause there's no shit here, man. Not tonight. Not for you, see? *Pas de dope, bébé,* dig?" She motioned me to lie flat on my belly, piling on top of me half of the rags that made up her bed.

"I dig, *sale putain,*" the cop responded, entering and placing a hairy hand on each of her shoulders. I could see, in the instant before my eyes were completely hidden, that he bristled all over with crinkly black hair; not only on the backs of his hands, but the nape of his neck, his shoulders. And his face was blue up to the cheekbones, as if in three or four days he could have grown a bushy beard that would have covered everything but his forehead and eyes. As Wog fashion dictated, however, he wore only a hairline mustache, touching which tenderly, he said, "We make zigzig, *hein?*"

"You want dope, man," she said, trying to pull free, "or you want me, you give me bread, see? Big bread. *Fric.*" She rubbed her thumb and forefinger together, to make her point clear.

"Pas de fric, bébé," he answered, releasing her in order to shrug and spread his arms wide, palms out, showing how empty they were. *"Mais, c'est égal.* I have big prick. *Magnifique. Formidable."*

"Don't try to shit me, buster, I been there before. Man, I seen bigger pricks on a cactus. So blow." She stretched out her right arm to give him the finger: an obscene gesture, inherited by her tribe from the twentieth century, made by extending the third digit while all the others are kept closed. But he knocked it down before it had reached shoulder height; then, drawing his own back, slapped her hard in the face, three times.

Her head bounced with each impact, and the overlapping marks were visible, very red against her pallor; but she made no sound.

70

"You want to go to headquarters, *hein?*" he asked. *"Tu sais qu'est-ce que nous allons faire là-bas? Pas moi seul, tu comprends, mais tout le monde.* And you crawl home, *bébé, le cul tout sanglant. Tu comprends qu'est-que je te dis?"*

"Je comprends, buster. But big talk don't scare me. Like when money talks, I listen, Wog-boy. Otherwise, no dice. You gimme bread, I give you dope. OK?"

"OK, *chérie.* I give you big bread. You give me big dope. Zigzig, too. *Ça va?"*

"Ça va. But real WC Credits, man. None of that Wog toilet paper. I already wiped my ass today."

His "bread," as it turned out, was in his own tent, a half mile away; wrapped up in an old pair of *gotchkas,* no doubt, or buried in the dirt to protect it from his comrades, who stole from each other incessantly for survival and prestige.

"It's not that he needs the dope, man," M-M informed me, once he was gone. "He's got a stash like the Central WC Bank. But like he's always gotta keep ahead. 'Cause he's the big dealer, dig? I only seen him do dope himself once, and then he puked it right up. He can't hold it down for shit, man. I shoulda remembered that."

At that point, she explained to me why she had not felt worried about bringing me back with her, figuring the cops were all taken care of, though forgetting Dodo, of course. It seemed that the police in the area had gathered in her camp for some sort of a bash; to celebrate the anniversary, she thought, of a big victory of the Yitts over the Wogs, or vice versa; consequently, they were all "zonked out" on Learyum-D, the Privileged Drug of her Cult. "D-Learyum," the anti-Freaks call it: those "straights" to whom the Hypsies refer to in contempt among themselves—being as sure as anyone that, despite the poverty and squalor in which they live, *they* are the Chosen People. And why not?

"Man," she concluded, "you shoulda seen them poor cats. Like all the pigs in the world are laying out there right now, eating dirt and flapping their arms and yelling, 'I'm flying, I'm flying.' Totally freaked out, man. They just keep yelling, 'I'm flying, I'm flying,' till somebody else says, 'You're flying, you're flying.' Far out, man."

Once she started the story, it seemed as if she could not stop, going round and round the same few facts, laughing like crazy.

"OK," I broke in, "great. They're all down for the count except Dodo. But what do we do about *him?*"

"And then they start all over again," she continued, not listening. "Like one dude goes, 'I'm flying,' and another dude goes, 'You're flying,' and—"

"Look, Melissa-Melinda." I call her by her full name only when something really matters; so she stopped, letting me finish. "I'm in trouble, bad trouble. I need help."

"I know," she answered, kneeling down to embrace me right through the rags. "I mean like every fuckin' body in the world knows. And tells every fuckin' body else. But why the hell don't you stand up? What are you, some kind of jellyfish?" She kept hauling and tugging; but I could see no point in standing up, because in a little while, Dodo would be back. "Why do you think I done it in the first place, man? I mean, give the fuzz all our good dope. Like it's for *you,* man. So you won't get busted. But, like I say, I forgot that fuckin' Dodo."

Half rising, I kissed her hard; and for a minute she responded, opening her lips and letting me feel the flickering tip of her tongue. Then, abruptly, she shoved me away. "Cool it, man," she said, unhooking my arms from around her neck. "I mean, don't let's make a big deal of it. I don't want to see *nobody* in some Wog-slammer. Shit, man, they'll break your balls, they'll eat your liver, they'll— But we got no time for rapping. So, listen good."

Crossing the tent to another pile of rags, indistinguishable from my own, she drew out from under it a long wooden club, polished smooth, and narrowing down from the end as big as a man's thigh to a fist-sized handle—something like those so-called bats used in the twentieth-century game of baseball. Protruding from the thick end of it was a spike, rusty but sharp, and as long as my little finger.

"Look, baby," she said, "like this is a heavy, but when that weirdo pig comes back, you gotta konk him with this shillalie. That's what my old man used to call it, 'my quote-unquote shillalie.' And he oughta of known. 'Cause it was his."

"I have to hit him with that thing?" I said weakly. *"Me?"*

"I ain't talking about nobody else, baby. Or maybe you think we oughta call the cops? Shit, man, I don't want to bug you, but that's how it's gotta be. Or *else.*" She hefted the club high in the air and swung once, straight from the shoulder. "Right on the back of the head, man. Or even better, just where, you know, his fuckin' skull turns into his fuckin' neck. Like I'll take care of conning him. But you gotta hit him and hit him right. The first time, man, 'cause there ain't gonna be no second."

"The first time?" I said, just to be saying something. But I found myself wishing I were a thousand miles away, or dead; or, best of all, that I had never been born.

"What I mean is, he packs one of them new-type Blasters that turns all your juices into ice. Like your snot, your sweat, your jism, your blood, man. So—"

She gave me no chance to answer, stacking the rags back over me again, the first fistful almost into my mouth. But even if she had let me, how could I have explained to someone used to a world in which violence was as habitual and routine as sex that even imagining an act of aggression made me sick. I had never struck anyone in my life, except once or twice in blind fits of rage, which had turned immediately into tears and contrition; since, in my country, men are trained from earliest childhood to consider violence the prerogative of women.

"Can you see out OK?" she whispered, rearranging my rags to make a peephole. "Just lay still, baby, and keep an eye peeled. He'll never know what hit him."

Before she had quite finished, Dodo was back in the entryway. I had been too scared to notice, but M-M must have been hearing for a long while his no-voice singing a popular song of the moment, which was still on his lips as he barged in.

> Oh, they don't wear pants
> In the southern part of France.
> They use dried grass
> To cover up their ass.

It was a recent revival out of the twentieth century or the nineteenth, a Golden Oldie, if there ever was one. And in his Wog-Frog accent, it seemed especially hilarious.

But he was proud of his performance, stopping and grinning, like someone waiting for applause. Always ready to oblige, M-M pretended to clap. "You oughta be on 'Songs to Jet By,' " she said. "You'd make it big."

"I do OK now, *chérie,*" he said, handing her a chit for fifty WCCs. "'Cause I don't burn nobody. *Et putain de dieu,* nobody don't burn me."

"It's real," she exclaimed in mock surprise, holding the chit up to the light.

"Me too, *bébé. Je suis* real, *aussi.* And you got the ough-day now. So let's make the big love, *hein?*" Taking her by the shoulder, he pulled her to him.

"Hey, wait a minute," she said. "Hold your horses, man. Like what do you want, instant delivery?" She laid both hands on his chest, not so much pushing him away as maneuvering him into position, so that his back was turned toward me. "Take it easy, man. Slow and easy does the trick."

But he had already dropped his *gotchkas,* those baggy sheepskin trousers worn by the Palestinian military, to just below his knees; and even from where I was, I could see he was more than ready.

"*Je m'en fous de toi, bébé,*" he said, forcing her down onto her knees before him. "*Et je m'en fous de ton* dope. *Plus tard* I take. Maybe you think I not know *où se trouve* your stash, *hein?*" He indicated where he thought her dope was with a backward toss of his head, and my heart leaped; for we shared a single hiding place, I and the drug supply.

Slowly, I rose to a kneeling position, then a low crouch, gripping the spiked club tighter and tighter in my hand, as I felt my terror turn to rage. *That dumb bastard,* I thought, *who understands nothing but dope and money and cunt, could end my quest forever without even knowing what he is doing. One blast of his Freezer and all my vital fluids will be ice, all men cut off for a century, a millennium, forever, from the Stars. By mistake. By dumb Wog mistake!*

I was on my feet now, my bat lifting higher and higher into the air, as if of its own volition; while, moving his hand from M-M's shoulder, the cop grabbed her long, tangled hair in his fist, and forced her head back, back till she opened her mouth to scream—then shoved his cock hard between her teeth. In and out. In and out. "Eat me, *putain,*" he yelled. "*Mange-le, merde de dieu.* Eat me like you done Mahmoud and Ihab and Dovidl and goddam every *salaud* but me. Eat me, *salope.* Aaaaaargh!"

In a minute, fifty seconds, he had come: his buttocks shaken by spasm after spasm, his head jerking crazily, like a balloon at the end of a string. Then he in turn fell to his knees, his forehead almost touching the ground. *"Salope,"* he began shrilly, his voice falling lower and lower, until his words could scarcely be made out, *"putain.* Filth. Disgust. Ah, *dégeulasse. On ne fait pas comme ça, tu sais. Pas les femmes honnêtes. Pas les filles Arabes. Putain de dieu. Salope. Ah, merde."*

He retched as if trying to vomit, but without success; then, forgetting the dope, stumbled out of the tent into the night. I could hear him for a long time running blindly, tripping, falling, picking himself up, running again; on his way who could tell where—to his wife, perhaps, or his mother, or his *copains.*

He seemed scarcely to notice Melissa-Melinda on his way out, though he had to push her aside to escape; since she stood hanging on to the tent flap with one hand, scrubbing her slobbered chin with the back of the other, and spitting his unswallowed seed out into the darkness. "I'll level with you," she said to no one in particular, not even looking around. "That's what they're all like, every fuckin' one of them. You, too, man." She still did not turn, but it was clear whom she meant. "No-good, uptight, hung-up sonofabitches. Why are you all into hating, not love?"

But I had crept back under my rag coverlet, burying my head in my arms, like a child trying to hide from a nightmare; because just before I had been ready to strike, an instant, a microsecond away from action, I had felt my rage dissolve into horror. And the club had dropped from my hand. Not that I found the sucking of cocks, like that poor Wog in flight from himself, a filthiness desired and detested, dreamed and abhorred. No, for us in Upper Columbia it is a Rite indescribably tender; never to be performed between blasé adults, but only teacher and student, or especially, mother and child. And even then only up to the age of ejaculation. Dear mother, you never tasted my seed. No one has tasted my seed.

Had I envied the Palestinian cop then for being able to come in the mouth of a girl as I can never do? Or was I too busy even then hoping and wishing, as I did now, that it had all worked differently: that he had turned and discovered me up on my feet, that I had killed him? Did I hate him only because I had not killed him? If he had seen me, challenged me, I might even have—

But such idle hypothesizing is, I know, the greatest cowardice of all. The point is that I did *not* kill him, that I did nothing. And even so, I had ended up safe, preserved for the quest by no act of my own, only the generosity of Melissa-Melinda.

"I'm sorry," I said, rising to face her, though not quite able to look her in the eye.

"Exactly what are you sorry about, man?" she asked, not looking at me either. "He really turned me on. I mean it was heavy, real heavy. Like I thought he would never stop coming. I mean, *wow!*"

Perhaps she even wept a little, but I could not be sure; and when I did not respond, she changed tone completely. "You shit!" she cried, "you turd-bird. You ball-less chicken. You didn't kill him."

"No," I said. "I didn't. I couldn't. I can't. I never killed any-one."

"And why the hell not?" she screamed, "why the fuckin' hell *not?*"

It was hard to explain, because in order to do so I had also to tell her the story of my life up to the point at which I had grabbed her by the hair as she tried to wriggle out under the wall of my tent, when I caught her stealing supplies. That was the first of our encounters; and it had ended, like all those which followed, not in words but in the simple act which was our sole bond.

But now I owed her my life, did I not—which is to say, what-ever of it still lay ahead. And in return, it seemed only fair to try to give her some sense of what lay behind. "See here," I began, "what you've got to understand is that I've been raped, too."

And I went on to tell her how our teachers in Upper Columbia would come into our dormitories sometimes after hours, into the chamber of the twelve-year-olds. They would be high on Syntho-Hash or bootlegged Meta-Methanane, and would force us to lie not on our backs as the Eternal Decrees dictate, but on our faces. Then they would strap on the great Perdurium Hyper-Dil-dos they were permitted in theory to use only on themselves, turning the vibration up to full and reaming us all, each one of them each of us. They would neither bind nor gag us, but we neither struggled nor screamed; though at first the blood would run down the backs of our thighs, and we knew that what they did was forbidden by the Guardians.

"We couldn't fight. Not didn't dare, *couldn't,*" I finished. "Not even cry out for help. But worst of all, I got an erection every time. And the last time, I even came. Tits alive, I didn't even know what it was. Only felt the warmth between my belly and floor and was scared. My First Ejaculation, what do you think of that?"

"Super," she said, "real cool." And I realized that she had been following nothing I said, maybe because I was forgetting to talk in the simple phrases we ordinarily used between us. Maybe because she never really listened to me, or, for all I know, anyone, simply responding to everything ritually, as she had whenever I paused, saying, "Crazy" or "Psychedelic" or "Wow" or "Groovy" or "Heavy, man, heavy."

Clearly, the whole thing had seemed merely fabulous to her, a dream, a fairy tale, an hallucinogenic "trip." "I didn't know you could rap so good," she commented, when she saw I was going to say no more. "Like I thought you were only into—"

"Fucking," I finished for her, feeling somehow bitter.

"Yeah," she responded. "So what are we waiting for? Ball me, baby. Don't just stand there with your teeth hanging out. Make me forget, man."

"Forget *what?*"

"It, man, *it.*"

"Why the hell did you let it happen, then, if you want to forget it?" My own question surprised me a little, considering what I had just been saying. But it didn't seem to faze her a bit.

"Because you let it happen, weirdo. Like you were suppose to kill him, dig? Kill him. Kill him. *Kill* him." Each time she repeated the phrase, she slugged me harder, right in the belly; the last time hard enough to spin me half around.

But I did nothing, though I knew she was waiting to be hit in return. Waiting.

"Man, oh, man," she said at last. "You really can't. You really fuckin' well can't. You weren't putting me on." This time it was she who carried me to the floor, pulling her sack of a dress up over her head as she went down, and reaching up under my tunic to grab me when we hit the dirt. "Most of the cats I ever balled woulda broke my ass for that. Some of them my arms and legs for good measure. And my father—I mean, wow!"

She went on then to talk about her father, who, if she was telling the truth, had not only been the first man to beat her ass, but the first to screw her, cornhole her, blow her, teach her to blow him. Meanwhile, her hand was stroking my balls and diddling my prick, as gently as a mother waking her baby to feed him. But I had stopped listening, aware that *this* baby was not going to wake up.

For the first time in my life, then, I realized I was not going to be able to satisfy a woman; and I found myself incapable of thinking about anything else. Maybe in your world, dear reader, the Sexual Technicians will have found a mode of reproduction which does not involve putting males on their mettle, over and over, until the inevitable moment when they fail—knowing that the woman with whom they have failed shares the knowledge of that failure forever. It is not for any of us life's greatest calamity; and certainly, at that juncture of my life, I had other concerns that outweighed it. But it was impossible for me to listen even to one on whom I knew my very survival depended—and especially when she talked about her sex life with someone else.

Yet I was intrigued as she began to explain how sometimes she and her father and his current "old lady" used to make it together. First she and the old man would "ball" for a while, she said, while her acting stepmother looked on. Then that stepmother and her father would take a turn, with her standing by; then she and his old lady, with her father on the sidelines. Only when they were sufficiently "turned on," fucking and watching, watching and fucking, would the three of them do it together. "Until," she told me, "you couldn't tell where one of us stopped and another began. It was like a pretzel, man, or a Moebius strip."

In the end, however, it had all turned sour for her. Not because of any "hang-ups," but because finally it came to her that her old man had been playing games with them both. "I mean, he was using me to put the old lady down. To make her feel old and uptight, you dig? Like she was always copping out before him and me were finished. Cool, huh?"

"What's so cool about it?" I asked, not yet sensing her tone.

But she didn't even trouble to respond. "And he was using her to put me down. To make me feel young and stupid. Like I couldn't get enough of it ever. But him, he was the cool one. You get what I mean?"

I wasn't sure that I did, but "Yes," I said. "Yes."

"I mean he was a shit, man, an A-number-one rinky-dink shit. Would you believe it, he dyed his hair? Like even on his chest . . ."

"Lots of men do," I answered stupidly.

Now it was she who was not listening to me. "So I split. Cleared the hell out. Because I don't let nobody put me down. Never. Not even if he is my father, and getting old and scared. Like you, man." And now she stopped and waited. But for what? What was I supposed to say? That I wasn't old? Or that he wasn't? Or that nobody ever grew old? Or what?

"Well, say something, for crying out loud. I was right, wasn't I? What the hell else could I do?"

"Nothing," I said. "There was nothing else you could do." But all I was thinking of really was my cock, which at that point hung between two of my fingers (I had thought, *Well, why shouldn't I encourage it a little?*) like a hunk of limp spaghetti.

At least I was turned away from her, so that she couldn't see it; but she had kept prodding and pushing. At that very moment, in fact, she managed to shove her arm through the crook of my elbow, so that her fingers were intertwined with mine. "What's with you, man?" she said. "You trying to hide something?"

"I've got nothing to hide," I answered, rolling over so that she could get a good look at my limpness. "Nothing, as you can see." It was as if I had no other word left but nothing, nothing, nothing.

"Well, don't let it bug you," she said. "It's no big deal. An old dude like you, you got to expect it. But I can dig it. And like I say, I don't put nobody down." She kissed me then, right on the poor dead head of it. "And I'm tired. Shit, man, am I ever tired." She eased her body back against mine, her shoulders and spine against my chest and belly, her head fallen backward so that it rested in the hollow at the base of my neck; and her buttocks snuggled against my lifeless penis. Reaching around her I could feel just under her left breast the erratic thumping of her heart. "So we'll sleep, right?" she said in a low, dreamy voice. "It'll feel good for a change. Real good."

She must have meant every word of it, for her sentence ended in a snore. I could feel her body jerk once, hard, as if it were trying to escape my embrace; then she relaxed completely.

But I lay there tense and wide awake; though I tried to match my breathing to the regular intake and release of hers. I was sure that if only I could get the rhythm right, I would sleep, too. But nothing worked.

It is not because I am old, I told myself, *that I have had my first fiasco.* And what is old anyhow? At fifty the seed still rises copiously from the testes, and blood rushes from brain to penis on cue. We males are not born with the biological clock that ticks off the age of women, whether they be Mistresses or slaves. At sixty and seventy we become fathers still; at seventy we have not yet given up masturbation; and at eighty we die with hard-ons, embarrassing our nurses and adoring grandchildren. Only the heart shrivels with the years, not the cock.

Had I not been erect up to the moment the Palestinian policeman had exploded in her mouth, and even immediately afterward, when she had trembled, I swear, not with fear or anger, but delight? No, my flesh did not fall until the club fell from my hand, and I knew I could not kill. Only hide and wait to be saved. But surely that could not be the cause either, since from my first day in school I had been taught that this was my masculine fate, that I could only . . .

I must have slept, after all; for I did not know where I was when I felt Melissa-Melinda's hand on my shoulder, shaking me urgently. "Is it morning yet?" she asked, though the sky through the tent hole showed as black as ever. It could have been no more than an hour since she had dozed off in my arms. "Is it light?"

"No," I answered. "At dawn I must leave you. But it is not time."

Still bewildered, she looked down at herself, then over at me. "Did you ball me, baby?" she wanted to know. "And was it good like always?"

"It was good like always," I said, wondering what she was up to. Was she just putting me on, or had she been stoned out of her mind from the start? "But I didn't ball you."

"No shit?" she asked.

And "No shit," I stupidly repeated.

"Then you gotta let me do my thing. My other thing. I mean, I don't want something for nothing, man. So let me read it, baby."

She grabbed my hand in the dark, then dropped it again quickly, shivering a little.

"Read *what?*" I said. "What are you doing anyhow?"

"Read your *hand,* you jerk, what else? I got real Gypsy blood in me. And, like they say, I was born with a caul."

"Forget it," I answered. "Whatever you could find there, I don't want to know. I've got troubles enough."

"You don't know the half of it, baby. I can see the bad vibes in the dark. Smell them. Something real heavy is coming down, man. And like you better dig it, or else."

As she spoke, she was flipping open the poison ring she wore on her right hand, shaking out of it onto her palm a tiny Stone. It was not a jewel, I could tell immediately, though it glowed bright in the darkness when she rubbed it once or twice against the upper part of her thigh. "That turns it on, man," she explained. "Body heat. Just like you and me. What a gas!"

"It's the middle of the night," I said, "and I've got a long way to go tomorrow. So why don't you leave me alone. Let me sleep."

"I don't see you sleeping, man. Look, this light don't last for long. So while we got it, let's use it, right?"

The whole tent shone now with a radiance not like that of the naked sun, or even of the stored solar energy we use for illumination in Upper Columbia. Of anything I've ever experienced, it was most like starlight here on the edge of the Desert, when there is no moon: cold and distant and intense, though without the slightest dazzle or glare. But it was different even from that in a way I find hard to express, seeming to come from inside my own head rather than from outside.

"Come on, lemme have your hand, man." She grabbed me by the right wrist, turning my palm upward. "And just relax. I ain't gonna bite you. Like I tried that before, and a fat lotta good it did me." Apparently she remembered our failed night now that she was fully awake. "Or you either. So I got to give you something to make up for that bad scene, right? Something for the road. Like a souvenir. To remember."

"Remember what?" I said. "But if you really mean it, which I doubt, there's one thing I'd love for a souvenir. One thing I could sure use where I'm going." I stabbed a finger out in the direction of the Stone, almost touching it; but she closed her palm over it.

"Man, do you know what that thing is worth? Like it's a PSSS, if you dig what that is. And I don't mean 'piss,' neither."

I knew what she meant all right; though I'd never been close to one before, and somehow I had imagined it would be bigger. What she held in her grubby hand was nothing less than a Power-Source-Solid-State, the superminiaturized model, in fact. Not yet released to the general public, it could be traded on the black markets of the most advanced nations for a power backpack like that of the Meta-Technicians, or a small lunar-range jet; while in the bazaars of the slave state of New Alabama, it was probably worth two strong men or a nubile girl.

"I know," I said. "But the question is, where did you steal it? And how long do you think it will be till they catch up with you?"

"I didn't rip it off from nobody, man. 'Cause I got it from a Yitt General, and if he stole it, he never told me. He *gave* it to me 'cause I use to know him, like they say in that country, once a week for a whole year. Meaning by 'know' what us ordinary people call—"

"I know that, too," I interrupted her. "But that's not the point."

"The point is that Yitt General, he respected me, man. And I ain't gonna give away nothing he gave me to some joker who don't."

"Meaning me?" I asked.

"Meaning you," she answered.

I didn't believe a word of her story, I must confess; figuring she must have drugged him and rolled him, since those Yitts are not famous for making bad bargains, especially with no-account girls. Or maybe she slipped it off his finger, kissing him good-bye—nice and easy, the way she is good at doing. I was sure that if that PSSS hadn't been too hot to fence, she would have swapped it long since for something she wanted more: dope or incense or Bedouin doilies for her dirt floor. Maybe even one of those autopowered Smellie-Feelie sets that were standard equipment that year in every no-mad's tent. In the end, it made no difference, one way or the other; since clearly she would not part with the PSSS, however she had acquired it.

"OK," I said, "if that's the way it is."

"That's the way it is, man, and that's how it's gonna stay. I keep the Stone, and you get your fortune told."

"No," I said.

"What a creep you are," she responded, tickling my palm with her index finger. "Come on. Please. Pretty please. Pretty please with sugar on it."

"Why not?" I said. "I've got no fortune left to tell. But that's no reason you shouldn't try. Besides, I've broken every other law on the books these last couple of days, so I might as well break this one, too."

"Why are you such a fuckin' clown, man. You know goddam well it's OK. Like it's our PA." It was true, though I had forgotten it, that Gypsies and Hippies both belong to the Church of Latter-Day Witches. And for that Cult, all kinds of fortune-telling, otherwise banned by Eternal Decree, are Permitted Actions: horoscopy, palmistry, medical diagnosis, phrenology, *I Ching,* necromancy, meteorology, stockbrokerage, card and tea-leaf reading, even practical clairvoyance, with or without apparatus.

But she did not finally read my palm at all, though she held it for a long time telling me how she had learned the "whole bit" from her Gypsy grandmother: tarot, cheiromancy, the "works." Then she began her routine in what have been the traditional fashion, jerking her head forward so that her long purple-black hair fell over her eyes, while she traced blindly with the tip of her right index finger the chief lines of my palm. Her nails were dirty and broken, but my hand trembled at their touch.

"Yes," she said, "oh, yes. Holy shit, no. No. No. *No.*"

Then her head was flung backward suddenly. Not as if she herself jerked it this time, but as if some force outside of her were tugging at it: a force she wanted to resist. Her mouth was open, like that of someone about to scream, the teeth yellow and flecked with spit. And her eyes, open now, were rolled back in her head.

"I can see," she began again, gripping my hand, which she had never released, tighter and tighter. Her voice was very low, almost a whisper, and sounded somehow like the voice of a stranger, though whether friend or foe would have been hard to say.

"I can see an old man . . . not you . . . not you . . . very old. . . . And it's like . . . I don't know . . . like he's seeing me . . . and you, too . . . like we're all looking at each other . . . like he's telling your fortune . . . not me. . . . And he says. . . . No, no, *no!*"

Her body jerked back and forth, back and forth, in violent spasms; her lips pulling back until her gums showed in what could have been a grin. And when the spasms subsided, her lids closed slowly, twitching as if her eyes continued to move back and forth under them.

"I see . . ." she started again, her voice louder, firmer, more like her own. "No, I can't . . . can't see. . . . Yes, it's a . . . a woman, a sort of a woman . . . but big. . . . Like a mountain, a cloud, a wave rolling over him . . . over the old man. . . . And now it's like they're balling or fighting . . . fighting and balling . . . rolling, rolling, like mountains moving . . . like waves moving . . . like rocks rolling. . . . Like water. . . . Only . . . only the old man is you, Jacob. . . ."

It was the first time she had ever called me by my given name, the secret name which I was sure I had never told her.

"And the . . . the woman is me, *me*. . . . Like they're everybody, Jacob . . . like we're everybody. . . . Only she's . . . she's. . . ."

"Black," I suggested; not even knowing whether she could hear me. Imagine it, Black! But that is the way my mind works.

"No color . . . none. . . . You can . . . like see through her. . . . You can see through her, Jacob . . . see into her . . . only behind her . . . at the bottom of her. . . . There's . . . there's nothing. . . . *Nothing!*"

I realized then that she had released my hand, and looking up, saw that her eyes had popped open.

"So, thanks for nothing," I said, figuring to settle for a bad joke; but I could not—suddenly wanting, *needing* to know what lay ahead. "Tell me more," I said. "You can't stop there."

It could only have been two, three hours until dawn. And I found myself trembling with the sort of chill that often, in a world of abrupt temperature changes, wakes me toward morning. But worse. So that this time it was I who said, "Please!" and she who said, "No!"

"No, no, no, *no,*" she repeated, squinching her eyes closed under the dark Gypsy brows that met over her nose; and shaking her head violently like a wet dog. "I won't, man. I can't. Not ever. To hell with my grandmother."

She closed my fingers down over my open palm, squeezing

them tight with her own, which were trembling like mine. "Never. I wish I was dead." Was she crying a little, I wondered, peering at her through the fading light. But why was the light fading? What had happened to the PSSS? Only asking those questions, did I realize that she must have slipped something into my hand, closing it. And that something could only have been the PSSS.

It felt to the touch uncanny in a way I would not have suspected: tinier even than it had seemed looking at it, but also harder, harder than any object I had ever held. Moreover, its temperature baffled my senses, seeming neither hot nor cold, though somehow suggesting both; as if it were compounded of all that was most titillating at both extremes, without the presence of danger or the threat of pain. And it pulsed against the pulsing of my own veins, as if it, too, had a beating heart.

"But I can't really take it," I said, trying to open my hand. "When I asked you for it, I was only—"

"Keep it," she answered, pressing my fingers down even more firmly. "'Cause you need it worse than me. Like you need it worse than anybody. No, man, I *mean* it." She had released my hand temporarily, but only in order to strip the poison ring from her middle finger; and to make sure I understood, kept wagging her head back and forth, *no, no, no!* "And you better glom onto this, too. To keep the Stone safe, dig? Like one of them crazy Wogs would kill his own grandmother for something like this. Before breakfast. And he don't even have to be crazy. I dig you don't know what's flying, but believe me, the shit is going to hit the fan. Hey, look, man, it *fits.*" She had tried it first on the little finger of my right hand, then of the left, which it really did fit—a little tight, maybe, but there to stay.

"Better vibes on the other hand, man," she said. "But it's cool either way."

"Yeah, cool," I responded, hating myself a little, as always when I try to talk her argot. The ring embarrassed me, in any case, making me feel like a character in one of those twentieth-century novels which, I must confess, I have come to read for pleasure, who has just got "married" or "betrothed." But it was like a girl, I felt, you understand, not like a man; as if I had just become a "bride." But of whom, I wondered, or of what?

"You'll regret it," I said, dropping the Stone into the ring and letting the lid *ping* closed. Knowing her, I was sure that she would—in a week, or a day, or even a couple of hours. . . . But I figured the best way to prevent it was to say it, to keep her on the defensive. "You'll live to regret it. But thanks—for now."

"Make it thanks forever," she said. "'Cause it's not cool just for now. With you and me, it's cool forever. Like *forever*, man."

I took her in my arms, then, kissing her on the forehead, both cheeks, the lips; and before I finished, she had gone limp in my arms, exhausted, hardly breathing; as if she had just run twenty miles, fifty, a hundred—one mile too many, in any case. As if she were really dead. But I could see the slow, shallow rise and fall of her ribcage as I gently lowered myself to the ground without releasing her or causing her to wake.

Not much more than an hour could have passed, however, when I felt her ease herself from my embrace; heard her get to her feet and move cautiously through the rubble that littered the floor of the tent, then take a step or two outside: to piss, it would appear, for I heard the sound of that, too. But I did not open my eyes or stir, desiring, until dawn broke, to relax as completely as I could, even though sleep continued to evade me. And so I felt without seeing the cautious movement of her fingers on the back of my hand after she had returned; heard the small sound of the poison ring opening, then closing again, as she took back the PSSS—leaving the ring, however, so that I would not notice it until I was long gone from her camp. How could I resent what I had foreseen and could, I was sure, undo? So I thought, instead, of the generous act which had preceded the theft, and of the uncustomary surge of affection which, I flattered myself, had prompted that act.

Did I hear her sigh then, or only imagine it, as she moved uncertainly about the small space she lived in, searching, I supposed, for a secure hiding place. I did not dare open my eyes at that point, though I desperately longed to; for even through my closed lids, I was aware of the glow that lit up everything around me—the PSSS being, I presumed, still warm. And I did not want, in any case, to let her know that I knew; for the advantage was mine now, clearly mine, as long as she remained unaware of what I had discovered. But not unless I could find the Stone.

I felt her lower herself into our bed of rags once more and

snuggle against me; so I threw an arm over her, like one who half-wakes and reaches out to be assured that his partner is still beside him. But I wanted really to check on her breathing. And when I heard it grow regular again, I rolled cautiously away from her body, then off our low couch; finally over and over across the dirt floor, until I felt myself touching the furthest tent wall. Only at that point did I dare very slowly to ease myself up onto my hands and knees and crawl through the blackness, patting the ground before me. From time to time, I would pick up the rags and the junk I encountered, hoping that she had not had time to bury the PSSS in the earth and that somewhere in the tent it continued to glow with vestigial heat.

Vain hope. To find it would take, I knew, not just patience and skill, but, in place of the time I did not have, luck—plain dumb luck. And I was, it seemed, fresh out of luck. I had no more than minutes to invest in the search; since my sole chance of escaping was to get out before the Wog policeman returned, or the other cops awoke from their sodden slumber, or M-M sat up suddenly in her bed. To get out *now*.

My heart leaped as she shifted over to her back from her side, on which she had been sleeping until then, her knees pressed against her breast and almost touching her chin, her arms clasping her legs. But she did not wake. And watching her with held breath, I could see at the juncture of her legs, now spread wide apart, the tiniest luminescence, a glow steady and unblinking, though small beyond belief.

Of course. Where else would she have hidden the Stone.

Gently, gently, I thrust the index finger of my right hand into her damp pussy, higher and higher, until, on the verge of despair, I felt it, had it. Then even more gently, I drew it out, my eyes never leaving her face and her breasts, which continued to heave regularly. She smiled a little at the point of deepest thrust, even wriggling slightly about my finger. Only at the very last instant, something—perhaps the scarcely audible *plop* as the final suction of her labia broke, or the pressure on a particularly erogenous zone —half-woke her. The whole upper half of her body rose stiffly and abruptly, like a puppet jerked to attention, and her eyes sprang open. "Right *on*," she said, her voice making my heart leap, my stomach drop.

But she could see nothing, I could tell even from where I stood pressed back against the tent wall, breathing hard, the Stone clutched in my hand. Then, as quickly and rigidly as it had risen, her body fell, racked by a snore as her head hit the pillow of rags once more. And she slept on without even moving while I tiptoed to the door of the tent, where, looking down at myself, I discovered that I had grown hard again.

Imagine it, dear reader, hard at such a moment! And believe further, that, creature of habit, I was tempted for one moment to return and throw myself on her where she lay. But discretion triumphed over lust and pride; so that, instead, I stepped out into the coolness of almost morning. There was no sound in the camp, the drugged policemen flying silently off somewhere in the semi-dark, if, indeed, they still flew at all. And I, I knew with a sinking heart, was alone now to the end. Checking the Stars for direction, I headed due south toward the Desert, the Scroll and the terrors Melissa-Melinda had not dared to tell me—my erection pointing the way.

SEVEN

I was a long way from home free, however; since a venture deep into the Desert posed political problems, as well as physical and logistical ones. Though the sovereignty of much of the region was still in dispute, the particular area I sought had long been under the control of the Free Socialist Republic of the Negev, a state officially at war with Liberated Palestine, from which I was starting. Ordinarily there was no difficulty in slipping across the ill-defined borders which separate the two. Actual hostilities had ceased years before, and neither nation had fixed checkpoints or sentry posts, only patrols crisscrossing the region in irregular patterns to make sure that the papers of all travelers were in order and that they carried no contraband. But a small bribe, whether WC Credits, or pornographic filmstrips, or dope, could buy entry into either country, even for refugees without passports or smugglers caught in the act. As a matter of fact, the Acetylsalicylic Acid used by my own Cult was especially prized by both sides; and I was well supplied.

At any other time, then, I would simply have moved ahead by the most direct route, running the risk of being stopped and searched, maybe even hassled a little. But this time, I feared that a general alert might have been beamed to the gendarmerie of all Seven Nations, offering a reward for my arrest greater than I could match out of my remaining store of our Privileged Drug. So I decided, after all, not to proceed due south. Instead, I would swing westward a bit, in a detour which would allow me finally to follow the so called Heartbreak Trail back to the point where, according to the 3-D Lasermap in my head, the cave and the Scrolls were to be found.

The local military refused, except under duress, ever to traverse that linked series of dry gullies and arid lake beds—not even in their Puddle Jumpers, which make an approaching patrol look like a horde of locusts. And I could not blame them really; though I proposed, having no choice, to travel that terrain on foot, trusting that my aging body would carry me through. In Upper Columbia I would never have dared to undertake such a journey, even if I had been granted permission by my Superiors. But five years in the field had toughened a physique naturally superior, despite its smallness of size, to the flabbier frames of the Wogs; many of whom were, in fact, no taller than I. I did not doubt, however, that the terrors of the Heartbreak Trail were genuine enough, though exaggerated by that paranoia endemic among cops and soldiers everywhere. Of this I had been assured by some of my own fellow archaeologists, who had ventured into its draws and canyons to make exploratory digs.

The chief menace, I gathered, was the lack of water, there being apparently not a single rivulet, spring or well along the more than one hundred miles of the trail. Like everyone else engaged in archaeology, I was equipped, however, with those government-issue, double-bonded Hydrogen Caps, which turn into H_2O immediately on exposure to the oxygen present in the atmosphere. Moreover, I was not afraid of snakes and lizards, even the oversize variety which reportedly abound in the region, and terrify the local constabulary more than the drought. Despite rumors to the contrary, I firmly believed that even this backwater of civilization had been cleared, along with the rest of the world, of all poisonous or man-eating pests. Indeed, I myself had seen from time to time the low-flying, unmanned Sprayjets of the WC spewing overkill doses of APT on the neighboring hills and meadows.

The Eighty-Year War over the use of APT, which is to say, Anti-Predator Toxin, had ended long before I was born. And it had not, in any case, ever involved Upper Columbia, which was one of the first five states (there are still fewer than fifty) to achieve a totally controlled, meta-natural environment. I had, therefore, never encountered, before my exile, any beast lower on the evolutionary scale than *Homo sapiens sapiens,* not even in robot form. Proto-cats and para-dogs had, it is true, been a fad in the time of my great-grandparents. But they had been pulled off the streets by roving mobs and melted into scrap during the period of anticybernetic reaction which followed the Great Humanoid Fiasco of 2411. Vestiges of the rage that scandal had engendered still smoldered in my father, whom I remember saying, doubtless in imitation of his father, who in turn was echoing his, "Goddam it, computers should look like computers. Or how the hell can you keep them in their place?"

In all seven of the post-Israeli states, however—except for Lydda-Beirut, the single domed hydroterran cluster of the region—there still lived certain species of the lower fauna which, at first, I could not believe were truly harmless. In fact, I still find it disturbing to share my sleeping space with some uninvited guest of that order, say, a desert rat. And I have yet to be persuaded to pat even the fuzziest and gentlest of those puff lemurs from the hills of Galil, which the Palestinians keep for pets. But leaning over backward, perhaps, I will not countenance gossip about the persistence of Gila monsters, scorpions, copperheads or cobras, here or anywhere else. Except, of course, in the three great extraterrestial zoos, in which a pair of all the major species of the killers and eaters of man (except, of course, man himself) are kept.

I myself would favor, timid soul that I am, the abolition of even these few refuges. I realize, however, that they are a necessary sop to the sentimentalists of the Pro-Predator Party: the so-called Wolf Men, who remain strong to this very day in Wallachia, New Bengal and the United States of Southern California. All pretense of maintaining a natural habitat for such ravenous beasts was, in any case, abandoned after the animal uprising in the zoo on the Artificial Satellite of Neptune. Moved by agitators who have never been identified, the Neptunian predators broke loose and ate not just their keepers, but a party of visiting schoolchildren. They terrorized the whole satellite for more than a month, in fact, until they were subdued by an armed expedition jet-dropped from the Bubble Colony on the Mother Planet. Since that time, not only on Satellite-Neptune, but also at Venus-B and Luna-Mercury, such dangerous creatures have been, thank goodness, kept enclosed in a double force field, too intricately overlapped to allow the escape of a single hydrogen molecule. So there is no way left by which a population of predators could be renewed.

Consequently, I did not believe in the presence of venomous reptiles along the Heartbreak Trail, any more than I believed the even more fatuous tales told by wildcat prospectors to gullible greenhorns about open ore deposits in the Desert—mixtures of plutonium, uranium and curerium-2, which drive travelers mad by increasing beta-ray production in the brain. Yet, I must confess that I did not relish the thought of trekking mile after mile through waterless wastes; the only sound in my ears, except for the intake and release of my own breath, the slither of scaled vermin over lava and rocks. And so I was glad that my detour would take me within earshot of the Jerusalem Fun House and Amusement Park, to which visitors come from all quarters of the globe, including hordes of gawking provincials from the boondocks of Mercury and Uranus

My route did not take me quite close enough to see even the glow of its multicolored deuteron hoardings. But I could make out, at one point, the screech of the frictionless roller coasters, scooting in a few seconds from heights higher than Everest to underground caverns deep as the periphery of earth's core; and the clash of hundreds on hundreds of Perdurium free-fall bumper cars, meeting head on at the speed of gravity, thirty-two feet per second per second. I was not quite sure whether I could really hear the music from the free-form Dance Hall floating in the quicksilver pond, around which everything else rotated faster and faster as the night wore away. Cued as it was by the random movements of anyone entering the Hall, or passing along the moving roadway beside it, even by the motion of a bird, a plane, a child's kite in the air overhead, that music was as random as a dream: a part of the total ambience, like any noise in the street.

But I imagined I heard it, then went on to imagine what we still call the dancers, though they no longer move their bodies in time to an external beat, as remained the custom up to a few decades ago. They respond instead partly to their own peristaltic rhythms, partly to the pattern of sound improvised by the Synthesizer, partly to the play of light from a Color Organ, somehow synchronized with both. Motionless to the onlooker, they approach an invisible climax, made manifest when, sooner or later, they fall to the floor unconscious. It is considered chic this year to "dance" thus in configurations of three; and after long practice, some triadic groups manage, without ever touching or looking, to black out simultaneously.

I had no desire to enter the Park, or even to get closer than my travel plan took me, having already visited it twice during my five years' sojourn nearby. I wanted only to experience, vicariously, people much like me crying out in pleasure or, for that matter, in boredom and disgust. And thus to be reassured that not far from my present loneliness, nor impossibly distant from the Desert places I would soon tread, there was a habitable and inhabited world. I wanted, not companionship, but the knowledge that such companionship existed, for others, if not for me. Even when I had entered the Park earlier, I had not danced or gone on the rides: not even the newest attraction, called There and Back, which promised "a peek at the future," and was doubtless a fake. It had seemed enough to me even then just to look; almost too much to bear when total strangers would touch their flesh to my flesh, saying, "Excuse me," or "Hey, I'm sorry," or "Why the hell don't you watch where you're going?"

There was nothing left of the ancient City that had once stood here and which, during the centuries of my expertise, had been rent by strife based on the preceding two thousand years of bloodshed. That strife, the World Council decided finally, was too intimately connected with the forbidden God Cults of Judaism, Christianity and Islam to be any longer endured. Moreover, Jerusalem had become a pesthole: its streets congested and its air foul with the fumes of the combustion engines, then used for short-distance transport and private acts of aggression.

Consequently, some three hundred years ago, in accordance with a decree promulgated by the WC and ratified by two-thirds of its member states, wave after wave of remote-control Crates, filled with jellied fire, were hurled into the smoking center of the City: an appropriately obsolete end for so obsolete a survival. For three days and nights it burned, until all of its bitter past had been fused into a heap of smoking slag, like Sodom and Gomorrah of its own legends. A hundred years after that, when the slag had become ashes, and the ashes soil from which grass began to grow, Liberated Palestine built on the site a Fun House and Dance Hall; and, if rumor be true, an underground brothel for traveling bureaucrats.

But throughout, one Wall of the hundred thousand that had been Old Jerusalem remained. Some say it was left standing in accordance with a plan of the WC; but others argue that it survived despite their efforts—including attempts at demolition with lasers and nuclear explosives. Whatever the truth of such speculations, the Wall, I know, is still there. I have visited it myself in the

Perpetual Enclave maintained by the Recreation Department of the World Council, who have planted a double row of cypresses around it and built a fountain to play eternally before it.

Even as a tourist, I had found it intriguing; and so I asked Regional Headquarters to petition the Palestinian Government to let me return with a Multi-Level Scanner and an Atomic Chronometer. To my surprise, I was refused permission by authorities worried about the intrusion into this no-man's land of religious Yitts, to whom the Wall is sacred. And they found my name suspicious enough to justify a denial. As if "Jacob" were not, after "Vladimir," the most popular male name in my country, from which the last practicing Jew was exiled a century and a half ago.

Being stubborn, I returned three days later, though without the Atomic Chronometer, which would have set all the Radiation Counters in a ten-mile area clanging. I carried only my Multi-Level Scanner, disguised as a 3-D Superpolaroid Snapbox; so that I shall never be able to verify the antiquity of the Wall reliably. Yet it proved impossible to stand before it without feeling in the marrow of my bones the chill of death and the thrill of survival, the ambiguous shudder of the past. I found myself trembling and weak in the knees, so that I leaned with both hands against the ancient stones, my eyes cast down to my feet and the carefully tended turf on which they rested.

I do not know how long I remained in that position; but after a while, I became aware that someone who stood to my right was whispering into my ear. He was a little man, smaller even than I, with a long, sensitive nose, watery eyes and the faintest suspicion of a hump. It was only after he had gone that I realized he must have been one of those crypto-Jews, who so trouble the Palestinians, and that the language in which he addressed me, convinced by my visible emotion that I was a coreligionist, must therefore have been Yitsch. But I understood only the final word which he spoke, turning on his heel, since it is also Hebrew, which I have studied. And the contempt with which he spoke it would have made it comprehensible to a child of three, whatever his native tongue. *"Goy,"* he said, and moved away through the gawking crowd, in search of a real fellow believer.

But if I am, indeed, a *goy,* a pagan, an outsider, why was I so moved, standing before what as an archaeologist I knew must be all that is left of the Great Temple of Jehovah? And why, sitting on a grassy knoll five miles away remembering it, was I moved once more—this time to tears? Is it possible that the whole White population of Upper Columbia is descended from Jews with non-Jewish wives, who made up the ruling class of North America just before the great Revolutionary *Putsch*? Or is it only that all slaves in whatever Egypt (to borrow a metaphor from the banned Scriptures of Judaism), become in some sense "Jews"? The true Jews, which the descendants of Abraham, Isaac and Jacob, my namesake, cease to be whenever they play the part of the oppressor rather than the oppressed.

Such thoughts did not occur to me when I actually stood before the Wall and raised to my eye my disguised Infrared Scanner. Fortunately, there had just been a general power failure, and so the customary *son et lumière* display was interrupted: those three-dimensional pictures of the Space Pioneers, who seem to move back and forth along the Wall in an archaic garb which onlooking children find hilarious; and the medley of the patriotic songs once sacred to the old United States and the former Soviet Union. To make the setup even more favorable for me, it was the dark of the moon, so only the transistor-powered patrol lights from the Palestinian Superchoppers overhead cut through the darkness from time to time.

In the end, I was disappointed, however, for I could discern no really ancient inscriptions beneath the phosphopaint: no Akkadian, no Chaldee, no Old Testament Hebrew. I am not an epigrapher, of course, and it is possible that more sophisticated equipment would have produced better results. But what I did find were four legible inscriptions of quite recent origin: one in twentieth-century Hebrew, one in the dialect from which Melissa-Melinda's argot has descended, two in Early Modern English, which was the *lingua franca* during the rise and fall of the Second Israeli Commonwealth.

The first was historical, reading in English, or perhaps American, "KILROY WAS HERE": a rallying cry, apparently, of the "Allied Forces" in the world's last Great War, which ended in 1945. The second, in Neo-Hebrew, was theological and from approximately the same period, though it alluded to events two millennia old: the mysterious execution of the pseudo Messiah, Jesus. "WE DID SO KILL HIM," it runs, apparently claiming the credit for the Jews. The third and fourth are political, though they verge still on the theological. "HANDS OFF THE MOON," reads the third; and the fourth, representing anti-imperialist attitudes of nearly a century later, says, "MARS SUCKS."

But the first word was so blurred that I sharpened focus, layering in until I could see that it had been changed twice, reading one layer down, "MAO SUCKS," and a layer below that, "GOD SUCKS." "God" means, once more, I presume, the Jewish Jehovah, and "Mao" is the name of a Chinese revolutionary who died toward the end of the twentieth century, dismaying many who had believed him immortal. It was a meager result for an investigation I had begun with high hopes; and it left me unsure whether the Wall may not have been counterfeited less than five hundred years ago by the Tourist Board of the Second Israeli Commonwealth, or put together out of old stones by the Palestinian Military as a trap to catch crypto Jews.

Forgive me, dear reader, for having taken so long to get myself to the Desert. It took me a long time in fact to reach my destination: a long, dreary time that I am not anxious to describe. Yet I was not then as reluctant to leave the pleasant hillside above Jerusalem, as I am now to leave it in words. Despite my own forebodings and the warnings of Melissa-Melinda, the small boy's heart in my aging breast thumped in anticipation of the new, the unexplored, the truly unknown.

I do not want to make excuses; only to remind you that after fifty, one is likely to feel intolerably confined not only by the routine of work and pleasure and continuing family relationships (in my case, *non*relationships), but also by the more insidious habits of waking, washing, eating, tending to the body's needs, going to sleep. For a little while in childhood, the body itself is an adventure, which is to say, an unknown territory. And for a little while longer, one's mother seems such an adventure, along with the home which is her extension; then the streets outside one's door, one's first friend beyond the home; then one's first teacher or first lover; then the next and the next and the next. . . . Every quest, therefore, no matter what its avowed end, is a quest for childhood: an attempt to return to the place from which one can set out for the first time. A snare and a delusion, as I have come to know.

Yet I find I regret nothing as I sit here with this page before me, the Priest's manuscript neatly piled at my feet, and the sound of the rain outside only enhancing the security of the dry cave I inhabit. For this instant the distant rhythm of the continuing downpour soothes me, lulls me . . . until I find myself thinking: *All things are possible, all things are possible, all things are possible still.* . . . It is a sign that I am beginning to dream, that I am falling asleep. So I force myself awake, wanting to lose nothing of what lies ahead, no matter how grim it may be; desiring only to be fully aware when the terror yet to come climaxes the terrors—and the triumphs—I have already lived.

How soon after setting out, however, the sheer slog of it wearied my bones and constricted my heart: the unremitting sun overhead, and underfoot the merciless stones. Hearing the word *Desert,* I had thought of dunes and sagebrush, cactus and shifting sand. And, indeed, from time to time, even on the Heartbreak Trail, there are gullies graced with vegetation and gritty sand, which seem a benediction in the petrified wilderness. But chiefly there are rocks and boulders and pebbles, sometimes a kind of rough gravel, especially hard to traverse.

It is all broken and gray and unlovely, cruel to the feet that tread it day after day, cutting the toughest boot soles to shreds, then blistering the exposed flesh. The two spare tunics I had packed, I tore into strips to wrap around my poor feet. And those strips, red as my unstaunched blood for an instant, in another would turn gray as everything else in the world through which I endlessly walked: the stones, the distant bluffs which seemed never to get closer, the sky itself through the haze of rock dust I stirred with each step that I took.

In a little while, I was as gray as the world around me: my eyebrows, my mustache, my beard, the hair on my head, my ankles, my thighs, my fingers and toes. And as dry, for there was no water anywhere, no water ever to wash in. True, there was the precious stuff I distilled at dawn and at dusk from my Double-H Tablets, but that I saved entirely for drinking. Early in my trek I would occasionally have an irresistible impulse to bend down and touch the gray rocks with my gray fingers. And each time my teeth would be set on edge, because they were not only as hot and as dry as I had expected, but indescribably—*dead.* I do not know how else to say it.

After a few days, when I was on the verge of total despair, perhaps even of turning back, calluses began to form on the soles of my feet, and the pain abated a little. But even before that, I had been learning to dream myself out of that infertile waste: to imagine myself strolling along the pediroads of my native place. There I would have been not so much strolling as letting myself be carried along. Our streets move with the will of the walker: letting him stand still if he likes, or, if he pleases, ride with them, adding his speed to their speed. Even where those roads have been built on rock, they are as springy as the springiest natural grass; and where they span vast areas of water, their surface is like the skin of a living creature, pliant but firm over the hydroponic plantations in their depths.

True, sometimes the power fails even in Upper Columbia, though not with the monotonous regularity of such events in the Seven Nations. And then we sweat a little and curse the technicians. But chiefly walking was for me in my childhood, my youth, my early maturity, more like swimming or floating in this part of the world. Except when, for the sake of my muscle tone, or at the order of Megan, who found me too flabby perhaps, or was moved by strategic reasons to say so, I went to the exercise treadmills.

Such dreams, however, were constantly being interrupted by a granite outcropping over which I would stumble, or the sudden squawk of a falcon swooping down on a rodent, who would scurry for cover in a rattle of stones. And I would wake to the petrified nightmare of my journey from which I could never awake in turn; but through which I continued to plod like one who walks open-eyed in his sleep. Then, without knowing it, I would be dreaming again. This time of the simulated shade trees of my childhood: the computerized elms and beeches and oaks that would shed leaves and grow them; or change color with the change of seasons that no longer existed, except in the memory banks of Mother, the Mistress-Computer. How I loved you, immortal trees immune to mildew or borers or blight; and though your fallen leaves would melt at the first touch of the sun, yourselves safe forever from the greed of men.

But I could no longer dream my way out when the final terror began. An impact of stone that would send me sprawling, but no stone when I looked down. The harsh cry of a bird that would make me leap, but no bird when I gazed upward. The shadow of a cloud, turning sunlight to shade and leaving me chilled, but no cloud above me. The wail of a wolf in a place where no wolf had ever ranged. The voice of my little Jacob crying my name and his, though I knew, hearing it, that he must be dead.

It is the radiation, I told myself, the plutonium, uranium and curerium-2 of the prospectors' tall stories. It is the sun on my uncovered head, I said to myself next, the glare and dazzle playing tricks with my eyes. These are mirages, I assured myself then, which everyone has always seen in deserts; distorted reflections from earth to cloud to earth of things which exist elsewhere. Or perhaps, I thought, they are hallucinations, caused by the Leary-um-D which M-M must have dropped onto the tip of my tongue as I slept. Everyone knows that Hypsies drug the unwary "straight dudes" they lure into their tents with promises of sex. Just as everyone knows that Gypsies steal babies, Amerindians get hope-lessly drunk on the smell of a bar rag and Upper Columbian Males have the longest cocks in the world.

Or could it be, I speculated further, the effect of some jimsonweed I must have swallowed without knowing it, when I stumbled two days ago into a patch of it? Or is it a series of 3-D lasar projections, tuned into my Electro-Neural Grid by the Me-ta-Technicians, for ends known only to themselves? Or by the enemies of the Meta-Technicians, for reasons even more myster-ious? After all, it might be just nerves. Or magic, whatever that is. Or demonic possession. Or something I ate. There are always ways not just of explaining, but of explaining *away* such things, are there not, patient reader; perhaps more of them in your time than even in ours. But none of them helped then, since the world around me continued to seem crooked, askew. And everything in it howled and gibbered and shrieked, not just birds and beasts and reptiles, but cactus and furze and gravel and stone. And, after a bit, so did I.

Only sleep was a refuge; for whatever troubled me then, I did not remember when I awoke, feeling always somehow refreshed and glad for the first instant of awareness to be seeing the dawn again, the beginning of a new day. But then my waking nightmare resumed. And so I found myself sleeping longer and longer each day, opening my eyes to a sun higher and higher in the sky; until one day I rose to discover it at its meridian, and the next barely above the horizon. This time, however, the twilight was of dusk rather than dawn. *Good,* I told myself, *it is a sign which I shall heed: a message from somewhere letting me know that I must travel at night.*

Indeed, I had thought of doing so from the start; but it had seemed to me even worse to have to sleep in the glare of the naked sun than to walk beneath it. And there had been for three, four, five, maybe six days (it was hard, after a while, to keep track), no shade, no shelter. Nor could I dig myself any kind of refuge with the tools I had brought along to unearth the buried manuscript. My Auto-Digger was of the type able to bore only through sand or clay, not solid rock; since, if the projected map of the Meta-Technicians had not misled me, that was the nature of the soil at the mouth of the Priest's cave.

But the terrain had already begun to change on the lap before my longest sleep. And the next night I could see, by the light of a moon approaching full, a gentler landscape around me: a new kind of countryside in which clumps of dwarf trees alternated with humps and hillocks of sand. The only rock was an occasional outcropping, sometimes high enough to cast a shadow in which I could stretch out at full length. As close to sunrise as I could manage, I would camp under such rocks or trees: digging myself a deep hole, like some burrowing beast, and curling up for my day's nap on my self-inflating rubberoid mattress. Occasionally I would be roused from my slumber by an actual beast snuggling down beside me; and once or twice, a snake—to whom my hole must have been more of a trap than a place of refuge—fell in on top of me, slithering in panic across my face.

But on the whole, things worked better at night than during the day, for there was, after dark, a kind of fitful breeze. Moreover, the absence of sunlight helped heal my blistered lips and the burn on the back of my neck, which had failed to respond to the medication I had brought with me for such purposes. Finally, I was spared the reflected glare that had kept me half-blind from morning to late afternoon; and the sweat no longer ran constantly into my eyes, nor dripped annoyingly from the end of my nose. Even my cumbersome backpack, overloaded with my mattress, medicine kit, digging equipment, dehydrated food and especially the reams of paper I had felt obliged to bring, seemed if not lighter, at least not quite so galling where the straps passed under my arms. The reduced size of the load in its Perdurium sack had deluded me into believing that it would be easier to tote than it proved. But Shrinko Bags, though they reduce bulk by molecular rearrangement, do not diminish weight. I suspect in fact that the reverse may be true, though, of course, the Commercials they sponsor do not admit it.

If only there had been water: real water, bubbling up out of the earth to form a pool, or trickling down the face of a rock in a miniature cascade, instead of a chemical compound concocted in a folding metal cup, tasting of rust and chlorine. Somehow, knowing that what you drink is not rain from the clouds but H_2O prepared in a chemist's retort leaves your real thirst unquenched—the thirst which, after a while, is more of the spirit than of the flesh. But even if there had been water, there was still the horror to confront. To be sure, it was different at night, but fear dogged me even then.

With the shift from daylight to dark, the noises that plagued me would stop. And for a while, it seemed a sufficient blessing just to be free of the grunting and yelping and howling and screaming of creatures panicked by a world gone utterly *wrong*. But before long, the unmitigated, unbroken silence palled, too; since not merely the cries which had terrified me, but all sounds had ceased, except for that of my own faltering footsteps and my own labored breath. When I stopped and suspended my breathing, however, I could often perceive, or perhaps only fancy I perceived, on the margin of hearing, the faintest of susurrations—almost inaudible yet at the same time all-pervading, vast. As if the earth, or something larger than the earth, were exhaling and inhaling. Sometimes, however, I could not hear even that; only feel the silence, thick as blood, as honey, as mud, as cooling lava.

Meanwhile, all around me there were shapes and forms, tantalizingly familiar, though remote at first, hovering on the periphery of sight as the susurration hovered on the margin of hearing. But as the nights passed, they drew closer and closer to me, or rather I seemed to draw closer and closer to them. I had the sense, though in fact my pace did not alter, of moving ever faster: like a child whose step quickens until, without knowing it, he is running in an effort to catch up with some heedless adult. When I drew near enough, I could see they were naked, these compellingly real forms, which yet, I realized on some level, did not exist at all. And their backs were always to me.

I never saw them as if from in front or in profile, but only from the rear. And after a bit, I recognized them by their bare buttocks: the huge and glistening black nates of Megan, the meager golden-brown rump of Marcia, Melissa-Melinda's generous ass, pale and freckled, the muscled no-nonsense backside of my mother. There were others as well who came and went, while these constituted a

101

kind of unchanging cadre: all of them women whom I had known casually or well, with the exception of one tight boyish behind, which I knew must be that of my small Jacob. But how he had grown since I saw him last, being now tall and skinny, surely a head taller than I.

I never, as I say, believed for a moment that they were really there. Yet I could not help feeling that the flesh before me would respond to my touch, seeming not ghostly or airy, but solid, togged toward the earth by a gravity even greater than ours. And I grew excited, I confess it, watching those bodies apparently grosser than my own, those buttocks I loved, highlighted by the sheen of a Desert moon. What turned me rigid and swollen, however, was something different from any desire I had known before: a longing conscious that it could never be satisfied; an intolerable tumescence aware that it could never explode into pleasure, or subside to rest.

Finally, I was able to stand it no longer. Squatting down on a great polished slab of black stone, basalt or agate, I grabbed my penis in one hand, bracing myself with the other, the pàlm flat on the ground; and masturbated once, twice, three times, so quickly I scarcely believed it. I had forgotten where I was, who had sent me, what I was seeking; knowing only the tension that racked me like dying itself; then the momentary relief as my warm seed spurted into the air; then the tension again. But I woke from my trance, fell back out of my ecstasy, when only dry spasms shook me on my fourth try, each spasm an unendurable pang. My penis was sore, rubbed raw by my cracked and calloused palm. My semen had dried to a scum on the back of my hand. And above me, the moon looked on in apparent mockery, perfectly round. At that precise moment, I realized then, it must at last be full, though I had thought so for the two nights before; and its circular face was the face of an enemy.

"What am I doing?" I cried, breaking the silence with speech, as it occurred to me I had not done in all the time since my night marches had begun. And at the sound of my words, the naked bodies, the phantasms, the projections of my anguish and fear, vanished forever.

Able, then, to deal with something besides my own terror, I consulted the map in my head, letting myself hear again the voice of the Signalman recite in replay the landmarks en route, the coordinates of the cave. Checking the data he had supplied against the features of the landscape I could begin to make out, for it was dawn, I realized that scarcely more than a day's—or rather, a night's—journey separated me from the place of the Scrolls. My heart pounding in excitement as my legs buckled, I flung myself down without digging a hole. I was too exhausted even to unpack my inflatable mattress; my body worn to the point of collapse by the long march of thirteen, or was it fourteen days, and the multiple orgasms of just a few minutes before. It took me forever, it seemed, to fall asleep. And I awoke, unrefreshed, long before sunset, to find my head full of fantasies, madder, I fear, than the nightmare visions which had plagued me, though more hopeful.

I forced myself to lie still until the afterglow faded from the western sky; but my eyes kept opening against my will, and I could not relax. I would need to recoup my strength, I knew, for the final lap and what must follow: the deep exploration of the subsoil, and the delicate excavation of a manuscript too fragile perhaps even to lift from its hiding place. Would I have to read it *in situ*, projecting it line by line onto a screen suspended above it, and unrolling it as I went with calipers more sensitive than any human hand? In any case, there was no hurry now, since twelve hours would make little difference to the state of a parchment already twenty-five hundred years old.

Once full darkness had come and I had risen to my feet, however, I must have doubled the pace at which I had been moving till then; for by midnight I found myself on the crest of a long, easy slope which I had been climbing for an hour or more. And there before me, distinctly outlined in the light of a moon almost as bright as that of the previous night, was the cave and the bank of sand I had seen in the 3-D projection of the Meta-Technicians. When I broke into a run, however, trying to hurl myself over that crest and down into the hollow I had toiled toward through so much grief, eager to be there at last, to be done—I found myself hurled backward hard enough to set me tumbling head over heels.

But by what? A sudden gust of wind of more than hurricane strength? No branch moved or needle quivered on the scrub pines that grew along the spine of the ridge. A double force field, invisible and unbreachable, like those which fenced in the predators at the extraterrestrial zoos? Nothing registered on my Infrared Scanner when I lifted it to my eye, nor did the pointer of my Radiation Counter budge when I held it as close to the unseen barrier as I could.

I would try again, I decided, whatever the cause—but this time at full speed and with the strength added by desperation. Once more, however, I was repelled; though it seemed now as if something were holding me back from behind rather than stopping me from in front, as if I had reached the limits of an invisible leash. But I was not yet discouraged. I would make a third and final attempt, I told myself, and only if this failed, too, would I sit down and figure things out. Perhaps I should have done so to begin with, but how could I sit with the cave in full sight; seeming through the clear air (on this side of the hill, there was no haze at all) close enough to reach out and touch. So once more I rose to my feet, and. . . .

I must have dropped in my tracks and slept before I could act, since the attempt I began waking, I finished in dreams; hurling myself again and again and again, I thought, against that unbreachable barrier. It was an effort which turned imperceptibly into the struggle to extricate myself from sleep and a series of new nightmare horrors in which I seemed at first to be tossed back and forth by creatures too huge to be seen as a whole, yet who tittered and screamed like children at play. Then I felt myself spread-eagled by powers without substance or form, who grabbed my arms and legs, tugging and hauling until it seemed as if my joints would be unhinged. And all the while, they whimpered and moaned, as if for me who suffered—or themselves who had to inflict such suffering.

I say "at first" and "then," because I can only relate serially events which occurred in my dream simultaneously and, as it were, forever. Neither torment, I am trying to say, occurred once and for all, but both over and over. Over and over and over, until the sky which seemed to be not only above, but also beneath and before and behind all of us, splintered and cracked with the noise of thunder. And I was alone. Falling. Falling. Falling . . .

I suppose I must have rocked back and forth in my troubled sleep, as I always do when I am deeply distressed, but this time crashing again and again into a great granite boulder at whose foot I found myself in a pool of blood when I awoke. There were welts on my forearms and thighs, and a trickle of blood ran still from each nostril into the corners of my mouth. Every bone, muscle and tendon in my body ached; but it was the little finger of my left hand which pained most: the flesh swollen almost to bursting, from the ring, which was red-hot, to the blackened nail.

Yet it seemed to me worth it when I discovered that during my sleep I had somehow rolled over the crest of the hill and lay now on the other side of the barrier. I took first one tentative step forward, then another, and another—hardly daring to believe that I could move ahead without hindrance. I was incredibly tired, more tired really than before my strange nonsleep. But calling up my last reserves of strength, I ran down the slope to the mouth of the cave and threw myself upon the spot where, if the Meta-Technicians had not deceived me, the Priest's manuscript was buried. For five minutes, ten minutes, I lay on that long-sought site, panting and exhausted, but as fierce in my vigil as a mother protecting a threatened child with her body.

Looking up finally, I could see, only a few feet from where I was lying, a small pool which I did not remember from the map of the Signalman; and I could not resist. Without even pausing to wonder when it had first bubbled up out of the earth—in the two millennia and a half between the concealment of the Scroll and the decoding of the signal from Outer Space, or in the couple of weeks of my journey—I shucked off the filthy tatters of my tunic and plunged in. What I dived into was yellow and sluggish, more mud than water really, and it stank of sulfur; but I wallowed in it like a sea creature returned to his element, and when I flung myself up on its bank, I felt clean.

I was not disconcerted by its unforeseen temperature, though it proved to be warmer than blood, as warm almost as the sultry air around me. Nor was I put off by the constant throbbing of its oily surface, which heaved and bubbled and broke to iridescence, dissolving the encrusted grime on my skin and soothing the universal ache of my joints. Afterward, I lay in the slant light of the rising sun until I was dry and sleep had taken me once more without warning.

I woke just after noon feeling refreshed and knowing exactly where I was and what I must do, knowing somehow that from now on all would go off without a hitch. And it did. I set my Infrared Scanner for the depth I had inferred from the laser projection, a depth which turned out to be right within half a centimeter; for there on my screen, first shot, was a blip indicating a mass of about the right size. Then I adjusted my Auto-Digger to stop some fifty centimeters short of that point, aware that the final clearing away must be done by an old-fashioned whisk broom held in experienced fingers. The dirt which the Digger removed made a pile seven or eight meters high; and sifting through samples taken at various stages, I discovered no trace of the dampness, the ground seepage that even in the Desert could have reduced the Priest's parchment Scrolls to illegible pulp.

I was confident now, but taking no chances; so that the moment the Digger signaled it had reached its preset limit, I filled the hole, as well as the air in and around it, with a colloidal suspension of Eternoplast droplets. How hard it is to believe that the sunlit air on which we thrive means instant death to treasures preserved against time by the airless dark; yet it is the archaeologist's first lesson. Waiting then the half hour required to fix the Eternoplast coating, to marry its molecules forever to those of the parchment, painfully and gently I brushed away the remaining cover of dirt. Then slowly, cautiously, I drew forth the double Scroll.

Its original wrappings had long since decayed, leaving only a few scraps of blue vegetable fiber and some shreds of silver filigree. But the parchment itself, though darkened a little by the passage of years, was not only intact, but still supple; and I could see at a glance that the characters with which it was inscribed were legible. Legible! Embracing the Scrolls in my arms like a Mistress, a Bride, I knelt on the ground in the posture of prayer; though I know no prayers, nor any power, except in myself, to whom I might pray.

I must at that point have fallen asleep again, my almost-prayer at the very verge of my lips; for I woke just before dawn to find myself still on my knees, but fallen forward so that my bent torso protected the precious Scrolls and my forehead rested on the ground. I could not have said whether I had slept for just a few hours, or through the whole succeeding day and most of the following night. Waking, I knew only that my head was clear, though my limbs still felt cramped and aching. The finger on which I wore the ring throbbed unbearably, as if the blood were trying to burst through the lacerated skin; and the circulation in my legs seemed to have stopped entirely. When I rose and tried, tentatively, to move them, I toppled over again, face downward. My whole body throbbed now in rhythm with the little finger of my left hand, as wave after wave of pain moved from the soles of my feet to the top of my skull, making me wish I could faint, or even die. It was as if a gigantic fist crushed and released, crushed and released my poor body—absentmindedly, I found myself thinking, rather than in deliberated malice. And I could not lose consciousness.

"Please," I said, "please," though I did not know whom I addressed. And I touched, feeling it a ritual act, the index finger of my right hand to the ring, which I could see was encrusted with blood. At this, the pain grew mild enough for me to get to my feet and plunge again (I was naked still) into the sluggish pond, which refreshed me a little more. It seemed, however, to have grown, since my first immersion, more metallic and heavy, a bit colder, perhaps. And the recurrent pulse that moved its sullen waters pushed harder against my sides, not so much laving my body this time as lifting it half into the air at each surge, as if trying to disgorge me. Despite the remission of pain, I grew progressively less comfortable, even finally afraid; so that I ceased fighting to keep myself under and let one last, slow heave cast me up onto the muddy bank. I lay for a long time in the tepid ooze, trying desperately to fill my lungs with the air which seemed to have changed, too; becoming thick, viscous, almost suffocating. Or maybe it was only that I had momentarily lost the knack (as I could remember having happened during my earliest years, though never since I had reach maturity) of breathing unconsciously, needing instead to will each suspiration, and having to struggle to establish a rhythm in sync with the motion of my blood and the beating of my heart.

At last, however, I succeeded in overcoming my strange hypoventilation enough so that I was able to pick up the Scrolls and stagger back into the cave, which turned out to be cool and dry, with a high vaulted roof and a floor of fine, faintly luminous sand. The morning sun defined an arc of brightness at its mouth: a kind of vestibule, reaching perhaps a third of the way back toward the rear wall. I could make out in the dimness an opening in that wall wide enough for a not very wide man to squeeze through. But though I am, in fact, just such a not very wide man, I was too weary to do more than walk to the back of the cave and thrust my arm in as far as it would go.

Though my legs had grown almost supple again, and even my ring finger merely throbbed and itched, just making the twenty or thirty paces it took to reach that cleft left me trembling and covered with cold sweat. My heart was pounding almost loud enough to drown out the subdued roar I could hear now through the cleft: the noise, I presumed, of an underground river. But I could feel only the brush of what must have been a wing, at which I clutched in desperation, not quite knowing why. I caught nothing, of course, though a frantic fluttering and thumping followed, then a twittering as of bats; and, on my side of the cleft, the dry rustling of what must have been hordes of insects. I could not see them in the half-light, but the sound was unmistakable; and I felt somehow comforted by such evidence of other life, however minute and alien and invisible.

I could no longer put off sleeping, I knew, even as I bent to place the Scrolls near the mouth of the cave, where the first light of dawn would touch them. I wanted desperately to unroll them, to begin. But I could no longer keep my eyes open. *As soon as my strength allows,* I assured myself, *I will unpack, sort out my dictionaries, find paper and pens. And when I am able, I will start my translation. After all, there is no hurry now. What has waited for twenty-five hundred years can wait a little while longer. If only I live.*

But I did not doubt really that I would survive—not at the level of dreams anyhow. No, even with the icy sweat running down my face and my heart thumping hard enough to trouble my sleep, I dreamed a glorious climax to my adventures. I stood on the platform of some Great Hall, reading aloud to row after row of enraptured listeners my completed translation. The Meta-Technicians sat in the front seats, their mysterious Superiors in darkened boxes on either side of the auditorium. And the rest of the world, the rulers and the ruled, the truly curious and the merely dutiful (was Megan among them? or my son?), sat packed shoulder to shoulder in the tiers that sloped upward toward invisible balconies. From time to time, cries of admiration and wonder would half-drown my words; and I would pause to acknowledge them with a smile or a nod.

But it was not only such childish fantasies which sustained my belief that I *had* to live long enough to finish my version of the Scrolls, which the Meta-Technicians would not otherwise be able to read. Like all proper Futurists, they make a point of their illiteracy, thus distinguishing themselves from the nostalgic and literate Priests who worship the past. Nor would the Simplex Audio-Print Transformers, which translate directly from printed page to spoken voice, as well as from language to language, have been of much use. Though they are available in the archives of all meta-urban clusters, none of them has been programmed to render into their auditor's native tongue texts written in the banned languages of the Forbidden Cults, chief among which is the Ancient Religion of Israel.

I was unsure whether the Meta-Technicians had promised to come to me when my quest was achieved, or whether they had directed me to find my way back to the *tel* beside which they had first told me of my mission. But weak as I was, I could not have retraced my frightful journey in any case. No, I told myself, it would be as much as I could manage simply to stay where I was and write—hoping meanwhile that, in this refuge hollowed out of living rock, this sanctuary from solar heat and lunar madness, I would, however slowly, recoup my strength. Then, if ever, would be time enough to think of travel.

Meanwhile, I must begin to take care of myself: to eat and drink regularly, for instance; and to establish again the routine of sleeping and waking by which most men are accustomed to pattern their lives. I had not taken food, I realized, for days; and for almost as long, I had drunk water only, on which the body thrives but the spirit is undernourished. My Perdurium sack contained enough supplies for another month at least, perhaps two, if I rationed them carefully. And so I moistened a little compressed and dehydrated bread, real wheaten bread for which I have an old-fashioned taste, with a few drops of the genuine grape wine, which I carried with me for similar nostalgic reasons; and I broke my fast. My throat closed, however, at the first mouthful, so that I heaved it up again in a puddle of bile. But when the dry retching which followed had stopped, I tried again and again; until, on the third attempt, I was successful. *I will live,* I told myself, the benediction of the wine mounting toward my head, *because I must.* Then unrolling the First Scroll, carefully, carefully, I began.

THE FIRST SCROLL

of

ELIEZAR ben YAAKOV ha-KOHEN

(written A.D. *4—*

translated by Jacob Mindyson

A.D. *2501)*

I remember still how it hung in the western sky, brighter than any star, brighter than the sun rising through the haze that hovered about the surrounding hills. But I do not remember when it came exactly,[1] whether in the earliest spring, as the astrologers claim; or at the midwinter solstice, as those mythologues assert who seek to assimilate all extraordinary events to the approach and retreat of the sun. I remember only hearing first of the event from certain farmers and sheepherders who were watching all night for wolves or changes in the weather, or whatever it is that such folk seek in the darkness. And they, of course, took that ship from beyond the stars as a star itself, a new star, and, therefore, a sign and a portent.

What else could it portend in a time of oppression to those who did not know that all times are times of oppression, except the coming of the Anointed One, that superman, man-god on a white horse; whom they, in despite of our admonitions, expected momentarily to deliver them from their suffering and ennui. How could they acknowledge what we Priests dare not ever deny: that there is no salvation from suffering and ennui except *other* suffering and ennui; plus, of course, the endless waiting which is our vocation. Not prayer and sacrifice which the people demand of us, and for which they support us in what seems to their poverty shameless plenty, but waiting for what can never come yet must be expected forever: this is our excuse for being.

For them, however, every day brings the promise of a new savior, another Son of David, Son of Man, Son of God—among

[1] Eliezar gives no indication of the year of which he is talking; but it is clear that the events described occurred at the beginning of the Roman Empire in the reign of Augustus: the start of what we call still—deprived of all religious connotation—the Christian Era.

whom we scarcely noticed at first the child [2] whose birth or conception was signaled by the coming of the spaceship. Birth *and* conception, I suppose I should say, for in his case those two events occurred simultaneously. Indeed, for the Messenger, the Malaach, who was his father, time is perceived only as one among the many illusions by which we all live here below, Priests and peasants alike.

But we Priests, having talked to the Messengers and to the Elim, the Masters who dispatch them, understand such matters a little; unlike the ignorant to whom Elim is merely one name among the many used to call on the Nameless One who created Eretz and Shamaim, the Heavens and the Earth. And the Messengers they consider similarly supernatural creatures, whose ships must consequently be taken for new stars announcing messages of hope. As if the Eternal had no other concern than broadcasting to us here below timely forecasts and warnings.

Yet we Priests are forbidden by ancient contract to tell what we know to our own people. And we must consequently endure the indignity—we who, since time began, have been manipulating the Urim and Tumim, to talk with the Elim, to call the Messengers—of being treated as mere hackers and burners of beasts. These days we scarcely dare, lest we be considered derelict, leave the Temple: that gaudy House of Worship, taken over by candlemongers, souvenir sellers and changers into our own money of the beads, feathers, shells and unworked ingots which the outlanders bring into our midst, to buy a blessing or to ensure the birth of male children.

Meanwhile, we long only to escape from the public ceremonies (I, at least, like my father and his father and his father's father, though not my accursed sons) to the Sanctuary, where without words we communicate with the Masters of Space and Time: learning to prepare our people for the fate, which, the Elim say, awaits them: the burning and pillage of the Temple and the

---

[2] Though Eliezar does not ever mention his name, quite clearly "the child" is that Yehoshuah, or Jesus, whom the Christian Churches in their heyday considered the Messiah or even God Incarnate. For several centuries after the founding of those Churches, Jewish scribes—either out of superstition or to avoid being charged with blasphemy—avoided writing his name; sometimes substituting the conventional code name Balaam, or, as in Eliezar's case, avoiding it completely.

scattering of their seed in alien lands. There, it appears, our last descendants, having forgotten their Past, will invent the Future, invent Science. I do not understand what that "Science" will be, except that it involves formulae rather like those of the Pharaoh's magicians, by whose aid humans will make ships resembling the vessels of the Messengers—ships for crossing space and time.

Not we Jews alone, who have been Chosen [3] by the Elim, but even the *goyim,* who believe in their bodies and love to pull levers, will be able to move thus, as freely as the Messengers themselves. Yet maybe in the end we will prove to be Chosen still: chosen, unlike the heathen, to move through the Cosmos without machines, to *think* ourselves from place to place, moment to moment. But this, of course, we can do even now; and indeed (why am I, even in my ninth decade, so slow to comprehend?) all "prophecies" of the Elim have served only to tell us that the future is no more than the present actualized, i.e., fully known.[4]

But why we, who were slaves, were Chosen in the first place remains a mystery. If, indeed, we were ever slaves to the High King, and there were ever such a ruler over a Swamp Kingdom, the Mitzraim of which our tradition teaches. It may well be, as the Elim sometimes suggest, that the whole pseudo history of our Enslavement and our Going Out [5] is a self-serving lie, or at best a parable. But what then of Aaron and Moshe and Maryam, the first my presumed ur-ancestor, and the others the brother and sister with whom he had so much trouble: the angry one who was not permitted to enter into our Holy Land, and the vixen finally smitten with leprosy for her spite. The Elim are always trying to deprive us of whatever in our past is attributable not to them but to

---

[3] The notion of the Chosen People, though it sustained first the Hebrews and then their descendants, the Jews, in times of trouble, became finally a stumbling block to them; a weapon in the arsenal of their enemies, who tried throughout history to destroy them—as if to prove that it was really *they* who were chosen.

[4] There is a certain antirationalist bias—before the invention of rationalism—in this Priest, which leads him not just here, but throughout his account, to needless and annoying mystification.

[5] The Arch-Priest refers here to the central story of the so-called Five Books of Moses, the first five sections of the Hebrew Scriptures, which tell of the enslavement of the Ancient Israelites in Egypt and their escape under the leadership of Moses and Joshuah to Palestine, which they then conquered by force. A bloody and unedifying story!

the Nameless One, the ur-Father who made us a nation of Priests long before the first Messengers came. It is envy which moves them, for they are ridden by passions baser than those which possess us humans.

Have I not myself met and spoken to travelers returning from Mitzraim, who have climbed to the top of the giant tombs our forefathers helped to build; and watched from there the descendant of the Great King carried in a jewel-encrusted barge down the Great River, which each year swallows the land and disgorges it again at the will of the Cow Goddess they adore? It was the image of that Goddess in the form of a golden heifer which Maryam persuaded Aaron to set up in the desert, convincing him that the fire of YHVH had consumed their brother—and that the Father having turned his face aside, they must seek favor from the Mother.[6]

But travelers also lie; indeed, who can distinguish fact from fancy even in those zealously guarded records set down by his father's father's fathers? Some matters we must accept on faith, but in the realm of probability it is advisable to choose the more probable over the less. And is it not most likely that we were initially Chosen precisely because we alone in the world bathed by the Inner Sea did not bow down to the Cow Goddess?

Everywhere around us the nations enjoined their daughters to fuck on the lintel of their temples no matter what stranger willing to proffer a penny to the priests of the White One. Everywhere around us, those already deballed priests cut off with a silver sickle, representing the moon, the balls of acolytes, doomed thereafter to watch without sharing the sacred orgy on their doorstep. Everywhere around us, weeping mothers offered to the open mouth, the gnashing teeth and lolling tongue of the Dark One their own babies.

But we rejected all three abominations: temple prostitution, castration of the priesthood (among us, no one who is not fully a man can preside at the altar), infant sacrifice. And we forbade our women to go out into the fields like beasts in quest of beasts; even

---

[6] Here begins the major theme, the obsessive concern of Eliezar, who the reader should be warned cannot be taken without caution when he purports to describe the Cult of the Great Mother, about which, in fact, there is little reliable information.

as we forbade them to choose from among their number a god-dess-surrogate who would ride down, bare-bottomed and panting, a score of men prone in the first furrow turned by the plow, in order to ensure the return of the wheat.

It is for this rejection that the Elim first chose us, as they like to remind me whenever we speak together. I say "speak," though we communicate without words. I touch the Urim and Tumim in the prescribed fashion. The Elim respond by touching the knobs or foci of possibility which correspond to knobs in a world where there is no disjunction between things in themselves and the awareness of things.[7]

Sometimes the Elim are, how shall I say, loose-lipped, indis-creet; as if—to put it in earthly terms—they had drunk too much wine. And at such moments they tend to betray secrets, sure, perhaps, that their human interlocutor is too gross to understand; and in any case convinced that they have nothing to fear, since there is nothing we can do to change their plans. On such an occasion, I first learned of the War which is their central concern: the age-long conflict between the segment of space they have preempted, and another possessed or controlled by beings who correspond in ways I do not pretend fully to understand to what are called in our world women. They do not always refer to those Others specifically as female, sometimes calling them Darkness, Evil, even Nothing. But when they are most unguarded, or most befuddled by rage, which seems to operate for them as chemical intoxicants do for us, they say unmistakably: "Cows," "Bitches," "Cunts."

Once, one of the Masters hinted that the very existence of sexuality, as well as the consequent conflict of the sexes, on what they insist on calling the third satellite of the sun, is only a byproduct of their larger Cosmic War.

"But the earth which I inhabit by right and on which you are an intruder," I was moved to protest, "was created *before* the sun by the Ancient of Days whom you refuse to acknowledge, though only by his permission could you be here."

[7] At moments like this, one is tempted to believe that the rhetoric of the Arch-Priest conceals not secrets too lofty for ordinary language, but merely his own pretechnological ignorance.

"I am not 'here,' " he answered. "Not anywhere, which is to say, not in any 'where' you could possibly comprehend."

"The point is irrelevant," I rejoined. "What I am trying to say is that from the beginning, we have been—"

"I will tell you a story," he said, "a kind of bedtime story or nursery tale, of which your people seem inordinately fond. And you must write it down, as we have taught you to write, relieving you of the burden of memory. Then you can add it to what you call, having no other, *the* Book."

"I am not a child," I responded, "but an ancient servitor grown gray attempting to satisfy two unreconcilable wills, and I shall not—"

"Write," he cut me off again. "Listen and write, so that later you or your sons will be able to say, as you love to do: 'It is written.' Are you ready?"

His "voice" had, as it were, risen; which is to say, had become an almost intolerable pain at the base of my skull; but I did not answer, simply let him continue.

"Write," he went on: " 'In the beginning the Elim created the male alone, calling his name Adam.' " 8

This I could not abide, crying out, "You say what is not so; for it is already written, 'Male and female created he them.' And this means, first"—I paused, ticking the point off on my middle finger, about which we are accustomed to wrap the strap of our phylacteries—"we were not created in the beginning at all, | but | on the sixth day. And second, created in his own image not by you but by the One whose Name is four-fold, signifying male-female/male-female." 9

"Speak then the name of the One who is four, being twice

8 The somewhat tedious rigmarole which follows is a possible explanation of a problem which concerned scholars who were also Christians or Jews from the eighteenth century to the twenty-second: namely, the fact that in the Creation story which begins the Scriptures of the Jews, there are not only contradictory items (a statement, for instance, that man was made before woman, alongside an assertion of their simultaneous creation); but the name of their Creator is sometimes given as JHVH (Jehovah?), sometimes ELHM (Elohim?). I have taken the liberty of shortening Eliezar's account drastically.

9 An esoteric point probably not worth, from any practical point of view, even explaining. But certain mystics among the Jews associated the *heh* (H), which is the second and fourth letter of the "Holy Name," with the female; the first and the third, *yod* (Y) and *vav* (V),

male and female. Tell me, please, his name," the El challenged, a familiar gambit. "What is he called?"

"He is called nothing. He has no name. And this you know well who forget nothing."

"What has no name does not exist," the El responded. "Blot out the lying text and write instead: 'And the Elim created man out of the dust of the ground and called his name Adam after the dust from which he was made.' Only what is named exists. Dust exists, man exists. Write."

"What is written cannot be expunged," I said. "The text is forever: 'Male and female created he them.' "

"And so he did," the El responded, "as you can see by looking over your own shoulder. For behind you are female—curved and penetrable, alluring to other males—whatever you may be before. As one of our first Messengers discovered, when, assuming the guise of a human male, he aroused the lust of the catamites of Sodom and Gomorrah. Only in this sense are you double; which is to say, like us, the Elim, to whom all things are possible, sexually as well as metaphysically."

"All things but love," I rejoined; for I could hear the other Elim making their equivalent of a titter.

"Love is not a name, old joker," the El answered, "and therefore does not exist. Only fucking and being fucked. Fear the Elim, for that is the beginning and end of wisdom."

It is useless to try to argue with them, bullies that they are, leaving me always feeling like a twelve-year-old who has challenged his father. But like such a twelve-year-old, I did not know how to stop. "But why were we sundered then?" I continued. "Why were our two halves divided in the Garden?" [10] What could I expect but another lie, one more evasion?

"It is because she who is called in your legends Lilith straddled the lonely Adam in his sleep, riding him like a horse or an ass,

with the male. The basis of all this is childishly obvious; since, written in Hebrew script, the *yod* and *vav* resemble a short and long penis, while the *heh* suggests the shape of the female pudenda.

[10] In order to explain both versions, the J-Version and the E-Version, as they were called by later scholars, the Jewish sages taught that the first human creature was an androgyne, whom later God split down the center.

in order to rouse his flesh for the first time. When he awoke she was gone, but he could behold still in his swollen flesh the first miracle, the only true miracle: the turning of a snake into a rod."

"Stop," I pleaded, covering my ears against the blasphemy, but longing secretly to hear what the El would say next.

"The consequences of all this," he continued, "we could not foresee, since the will of the abominable Other had entered; but we saw it was not good. And so we split down the center the fallen Adam, doomed forever to seek unity with the female—cleft him as he lay exhausted by his first expenditure of seed. At the very moment of separation, however, we lopped from his sundered female half the Serpent which had learned to become a rod; and condemned it to eat dust for all of its days. How could we know that in the ripeness of time it would climb into the branches of the tree which stood in the center of the Garden, and—"

"Enough," I shouted, this time meaning it, "or I will tune you out, shut off our connection forever, as you taught my fathers to do in the beginning." I spoke at a venture, not sure I could accomplish what I threatened; since I had no way of being sure that the Elim had not been deceiving us with the assurance that communication between us could be terminated at will by either party. But I could feel the consternation of my listeners, so I was emboldened to go on. "You yourself have taught me that we were not made of dirt but of the endless play of possibility; that man is a statistical average calculated in a Mind which, as you keep informing me, does not exist. Why do you speak to me now in the language of childhood, the language you have taught me to distrust?"

"It is a parable," the El answered, as always at such a juncture. "Let those with ears hear."

"It is bullshit," I roared, "bullshit from outer space." [10a]

"Which your revered fathers would have called Revelation," the mocking nonvoice continued; but I was already turning the dials. "Turning the dials," I say, knowing that the phrase is only a primitive way of speaking; "actualized certain potentials in the

[10a] The actual Hebrew words of Eliezar at this point are incomprehensible to me—perhaps because they are too obscene and colloquial to have been recorded in lexicons. Assuming this, I give a modern equivalent.

solid-state transmitter," the Elim would have put it. Yet, as I touched the Urim and Tumim, I thought: *"Right. Left. Left. Left. Right,"* like one turning a dial. For one instant I was tempted to add the final *"Left. Left. Right,"* which, I had been told, would cut us off for all eternity; or, to put it another, even more primitive way, kill God. But what does it matter, since any way of saying anything is, according to the Elim, a parable, i.e., bullshit once again.

I did, however, sit down to write, as I had been bidden, the story of Creation, serving as ever two Masters. But to attest my faith in their ultimate unity, I set down both accounts: not attempting to reconcile, but merely intertwining them, regardless of their contradictions. Perhaps I hoped thus to suggest a truth I was not subtle or simple enough to perceive, in a form available to all; even to those I am sometimes tempted to despise, because they believe that we walk beneath an inverted bowl fretted with fire, and that the Nameless One once walked with us in the cool of the evening in the guise of an aged man.

I have, however, played a little trick with my sources by switching the Divine Names in the two accounts, and, as a final twist, adding an "H" to Elim, without which that name would have to be rendered in our vowelless script by three consonants. But four, not three, is the number of Divinity. . . .[11]

Pointless *pilpul,* my father would have said at this point; for he had little patience with etymologies or juggling interpretations of the text. But if the Elim speak the truth, the Jews of the future, forbidden soldiering and agriculture and temple sacrifice, will have to spend their time, lest they perish of ennui, in exegesis of such texts as these. So for them I leave my version of Genesis, along with this garrulous apology. Both arise, I suppose, from my own boredom, which I do not understand; since I have a hundred decisions to make within the next few days, on one of which at least the fate of my entire people may depend.

To refresh myself, then, I will go for a little while into the Sanctuary, though not this time to converse with the Elim. The

[11] I have abbreviated the passage immediately preceding mercilessly, or rather mercifully; but I have left enough of Eliezar's exegetical horseplay to indicate how humorless he in fact is. The priestly vocation is, I fear, inimical to true wit.

eastern wall of that room can, when I choose, be made to "disappear," i.e., the motion of its basic constituents slowed down until the human eye can, as it were, see around, through them. So, at any rate, a Messenger once explained to me, revealing that what I had always regarded as just another wall was, in fact, an "Omni-Directional Space Scanner": their gift to Sholomo ben David on the day he completed the Temple.

I go often to meditate before it, when it is necessary for me to put my concerns into their proper scale; but today the experience promises to be special. It is a Tuesday, which is to say, a day of obligatory fasting: the third consecutive day, as it happens, on which I have gone without eating—not because I had intended thus to sanctify the two days before it, but because in my perplexity over what should be done with the Son of the Messenger, I had forgotten to take any meals. Three days of fasting, however, are sufficient, at my time of life, to induce in me vision and ecstasy. I will, therefore, not be able to tell whether I am seeing or hallucinating the births and deaths of stars in a Cosmos whose unsuspected vastness still creates in me a kind of inebriation.

Never mind. Though out of my rational mind, I shall not forget that I am watching only the image of an image in the mind of the Eternal. And I shall remember, too, that the heavenly bodies I behold are not lights hung in the Firmament to guide us in our wanderings, as my ancestors believed. Only other worlds in which, perhaps, other Arch-Priests are contriving mythologies to make endurable the meaninglessness of things. Consequently, I shall say for them as well as myself—for those among them who pray with me, and those for whom prayer is not yet or never to be invented: *Blessed be the Name that must remain unspoken.*

Rereading what I have written so far, I discover that it is one long digression. But to digress is the habit of old men, forgivable at worst, at best—I am told—actually charming. The trouble is that for too long I have talked only to myself, and I do not demand of myself that I stick to the point. In any case, to whom else can I talk, excepting always the Elim, with whom real conversation is impossible? My sons and my grandsons, my only real peers, are engrossed in the nominal business of the Temple: the examination of birds and beasts to make sure they are fit for the sacrifice; the required ransoming and ritual cutting of newborn males; and especially the delicate negotiations with our oppressors from Overseas, necessary to ensure our survival. I do not blame them, for they are busy with matters which mean profit and loss, if not actual life and death to us all. Moreover, they find my endless chatter not, I suspect, wisdom, but senile maunderings.

Perhaps they are right; for I am less and less aware these days of the difference between seeing and imagining, waking and sleeping—almost, living and dying. It is time, then, to pass on the secrets entrusted to me by the Elim, secrets which can only be told one to one, father to son. Tomorrow, therefore, I shall call to me the oldest of the lot (what is his name? there are so many) and explain to him the nature of the Messengers, the function of the Urim and Tumim, the true status of the Elim, whose pawns we are in that Cosmic War of Super Kings and Queens, which the board game we have inherited from the Swamplanders symbolizes. Perhaps I shall invite him to play a game of Chess with me and begin from there. If I could only believe it matters. If only, at least, I could recall his name.

But it is the spaceship I was writing about, that ship which glowed above our hills for three days and nights, throbbing, throbbing. I can feel it still in my aged bones, like the tremor of an earthquake, the surge of the sea, the beating of my own heart in fear or passion. But I cannot remember the name of the hamlet in the Galil [12] over which it hovered and in which the Boy was born, any more than I can remember the name of my own oldest son. Never mind. These days the followers of the Boy manage to attach his nativity to all the places associated in our Scriptures with the coming of the Anointed One, even inventing for him a journey into Mitzraim, since it is written: "Out of Mitzraim I have called my son."

But at that point, it was only certain tribal chieftains who paid attention to what they took for a celestial beacon; coming out of their mountain fastnesses to see what it might portend. Kings, they called themselves, these idle busybodies; though they ruled

[12] It is, of course, Bethlehem—or, alternatively, Nazareth; the "sacred" text of the Christians being about as contradictory as those of the Jews—as, indeed, the Priest here indicates.

over no one except their sons and daughters, and a handful of poor relatives, feeble-minded or widowed or unmarried, who served as their attendant slaves. And they bore in their hands for the child, whom their Shaman told them they would find, what gifts they could afford: withered fruits and nuts; but chiefly those broken crystals which, cast into the fire, make a fragrant smoke in which the offensive smell of unwashed bodies is lost—the smell of our common mortality blurred to sweet indistinction.

Why do I permit myself to despise them? Barbarians that they are, illiterate as the sheepherders themselves and with no lore, therefore, except certain childish jingles they know by heart, they, too, were hoping for a King of Kings, an end to oppression, a recess from time and history. It is not necessary to love everyone, as the obsequious Essenes advocate, certainly not such paltry kings. But it is better to feel pity than hatred for those who are caricatures of what is best, as well as worst, in ourselves.

In any event, what they found at the end of their quest was the son of an insubordinate Messenger, or should I say rather, the by-blow of that intolerable girl whose name I do not forget: that Maryam [13] through whom the Goddess may yet return, bringing with her temple prostitution, the castration of priests and the sacrifice, yes, the cannibalizing, of infants. I had realized that she would be a problem to us from the moment when her mother, Channah, whom I had known all of my life, brought her for presentation in the Temple, though she was a girl and not really of priestly blood; only collaterally, remotely related to us. It could not, I knew even then, be the doing of that mother herself, a simple woman accustomed to silence before her betters. She must have been put up to it by the child, who watched everything from the sidelines with prematurely, even preternaturally, sharp eyes.

"She will be a prophetess in Israel," Channah said, in the voice of a ventriloquist's dummy. "Like . . ." She paused, at a loss.

"Like Yael or Yehudith," I prompted her. "A woman of blood. A killer."

"Like Deborah," the girl whispered from behind her mother, who repeated the names aloud, "like Ruth and Esther."

[13] The reader must be careful not to confuse the two Maryams (or Miriam and Mary, as we have come to render the names), though the Priest includes both in his contempt: the sister of Aaron, and the Mother of Jesus, born some one or two thousand years later.

"A *shikse,*" I said, referring to Ruth, of course, "and one who married a *goy,*" meaning Esther.

"Say rather the grandmother of kings and the savior of her people," the girl rejoined, speaking for herself at last; and moving as she spoke until she stood against me, the top of her head reaching only to the jewels of my breastplate.

"Be quiet," I shouted her down. "And go home. It is better to be a good wife and mother than a prophetess in Israel."

"I will not be quiet," she answered, losing her lofty tone and becoming the little girl she was. "I will never be quiet. Never. Never. *Never!*" Then, raising her small fists as high as she could, she beat them against my chest.

But taking both of her hands in one of my thick-veined, liver-spotted own, I led her toward the exit, feeling her passion in the pulsing of her blood. I swear from that day I loved her, not as a child, but as a woman. "Go in peace," I said. "And peace go with you."

They departed then; but turning at the door, Channah insisted (afraid, perhaps, of being scolded by her daughter, if she left without the last word), "She will be a prophetess. It is why we called her Maryam."

It is impossible, after all, to deny that the name was well chosen; since her namesake, too, the first Maryam, sister of Moshe and Aaron, was also a troublemaker, a plotter and con-niver, whom the ur-Father blighted in the eyes of men for her refusal to accept the role defined for her by her sex.[14] There is an oral tradition among us that Maryam, in connivance with the Daughter of the High King of Mitzraim, inducted Moshe, our Master, into the mysteries of Isis. And it was the Oracle of that Cow Goddess, legend says further, who urged his marriage to Zipporah, a Black Priestess of the Mother Cult, for whose sake he did not circumcise his sons.

I know there are some who doubt such unwritten traditions. But how else can we make sense of that odd story in Torah about the Messenger who swallowed Moshe down to the navel, and

---

[14] Here also Eliezar's judgments must be taken with a grain of salt; since even his own Holy Books treat the first Maryam, whatever her weakness, as one more to be admired than despised. It is true, however, that she was at one point afflicted with leprosy for plotting against Moses.

would not disgorge him until his wife herself had hacked from their uncircumcised boys the bloody foreskins. From that moment on, the household of Moshe was no longer divided against itself; for the Priestess of Isis had capitulated in performing the ceremony of the *Brith*, the one Commandment of the Father on which all of the others are based.[15]

But the second Maryam, which is to say, our Maryam, has never capitulated—being as inexorable as the Bitter Sea which her name signifies. On that sea we Jews have turned our backs, leaving the governance of ships to the worshipers of the Goddess, and fishing only our inland waters. And so, too, I should have turned my back, while there was yet time, on the girl called with the sea's name. But I could not, G-d have mercy on me; for even as a child she seemed to me desirable. And such is the discrepancy of our ages, she remains for me still a child, or rather a child-woman, whom I yearn for still, though at forty-five she has grown shrill and haggard in the marketplace.

I am aware that we Priests are supposed to be immune to desire, cold by nature, like the first of our line. "As cold as Aaron's balls," the common people say, sniggering, when they think we are not listening. But the Unwritten Tradition hints that Aaron not merely impregnated his wives, as was his duty, with sons to serve at the altar; he also, in pursuit of pleasure, would slip into the tent of his sister to know her.[16] It was, to be sure, a custom among the rulers of the Swampland in which he was raised, for brother and sister to lie shamelessly together; but not custom alone drew him to his Maryam. It must have been, at least in part, her provocation, as it is in part the provocation of her namesake which undoes me, despite fasting and prayer.

Not that she ever confesses the game she is playing; far from it. In public she is icy and indifferent—not only rejecting me,

[15] It is hard to make sense of what remains of this gruesome story in the Jews' Book of Exodus. Apparently, though, it was Moses, who some have agreed was not even a Jew, rather than his surely pagan, and perhaps Black, wife, who resisted the Circumcision, so dear to the Priests. After all, it was the Priests who wrote or compiled all five of the Books of Moses—and they desired desperately to make Moses, actually often hostile to their ancestor Aaron, seem unequivocally on their side.

[16] I am no expert in the ancient lore and tradition; but this seems to me clearly a canard, a slanderous lie—told by one willing to say anything to promote the patriarchal cause.

which is, after all, proper, but any man able to possess her, including such as come seeking her hand in marriage. But this is, in the light of our Law, a sin worse than lust. From the start, however, she seemed determined to remain forever virgin. And it was in the name of that determination that she asked finally to be wed *nominally only* to Old Yussef: an impoverished carpenter left by a series of faithless wives with ten or twelve children, none his own; since for as long as anyone can remember he has been impotent.

It is now three decades or more since I first learned of Maryam's perverse resolution. She had just reached fifteen, an age at which most good Jewish girls already have a baby at the breast, but she showed still no inclination to marry. And so I called her to me to remonstrate with her, being not only her spiritual adviser but, as it were, an elder kinsman. "I need scarcely remind you," I began, "who boast, I believe, of your learning, that the First Commandment, given long before the other Ten, is 'Go forth and multiply and replenish the earth.' That law is incumbent not just on the Jews, since it was promulgated before our separation from the Nations, but on everyone not incapacitated in its performance by the will of G-d." [17]

We were sitting in the Great Vestibule, I remember, I on the High Seat, from which I had resolved not to descend lest I be tempted to touch her, she on a low stool I had set at a safe distance from my feet. But she rose and moved toward me with her first response. "It is not written," she said in a voice like velvet, "that the first Maryam, my namesake and model, ever bore any children at all. It was enough for her to care for her brothers. And therefore, I, too, am resolved to bear no children in the flesh, but to care for the offspring of the old carpenter, Yussef, whom I have chosen to wed precisely because he can never force me to break my vow. Surely this is no sin."

"To travesty marriage is the worst of sins," I told her, "not just against G-d, but against Nature as well. You are a young woman, comely and well made. . . ." I could not forbear looking,

---

[17] I write "G-d," without the vowel, to give a sense in our tongue of the pains Eliezar, like all his orthodox coreligionists, goes to in order not to take the Holy Name "in vain." Absurd scruple!

as I paused, at her breasts, clearly designed to suckle many, and to pillow the head of him who fathered them. "You have many fertile years before you, and therefore you must—"

But she would not hear me out. "I will suffer no husband to spill my maiden blood in the name of a Commandment," she cried, "not even if it be the First. I will be a Mother without being a wife, a Virgin Mother,[18] intact. I will belong to no one but myself and G-d."

I should have suspected by then that though she said "G-d," it was the Goddess she meant, to whom alone the notion of a Virgin Mother is neither blasphemous nor foolish. But she had placed her hands on my knees even as she made her case—perhaps at the prompting of that Goddess whom she secretly adored, perhaps only in response to what of the Goddess is embodied in every woman.

Then I was aware only that I needed to remove her hands from my body but could not; and so I rose to my feet to conceal my trembling. "Even as your husband will have shed his blood in the Circumcision, so you must be willing to shed yours in the sacrifice of your maidenhead," I managed to go on. "Only so can the Glory of the Everlasting be revealed, and the Ancient of Days enter into his Shekhinah." Ordinarily I am suspicious of such phrases, the cant of mysticism; but in my experience I have found them to move women.

Not so in the case of Maryam. "Forgive me, my master, but this is nonsense," she responded, falling to her knees and clasping my own in her arms, "the nonsense which men speak to men when they have escaped the skepticism of their wives and daughters. I remember rather the cry of a woman, the charge of Zipporah against Moshe: 'A bloody husband thou art because of the Circumcision.' I will have no bloody husband. I will be no bloody wife. There must be no more blood ever. Such is my woman's prayer."

---

[18] Church historians tell us that the dogma of the virginity of the Mother of Jesus (long actually believed in, quite literally, by the devout) is a relatively late invention. The Arch-Priest would have us believe that it existed in Mary's consciousness from the start. Such matters as these make me sometimes doubt the authenticity of the text—a problem to which I shall return later.

And to this I could only answer, "In blood, in blood, shalt thou remember." It is a phrase we repeat each time we memorialize the Promise of YHVH in the flesh of a newborn male, as she apparently recognized, crying out, "A bloody Priest thou art because of the Circumcision." [19]

How bloody she did not yet know, unable to foresee the blood destined to be shed someday by her son, being shed, in fact, even now as I write; and shed, be it said, with my permission and consent. Yet his death and suffering will be on her head as well as my own; for he has been caught between us, tugged at from one side and the other in a struggle we did not initiate and do not know how to end.

It had only begun then, our strange tug-of-war, as I sought once more to confute her, crying, "How can you talk of the remission of blood, you who are obliged to bleed every twenty-eight days in recompense for the sin of the first woman?"

"I will tell you a secret," she said then, her voice so low I could scarcely hear it. "It is not with me after the fashion of women. My breasts have budded, and the hair covers my secret parts like moss, but I am not, like other girls of my age, a slave to the moon. It is a sign."

She was, I suppose, mythologizing, which is to say, lying a little to justify what she felt to be her mission. Or perhaps she was only a little slow in developing, menarche still ahead of her. Yet I swear (and I am something of an expert in these matters, being consulted in cases of unnatural flux) that I could smell on her, pressed against me as she was in her urgency, the smell of a woman in the time of her uncleanness. And rage mounted in me, not just at the desecration of the Holy Place of YHVH, but at the *chutzpah* of the girl, her arrogance before me.

Before I could register my feelings, however, I had become aware of her head resting against my thigh. "I have never bled, father," she murmured, "never. Not from a scratch or a wound or a pulled tooth or the tug of the moon. I am *afraid* to bleed."

Her hair had fallen loose, blown about me by the breeze which springs up always in the evening, passing between the

---

[19] An adopted quotation from the imperfect tale in Exodus to which Eliezar has already referred, and which, precisely because of its ambiguity, becomes the *leit-motif* of his story.

columns of the Temple and dissipating the aroma of incense and sweat even in the remotest chambers. I could feel her rapid breathing, the warmness of her cheek, through the coarse robe I wore; so that, old goat that I was, my flesh rose against that robe like the Sacred Rod of Aaron. Even then, I had already entered my sixth decade. It was, in such a setting, at such a juncture of time, comic, even grotesque. Yet I found myself not laughing, but worrying about whether the girl could perceive it or perhaps had deliberately provoked it. If she were to raise her head only a few inches, I could not help thinking, it would touch my incongruous hardness.

But I went on as if nothing were amiss, Old Priests having for all contingencies old saws. "Do not be afraid of blood, my child. Before we are born, we float in a lake of blood and are nourished by it, as by milk or water or wine, or Manna from Heaven. Think of blood as the sustenance with which someday you will feed your own babies, quite as miraculously as YHVH fed us in the Desert." [20]

But her mood had changed suddenly and she evoked again the strange story out of Exodus, which apparently haunted her as it did me. "When the Angel of the Lord swallowed down Moshe, he did not free him until Zipporah, *shikse* that she was, Gentile and woman, had performed the rites of Circumcision with a stone snatched up from the roadside. I will bear a son to you, or to the grossest of your sons—to anyone you choose—if you will let me circumcise him with my woman's hand; for that was our privilege once, as even your garbled male version of the old story reveals."

I was not convinced by her interpretation, of course, though impressed by her exegetical skill—and by the cold fire of her eyes, impossibly blue beneath the tangled blackness of her hair. But I did not say so, being in any case too concerned with disengaging myself from her arms and lifting her to her feet. "You may marry the old carpenter," I told her, "but beware. It will be your punishment as well as your sin. Only go now, *go.* " And I covered my head with the folds of my prayer shawl in order to see and hear her no more.

---

[20] The reference here is to the Manna from Heaven, mentioned just above, with which their god allegedly fed the Children of Israel during their forty years of wandering in the Desert. It is reputed to have tasted to everyone like the food he most desired.

That night, however, I dreamed her naked and willing in my arms—as I dream her still from time to time. I who have not touched a woman in twenty years and who pray, lying down and rising up, to be delivered at last from the harsh taskmaster.

Such was, is (I have never spoken of her again but have watched her over the years) the woman who bore the son sought by sheepherders and tribal chiefs: the girl vowed to virginity whom that feckless Messenger took in an instant, at a whim, it would seem; though perhaps at the behest of and for ends known only to the Elim. Took her, at any rate, without a by-your-leave or a grunt, much less a declaration of love. So swiftly, she used to testify afterward in the meetings of those to whom her son seemed the true Anointed of the Lord, that her hymen was not even ruptured: like a bird without wings, a fire that left no ash, a word whispered in the ear without sound.

But these are metaphors once more, metaphors spoken by one for whom the distinction between the figurative and factual does not exist. Not because she is unlearned or stupid (G-d forbid!), but because she is mad; or maybe because she herself is a metaphor. Her stories, in any case, seem suspiciously like the legends of Yavan,[21] which she may have learned from some passing traveler, or perhaps even from the shifty Procurator of Judea himself,[22] who, my spies tell me, occasionally attends their meetings in what he takes to be an impenetrable disguise.

No, I am inclined to believe that the Messenger did not come to Maryam as bird or fire or word, but as herself; for only self-love could have moved her to surrender. In that guise, certainly, he appeared to me on the night before the spaceship actualized itself over our hills. It seemed then merely another in a series of erotic dreams; and perhaps I falsify now, treating it as something else. Yet I awoke after dreaming I had utterly possessed her, to find

[21] This is the form taken in Hebrew by "Ionia," and Eliezar seems to use it to mean all of Greece. I have merely transliterated it, however, rather than "translating" it as "Greece" or "Hellas," or whatever, to give some sense of how alien a place that Other Culture was to him.

[22] Pontius Pilate is another name Eliezar does not write. There can be no religious taboos involved in this case, however; so perhaps what motivates the omission is the Old Priest's reluctance to specify one whom he considered a mere tool of Roman power.

myself, as I had not been in a long, long time, polluted with my own seed. And at this point, in any case, I can no longer distinguish daylight reality from the nocturnal appearance of Messengers, or either from what I used to call "only a dream."

How I envy, in my time-bound, space-bound, reality-bound, flesh-bound condition, the freedom of the Elim and the Messengers not only to know the unreality of such distinctions, but to move back and forth across the boundaries they define. To be sure, there are risks involved in the ceaseless dissolution and reconstitution which such crossings demand: the metamorphosis of their essential selves into whatever form is viable in whatever here or there to which chance takes them. So at least the Elim tell me (self-pity echoing self-pity), whenever I cry out that I will serve them no longer in their absurd conflict with Woman-ness or Cosmic Cunthood, or whatever the Enemy is "really" called.

"Yin" is the term the Elim themselves seem to prefer, speaking of the Struggle between Yin and Yang,[23] as I gather they first learned to do in.the remote region of Kathai, one of the three places on this globe to which they have gone in search of allies, or better, pawns. Yavan is the second, and the third our own country, which we call simply Eretz, the Earth, the World; even as they call their home beyond the Stars Shamaim, the Heavens, the Sky. But this is confusing, since my ancestors used that same word for the Firmament, the translucent vault—as they thought—which separates the Waters Above from the Waters Below.

But never mind. The point is that to our land to Yavan the Elim came, as it were, on purpose. But in Kathai they seem to have arrived by mistake, a fortunate mistake, they insist; for in the works of the sages of that country, they found a clearer interpretation of what was at stake in their Great Struggle than they had been able to formulate for themselves. Nonetheless, the whole

[23] It seems to me highly improbable that a first-century Hebrew, Arch-Priest or not, could have any knowledge of the religious philosophy of China or, as he prefers to call it, "Kathai" (Cathay). Here as elsewhere, therefore, I am tempted to believe that I am dealing if not with a hoax, with a (twentieth-century, perhaps?) work of fantasy in a genre called "Science Fiction." But what am I to make then of the undoubted antiquity of the Scrolls? Or the credulity of the Meta-Technicians? Or the "message" they previously received from the Stars? Since such questions are beyond my competence, I shall continue to translate, and leave it to others to make final judgments.

event makes it clear that *they are not infallible.* It is probability only which they can perceive, statistical probability, as they have taught me to say. And sometimes after dissolution they are not able—as those probabilities have seemed to indicate—to refocus their consciousness, their existence, in modes appropriate to the place to which they have come. Sometimes, to put it in the language of men, they reoccur "nowhere." And when this happens, they are unable to return to their native Shamaim, but remain on the margin of actuality, persisting only as what we would call "haunts," "bogeys," "ghosts," or "monsters."

This last time around, however, some three decades ago by our calendar, their reckoning worked out to the last diminished fraction of reality. Their Ship reappeared, the Messenger descended; and extracting from me in the realm of dreams my hoarded seed (the last of my four wives had died in childbirth some ten years before), sowed it in the womb of the vanity-ridden girl who had vowed to remain forever virgin. Succubus and Incubus: these are the names which the common people give to the Messengers in the active and passive phases of such seed-gathering; believing, as I, too, believe, that it is pleasure which the Messengers seek with human men and women alike: the ecstasy of sexual release, unknown in their world, where, as they are accustomed to say, "there is no marriage or giving in marriage." [24]

But they seem also to long for offspring, pseudo sons and daughters. And for this reason they do not merely exploit our most shameful fantasies; but they transmit from one human body to another—even those forbidden to interbreed by Law and Custom—the seed they have thus extracted. We are enjoined against expending such seed outside of the womb to which we are bound in marriage. And, indeed, the Messengers themselves have been specifically banned from subverting that injunction by "knowing" the Daughters of Men, as they were accustomed to do in ancient times; thus creating what the old scribes refer to quaintly as "giants in the earth." "Let your young go to Yavan, if they

---

[24] A phrase actually quoted from the Christian "gospels," where it is attributed to Jesus, from whose lips the Arch-Priest perhaps heard it. He uses it here ironically, of course, giving it a wry twist, as he adapts it to his own theory of the birth of one who claimed to be the Messiah.

cannot control themselves," the first Priests told the Masters of Space; for they had learned that the Messengers are a kind of larval stage of the Elim, who do not conceive and bear, but bud and divide. "Let them hybridize with the *goyim* who celebrate such unions in story and song."

And for many generations the Pact was honored; the Messengers coming and going on their necessary business without molesting our women. It seems impossible, therefore, to believe that the Elim themselves were responsible for the events which culminated with the birth in the Galil (what could have changed their unchanging minds?), or that some unruly Messenger on his own contravened the long-established order of things. It must rather have been Maryam who triggered the catastrophe, invoking it by charms and spells, magic, in short: that perverse effort—conspired in not by women alone—to control daytime reality by wish, even as the nighttime reality of dreams is so controlled. I have long suspected Maryam of being a witch, an Ashtorite, who in the more rigorous days of our fathers (the law that a witch shall be put to death has become an idle threat in these degenerate times) would have been executed, stoned by an enraged community. And I, or he who stood in my place, would have cast the first stone.[25]

In fact, the Pact had been sealed with oaths so sacred that only a rebel of royal or priestly blood—or both, like Maryam—could have broken it without dying on the spot, which is to say, without willing his own death. Nor would the Elim have supported such rebellion; for cunning and ruthless though they may be, they are scrupulous at least—bound by their own word, as we are bound by the Commandments of the Everlasting. Only the devotees of the Dark Mother would have helped; smuggling the ill-fated girl out through the barred posterns of the city by night, so that she could go to the High Places to invoke the Power with a thousand Names: Astarte-Ashtoreth-Ishtar-Aphrodite-Isis-Kybele-Hecate-Demeter-Rhea.

---

[25] Again a snide reference to the gospels—and that strange injunction of Jesus against any except one "without sin," i.e., no one, casting the first stone. It is a hyperbole, I suppose, or the advice of one expecting the world to end. But even so understood, it makes (I find that here I agree with Eliezar) little sense.

G-d help me, I can see as if in a vision that self-declared perpetual virgin, too proud to yield to a Prist, kissing the bung of the anti-Priest of the White Goddess. She lies naked and spread-eagled before the Ho ned Buck, the Celebrant castrated in honor of the Mother—but permitted in recompense to wear at midsummer and midwinter the Double Dildo, allowed also to the Arch-Priestesses in a world where all distinctions dissolve: that two-pronged phallus of metal, which penetrates simultaneously anus and vagina, drenching both with a fluid colder than death.[26]

Perhaps, after all, it was as the Buck that the Messenger approached her—or rather as what that dread Hierophant of the Goddess merely symbolized: something icy and infertile as empty space, the true anti-Father. She would have experienced such a consummation not as a new experience to be sought or avoided, but only as an old one, already lived and remembered and dreamed, and now merely remembered and dreamed again. But this is foolishness; for the Messengers do not come *as* anything except themselves. It is we, unable to abide the fact that they are nothing or anything, who insist on *perceiving* them in ways congruous with our needs. So I, for instance, had always before seen the messengers as beautiful young men, lithe and golden, like the wrestlers in the gymnasiums, or the gladiators in the arenas of the pagans.

I went once to such an arena, for motives I did not dare explain to myself: though to those who asked, I mumbled something about wanting to bring back into our fold "the lost sheep of Israel." But I was neither titillated, as I half-feared I might be, nor horrified, as I half-hoped, at the spectacle of unclean beasts baited by unclean men, unclean men mangled by unclean beasts. What happens in the world of unredeemed Nature neither allures nor repels me. But I was balefully fascinated by a wrestling match between a huge Ethiopian, black as the pit of Gehenna, and an Israelite, son of a father who had been my childhood companion. Both men were nude, the Jew and the heathen; and I could not fail to notice that the former had had an artificial foreskin grafted onto

---

[26] The ceremonies described here by the Arch-Priest seem to forecast (or recall) those described in the confessions of the Witches, the hierophants of the underground revival of the Mother Cult, which reached a climax in Western Europe and America in the seventeenth century. Another suspicious item.

his penis, as I have heard the physicians of the *goyim* will do for a price. So the requirements of the Games demand.

Oddly enough, however, the Messengers appear to me always circumcised; though they are, of course, the ultimate Gentiles, not even present with the Seventy Nations of the earth when the Law was given to Israel at Sinai. Each sees what he wants to see— Maryam the lover she denied dreaming, and I the son I do not confess I long for: beautiful as a pagan but pious as a Jew. How different are the actual offspring of the four women I did not truly love, the sons who will inherit my mantle and my mission. Bandy-legged, potbellied, slack-mouthed, snouted like pigs and covered all over with red fur like Esau himself, they are as ugly within as without. Connivers and con men, how can they be inducted into the secrets of the Elim?

Would that the son of Maryam and the Messenger were the son of my body as he is of my soul—I who have helped bring him to this pass. Or do I mean would he were the son of my soul as he is of my body, since it was my stolen sperm which fertilized the egg from whence he sprang? I do not know what I mean, knowing only that he resembles neither me nor his mother; but the image, the version of the Messenger who sired him shared by his mother and me. Small wonder then that I have kept track of his every movement, surrounding him with agents, suborning those closest to him; and that at the important rites of his growing up, I have officiated personally, despite my resolve never to speak to his mother again.

It was I who held him in my arms at his *Pinyan-ha-ben,* his ritual ransoming from Temple service; I who wielded the Knife of the Circumcision on the eighth day after his birth, bending to suck the first drop of blood (it tasted like Jewish blood, I swear) from his tiny cock; I who blessed him with the threefold Blessing of the Priests when in his thirteenth year he came to us for his *Bar Mitzvah.* He sang his prescribed portion of the text like an angel, which is no surprise, angel being merely another word for Messenger; and he climaxed the whole event with a dazzling interpretation of the verb tenses in the Fifty-third Chapter of Isaiah.[27]

---

[27] A passage in the so-called Prophetic Books interpreted by Christians as a prophecy of the coming of Jesus as the Messiah, but read by Orthodox Jews as a description of the

How could I have suspected that he thought of the Prophet's "Suffering Servant" not as Israel, but as himself? I was too busy gloating (may YHVH forgive me) over the bafflement and confusion of the younger Priests, my sons and grandsons, who had come in mockery to test the dialectical skill of one, after all, still more boy than a man—a country bumpkin from the Galil. "Can salvation come out of Galilee?" the scholars of Jerusalem are accustomed to ask contemptuously.

Perhaps you are inclined to argue at this point that the Son of the Messenger should have been banned from all such rites to begin with, being excluded from the Community as a *momser*, the by-blow, as popular opinion has it, of a wandering Roman soldier. Certainly he should not have been indulged and pampered by the Arch-Priest himself—an old lecher, the same popular opinion believes, who might have sired the boy himself (and this time popular opinion is close to the truth), except that he could no longer, as the vulgar phrase has it, "cut the mustard." But the answer is clear, of course: the son of a Jewish mother is a Jew. There are some who would argue that such a view reflects a fundamental cynicism about women, leading to the conclusion that no man knows his own father. In my opinion, however, it is rather our inheritance from a time when it had not yet occurred to anyone to connect the joys of copulation with the messy business of bearing a child—a time therefore matrilineal at least, if not matriarchal.

In any event, in the light of Eternity and at the End of Days, I am sure that it is I who will be inscribed as his father, rather than that impotent old man who fostered him. Or even the absent and heedless Messenger, whom we must imagine pleasuring himself in far-off Yavan, where he descends upon some buxom *shikse* in the form of a bull or a swan or a shower of gold.[28] It can perhaps be said that I am his true mother as well, in the sense that I love him more warmly, less deviously than the female who, though she bore

___

Suffering Servant, Israel, redeeming the world. Both readings, however, subscribe to the theory of vicarious atonement, the salvation of the guilty by the suffering of the innocent.

[28] Here we must ask ourselves how a Priest in Israel could have come to know so well the "abominable" mythology of the Greeks; since each of his apparently offhand allusions refers to a specific myth about the loves of gods and mortals. My skepticism grows.

him, used him only to help restore the ancient dominion of Egg over Seed.

I watch her trailing behind him, always on the edge of the crowds that gather around his childish miracles, as he travels the road to certain death. And I observe her smiling ironically to herself when he cries over his shoulder, "Woman, go home. I must be about my Father's business." Quite obviously, she thinks he is her tool; even as the Messenger must have thought that she was his. And I who know the motives of all involved, except, perhaps, myself—have no way of knowing who will be victorious in the end, or, indeed, what in this context victory could mean.

Born outside of the Law though he was, the child of the Messenger was adopted into the Law by becoming, as we say without always realizing the full meaning, *Bar Mitzvah:* a Son of the Commandment which is also a Blessing. It is therefore right that I have, convening the Council, judged him under the Law. In the end, however, I was obliged, lovingly, regretfully, to surrender him to the lesser law of the one whom the pagans call Caesar; for he parried with the skill I would have expected questions aimed at convicting him of blasphemy. It was therefore right, too, that the courts of Caesar judge him in their way; though wrong for the Centurions of that far-off ruler to nail over his head a sign reading in their language and ours: KING OF THE JEWS. Had he been in fact a pretender, an aspirant to the throne on which the Greco-Syrian puppet now sits with our consent as well as theirs, he would have been (since the pseudogenealogies circulated by his mother proving royal descent are palpable frauds) guilty of *lèse-majesté:* a crime quite as serious as blasphemy itself.

We would, then, have been obliged to execute him in our way rather than theirs. "Cursed is the hanged man," we are accustomed to say, adding under our breaths: "And the lost heathen who hang him." We find it abominable that anyone, especially a Son of the Covenant, be nailed to the cross by a hired hangman whose name history will not remember. To us it seems more appropriate that the Community as a whole stone one they have found deserving of death: men, women and children heaving rock after rock in an ecstasy of common accord and responsibility; no one knowing which missile has finally killed him in fact, all knowing that all have killed him in intent. Had it worked out that way, once more I would have been proud to cast the first stone.

I am not saying, please understand (and I address particularly you who will read this in a future I have only glimpsed dimly in the Scanner of the Elim), that we Jews played no role in the death of the Messenger's son. Not only the Courts and the Law decide whether one who has defied them lives or dies; such matters are determined also by a shout in the street and a whisper in the ear—the people being especially good at the first, and we Priests at the second. But the primary responsibility for the execution (why are my eyes blurred? why does my hand tremble? what has undone me in a way which age itself could not?) rests with, as they say, "the duly constituted authorities." But this means with the Procurator of Judea:[29] a man who has never loved anyone, yet has desperately wanted to be loved by all, the people, the priests, even the Son of the Messenger. I consider it the worst of all disabilities for one holding high office—this desire for universal approval. And I speak as a man who has himself held high office for threescore years and ten, the life span of ordinary mortals.

I was suspicious of him from the start, this dutiful civil servant so dedicated to "doing a good job." Not that he was distant or arrogant, far from it. He bowed and scraped to everyone: to the rabble, to the Levites, those forgotten men of the Temple, to us, to his absent superiors in Rome, even to the Berserker [30] who sits so uneasily on the throne in Antioch. But what really gave him away was the ostentatious courtesy with which he addressed us, speaking in our own tongue instead of shouting at us in a pidgin version of his, like all of his predecessors.

"But what does he *want?*" we kept asking each other. And the answers were many: "He wants to feather his nest," "He doesn't know what he wants," "He wants to be loved," "He wants to survive in the history books," "He wants to be promoted, i.e.,

[29] Christianity, in the Early Church, at least, turned Pontius Pilate from the villain which Eliezar would make him to a kind of victim, a man not strong perhaps, but basically one of goodwill. But this clearly results from the Christians' desire to make peace with Rome, whose bureaucratic shell their Church inherited. Early Christian catechisms say, for instance, that Jesus was killed "by Pontius Pilate"; while later ones change this to "*under* Pontius Pilate."

[30] A puppet-king called Herod, whose name is also suppressed by the Arch-Priest, this time clearly out of contempt.

139

transferred to a more desirable post, closer to what he considers the Center of the World." How could he have known, for all his diligent reading of our records and prophecies, what only the Elim could have told him—as they told me, who could not have cared less: that this, our little Jerusalem, was the Center of the World; and that the Procurator would be remembered only because chance had brought him here.

Will it amuse or dismay him, I wonder, when I am long dead, and he has retired to some country villa in his native land to write his memoirs, to know *how* he is remembered? Not in the Seat of Judgment, or on the Rostrum addressing a crowd, but in the act of forever washing his hands. It is an oddly priestly gesture, borrowed perhaps from us; though for all I know, those who preside over his own native rites may perform the same symbolic act. Yet for him, I fear, the gesture which signifies for us the recognition that even the cleanest among us is eternally unclean, was only one more assertion of innocence. G-d in his infinite mercy forgive him, as I trapped in my tiny remnant of time cannot.

In the end, I find more palatable even that double agent, Yehudah: that creature whom my sons persuaded to act as a go-between, shuttling back and forth between the two worlds of G-d and Caesar, the upper and lower millstones between which the Son of the Messenger was ground small. Perhaps I sympathize with him, that orphan and outcast who belonged to nothing ever except in his traitor's role, because the part he played in our small drama seems analogous to my own in relation to the Elim. Finally, however, I *know* what I am doing, being in on the game; while he remains forever an outsider, as he rushes back and forth—pale and sweating—between the Temple and the Procurator's Palace, conveying the rumor and misinformation which will damn only him when the story is told.

All agents are, I suppose, double agents in the end, since it is love and belonging they seek on both sides. But few have become as deeply involved with the one they are hired to betray as has this unhappy Yehudah. For the last three years they have lived as intimately as a husband and wife, waking and sleeping together. How ill-assorted they seem, however. The Son of the Messenger always somehow distant, remote, and Yehudah sucking up to him, flattering him, finally, I am convinced, loving him, believing in his mission; yet by the same token, hating him, hating himself for hating him.

But Yehudah's special contempt is reserved for us, the Priests who pay him. I can read it in his eyes whenever he comes in secret to the appointed place of meeting, shuffling and bowing, offensively obsequious. Yet it was he who insisted on being paid, lest he have to confess to himself his true motives: the pleasure he finds in betraying what he loves, loving what he betrays. To be sure, my sons are equally adamant, insisting that it all be kept on a strictly cash basis, so that they can condescend to him as a hireling rather than recognize him as a brother.

I, on the other hand, can condescend to no one: not my sons, or Yehudah, or the Procurator. I have merely let happen what had to happen, what was plotted out of our time and space. But I know this is no excuse. One does not have to accept what he cannot prevent, since it is possible if not precisely to accelerate or delay such events, at least to *try* to accelerate or delay them. Instead, I have listened to the whining and sniveling of them all, as you (reading this in your secure and self-righteous future) must listen to my whining and sniveling. I do not try to exculpate myself—granting, even before I am challenged, that in a sense I do not quite understand, it might all have been different. But it does not matter whether I understand or not. It is enough to remember what the Elim have told me time and time again: that we, too, are the masters of possibility. Failing to live in the light of this knowledge, we are like gods who have abandoned their own creation. Like YHVH before us. But that is no excuse either.

Anyhow, it so happened (meaning—I know, I know—that I let it happen, willed it) that I was alone in the Sanctuary when Yehudah entered with his final report, in quest of his final payment. He did not receive, therefore, whatever the already mythologized accounts may say, his last thirty shekels; for I have not touched money for nearly half a century. "I will give you advice instead," I told him. "Now that it is too late for it to do you any good. But that is the nature of advice always."

"Spare me your old man's wisdom," he cut me off. "And pay up. Ass on the table, as they say in my trade. I have no time or patience for playing games with you, being beyond good and evil."

What could I do but laugh at this posturing; and, for once, he joined in, forgetting for that instant to feel sorry for himself, G-d be thanked for small favors. But he insisted on telling me in painful detail the story of the Passover Seder [31] they had held the night before, he and his so-called Master, along with eleven of the other faithful [32]—emphasizing what the Son of the Messenger had said over the *matzos,* the sacramental wine: calling the one, Yehudah claimed, his body, the other his blood. But who ever knows what to believe in such cases.

"This is blasphemy," he insisted, "true blasphemy at last, is it not?" He reached out toward me a trembling hand, from which I am ashamed to confess I shrank; his eye lighting up hopefully at the thought of having got the goods on his victim.

"What could be less blasphemous," I responded, "than a good Jew observing the Passover, honoring the festivals of his people even under the shadow of persecution? Never mind the metaphors of body and blood. Are not *matzos* and wine themselves metaphors? Besides, if we were to be judged for our metaphors, who among us would not be found guilty?"

I was in truth pleased that the boy had thus remained faithful to our Law till the very end. Long before, he had told me in private that not one *yod* (the smallest letter of our alphabet, and perhaps for that reason the first letter in the secret name of G-d) would, through his teaching, pass from the Torah given on Sinai; not even the tittle of a *yod,* which is to say, the spot of ink where the brush touches the parchment before the small curve of the letter is made. And saying this, he had knelt at my feet, as is

[31] This ceremonial event, which came to be known not as the "Last Passover Seder" but the "Last Supper," in order, apparently, to conceal the fact that Jesus remained all his life long an observant Jew, became a favorite subject for painters over the next two millennia. And it hangs still, in various versions, in the few remaining museums in our world. But it is an event which has ritual applications as well as aesthetic ones, since it provides the prototype for the Mass or Holy Communion.

[32] It is worth remarking, perhaps, how little attention the Old Priest pays to the Twelve Disciples, except for Yehudah, or Judas, and, just a little, Simon Peter, which is to say, Simon the Rock. John, "the beloved disciple," for instance, is not mentioned at all. For Eliezar, perhaps for all Jews, only this chief protagonist matters; but for the earliest Christians, his other followers, the actual founders of the Cult, are almost equally important.

proper, to receive the paternal Blessing. Yet it is I who shall, as is not proper at all, live to say Kaddish for him.

While all this was passing through my troubled mind, Yehudah stood before me, not looking at me really; but staring through me, through the wall behind me, through the world, as it were —waiting. "What are you waiting for?" I asked. "No matter how long you stand here, you will not be paid."

"I am going now to the Procurator," he answered. And when I did not respond, he added, "I kissed him. At the Seder. After he told us that one of us would betray him, I kissed him."

"Why not?" I said. And leaning forward, I kissed *him*, tasting on his cheek the taste of death, smelling on his breath the smell of death: his death and that of the Son of the Messenger, but chiefly my own.

How long ago that all seems to me: months, years, a century, forever; though in fact it happened only yesterday or the day before. But now I am the one who is waiting—waiting for the cry that will tell me my son is dead. It is to help pass the time (but it does not help really) that I am writing this account: for the record, for the future; though perhaps I will decide to destroy it after it is finished. If it is ever finished. If I do not die first.

I have refused to go to the Great Square for the crucifixion,[33] unwilling to watch the driving in of the nails, the trickling out of the blood and the sweat, the destruction of what is beautiful by those who are not beautiful. I will not even look out of the window of the High Tower of the Temple which faces the Square. I find no relish—as not only the *goyim* seem to do, but my own people as well—in the slow public dying of a Jew. I would have preferred the quick catastrophe of a stoning, which conceals what it destroys. I would have preferred. . . .

But I am falling asleep. *The moment has come. The roar of the crowd. It is done.*

---

[33] For Eliezar this event, more crucial to the mythology of the New Cult than even the Last Supper, seems somehow irrelevant, and is kept offstage in his account, to which only the Birth and the pseudo Resurrection are essential. More than his pity, I am suggesting, is necessary to explain his unwillingness to deal at length with the Death, over which all four of the gospels linger. Or perhaps I am being unfair. There is evidence of real compassion here, under the stuffy style.

EIGHT

I did not work through the entire text without interruption, as it turned out, though my strength grew with working. But I paused for rest and reflection after I had finished the First Scroll: the first part of the story of the Founder of Christianity as seen by Eliezar, the Arch-Priest of Israel. I must confess, I began by hating him for his obdurate rejection of the Female Principle, and even more for his lofty, condescending tone, his Jewish arrogance. Indeed, I hate him still—whether he existed in fact, or is only the invention of some writer of fiction, the unsympathetic hero of a hoax for which I may die. Yet I have somehow begun to identify with him in his foredoomed battle with Maryam, whose outcome I, of course, knew from the start.

As I finished transcribing the first section, in fact, my eyes brimmed with tears of an author moved by his creation to a deeper response than he has ever felt for real human beings. I had come by then to believe myself the true author not just of Eliezar's tale but of Eliezar himself. All translations, I suppose, add to such confusions, since they involve the reimagining as well as the retelling of events, which become in the process the translator's story. Moreover, this text was radically imperfect, and I had therefore to fill in the blanks by amending, extrapolating, improvising. Certain terms, finally, which I did not quite understand, I replaced with others out of my own culture: approximations or, at least, I hoped, analogues. But how could I be sure?

What possible use, then, I was driven to ask myself, could this quasi-fictional text be to the Meta-Technicians with their schemes for conquering space, achieving the Stars and opening a colloquy with Alien Intelligences in whom our world has long ceased to believe? Even if I had reproduced it exactly, the language of Eliezar would have remained too "primitive," too limited by his world view to be a reliable guide to action now. It would have required a subtler translator than I to find late-technological equivalents for the mumbo jumbo of pretechnological "magic" that Eliezar never managed to transcend. Besides, the Urim and Tumim, whatever they might be, were lost forever. And with them, I suspected, had gone any chance of communicating with the Masters of Space—except in the hit-or-miss fashion by which the Meta-Technicians had already managed it, without any help from the past.

In any case, they had not come to find me or the text: those absurd puppets, who I always knew would continue to pull my strings, though they themselves were manipulated by forces I had just begun to understand. Yet midway through my task, I was still waiting for them, like a child expecting his parents to deliver him from a grief, which, at some level, he already realizes is of their making, is them. Perhaps it was, more specifically, a father that I longed for, great baby that I was in the sixth decade of my life, having, as it were, just died and been reborn. And what sort of a father could I have imagined, a boy brought up in a gynocracy, except one who comes from Elsewhere to declare his son such a man as he has never seen outside of his own dreams, which is to say, a Hero?

As I write this, I have learned, however, that I was chosen, not as I had been deluded into believing to win the plaudits of men by freeing them from the limits of their humanity and their sense of loneliness in the Cosmos; but to compose for them, inside those limits and that loneliness, a dream of escape. It was not even my own dream but a gloss on someone else's: the translation into a new tongue of an old text, complete with footnotes and (as I see I shall have to provide before I am through) a glossary of unfamiliar terms. I shall be remembered, if at all, I am trying to say, not as a Hero, but as what used to be called a Scholar.

Yet I have been happy during these weeks in the cave, transcribing, editing, annotating. Exactly how long my happiness lasted, I am not sure, though I tried to keep track, knowing that with the return of the Meta-Technicians I would fall back into time. And I wanted to be ready. But I never managed to regularize my schedule of sleeping and waking, sleep jerking me over the border of consciousness into darkness and troubled dreams for periods whose length I could not estimate. And so I soon gave up any attempt to tally the days, content to judge the length of my stay by the slow diminution of my supplies.

It is hard to guess with any precision the amount of foods twice-shrunken for easy portage. And it would have been foolish in such a climate as I had come to inhabit, to take them out and rehydrate them except just before eating. But it seemed to me that considerably less than half of my original store remained when I had completed Part One of the Arch-Priest's account, and was preparing to begin Part Two. I suppose I should, therefore, have left writing for acting. But, despite my dreams of heroism, I had no plan of action, and no stomach for it. So like all men under such circumstances, I lied. *After all,* I would say to myself, in a tone which failed to convince even me, *the Technicians told me to wait, did they not; and true courage is to obey orders, even at the risk of seeming cowardly.*

But I was, I knew from the start, afraid to venture again into the Desert, or to cross again the unseen barrier at the top of the ridge. At moments when I needed a break from reading and writing, I would, however, stand in the cave's mouth, one hand touching the palpable reassurance of hard stone. At first, I would daydream about returning through that pass where I had suffered so much pain; then, I just looked—for an explanation, I suppose, some clue to what had so wracked my flesh. And finally, it seemed to me that I could discern a thin line of haze hovering just above its surface. Or rather, I believe now I was driven in my bafflement first to postulate such a line, then to persuade myself that I saw it. Certainly, I felt or intuited a radical discontinuity between earth and sky, the contour of the ridge and the air over it. It was as if two worlds, two media alien in every respect, had been forced into almost-tangency; leaving between them a gap of that primal nothingness from which they both came, and to which (like me) they would both return. But how could I have confessed such a perception, or formulated it even to myself? A "haze" I called it; and therefore I write the word down now, in what I intend to be a true record of my past, not as I have come to understand it, but as I lived it.

Even saying the neutral word *haze,* however, did not deliver me from the chills and nausea which assailed me whenever I looked too long at that nonspace above the ridge. And I would turn with the pleasure of one free at last from a nightmare he has come to believe he can never escape, to the slowly growing pile of pages that marked my progress. During the hours just before and after noon, I would sit near enough to the mouth of the cave so that I could work by indirect sunlight. And when it grew too dark, I would take the Stone from the ring and retreat to the innermost depths, where I would continue to write by its gentle glow until sleep overtook me. It was a routine which I came by imperceptible degrees to love, not as a means to be endured in the hope of some glorious end; but as a satisfaction in itself, greater than any I had found as a household pet, or an exile set to delving in foreign soil. For the first time in my life, I am suggesting, I felt truly at home.

Yet it was not until my long chore was completed that I could acknowledge how much more content I would have been had I been born before the Universities were closed in the last decades of the twenty-first century. In those days I would have been supported by the state for doing precisely what I did in my cave: paid *not* to venture into the Desert for any purpose except the compilation of such work as I was then engaged in. Two or three times, while I was translating the First Scroll, I dreamed that I sat at a "desk" in just such a University, lecturing a class of somnolent students about the Messengers and the Elim; and reading them relevant passages from the text. I would pause after each of the small jokes with which I punctuated my remarks to allow time for their dutiful laughter, tilting my chair back so that my head touched the "blackboard" on the wall behind it. Only when the bell rang to indicate the end of the "period" would I rise, and with a wave of my hand, "dismiss" them.

· Afterward, moving through the crowded hallways to my "office," I would smile down at their appreciative greetings or the questions they would stop to ask: less real questions than symbolic expressions of gratitude, assurances that they had listened well and would remember, even between bells, what I had told them. In my "office," my "secretary" would be waiting for me: super-Black, superbuxom, and mature to the point of rotten-ripeness—a super-Megan, in short, though without my old Megan's curt arrogance. "Yes, Professor," she would say. "Right away, Professor. Is there anything else for today, Professor?" Then she would busy herself with "taking dictation," abbreviated notes for reproduction on a primitive Gutenberg copying device called a "typewriter"; or with emptying the "wastebaskets," those receptacles for the detritus or excrement of the Gutenberg process, which have always seemed to me central symbols of twentieth-century life.

Needless to say, however, she would be ready at a moment's notice to interrupt whatever chore she was engaged in, and strip off the drab garment which covered her glistening flesh from neck to ankle. And when the whim moved me, I would signal her to do so, then to spread herself out, face up or face down as my fancy dictated, on my paper-strewn desk or the bare floor. Most satisfactory of all, though, was to dream her seated naked in the "swivel chair," as characteristic of the age as the wastebasket itself: her legs spread wide and hooked up over the arms, so that the hair-haloed pink target of her twat was fully exposed. Then, typically, I would wake to find myself alone in my dark cave. And I would cry out in anguish, or, rather, in the petulant grief of a frustrated child, wishing he had been born elsewhere or elsewhen.

Let me not be unfair to myself. It was not finally such dreams which made me wish I had lived in a twenty-first-century University, but the almost inadvertent hybridization of sexes, races and classes within its walls—which had, in fact, fostered such fantasies. Most of society had, by the close of that century, opted for mutual hatred rather than hybridization. And only a common contempt for the hybridizers had kept Females from destroying Males, Blacks, Whites, and the poor, the rich. Unfortunately, the impulse to hybridize had been unilateral, coming from Males eager to feminize themselves, Whites' desiring to become "niggerish," and bourgeois yearning for downward social mobility.

So also only the old, which is to say, the Professors, sought to emulate the young, which is to say, their students; while the latter rejected "maturity" as the culmination of all they most despised. Their rejection of maturity, however, meant the end of the University, which had been their breeding ground and nursery. Once that was gone, nothing lay before them except the open road: the long retreat from civilization which had ended in the camp of Melissa-Melinda.

The University, however, persisted for a hundred years in response to the demands of a new clientele: the offspring of poor, non-White parents, plus the less-favored daughters and wives of rich Anglo-Saxon Protestants and East European Jews, who succeeded in capturing all institutions of higher learning. But in three or four generations their descendants grew restive, at first vacillating between indolence and violence; then, in the late sixties of the twenty-first century, erupting in total rebellion, as their predecessors had almost exactly a century before.

This time, however, the rebels were led by non-White, Female Professors, who managed to. escalate local demonstrations into undeclared wars fought with weapons available in their laboratories. Their demands, however, turned out to be varied and contradictory. For "higher standards," on the one hand, and for the immediate expulsion of all "overachievers," on the other. For the banning of Cult observances from the campus, on the one hand, and in favor of replacing "Science" with "Meditation," on the other. For required chastity, on the one hand, and for universal sex initiation, on the other.

But it mattered little what slogans were shouted, since that revolt was directed, however unconsciously, against the Gutenberg skills themselves. From these the University had proved incapable of emancipating itself, despite attempts to substitute sensitivity sessions and multimedia presentations for lectures and books. Yet the vast majority of humanity had by that time proved itself unable or unwilling to read and write with ease or pleasure. At first, the underground discontent had expressed itself in indifference, evasion or breaches of classroom discipline on the part of the malcontents, at worst in habitual truancy. But all the while pressure was building toward a monstrous explosion.

Not until the Great Book-Burning of 2069, however, did all of this come into the open. It began with the firing of the Library at he Marilyn Monroe School of Women's Studies (formerly Yale University) by an Assistant Professor of Witchcraft. Refused tenure for her failure to "publish," she first kindled the flames, then flung herself into them from the rooftop solarium of the 125-story Parapsychology Building. In the next few days, her example was followed by hundreds, thousands, finally tens of thousands of her colleagues in all lands, who combined book-burning with suicide—not singly, as in the first instance, but in groups of twenty or more.

These acts were not the result of an international conspiracy. They were the spontaneous reactions of women who had always secretly despised the skills they fought to teach—hoping in vain that their students would deliver them from the trap of their own hypocrisy. Those students, however, continued merely to yawn, doze, scratch, stretch and whisper in impotent contempt. Until the teachers themselves had set the example.

At the climax of the Holocaust, libraries at some 650,000 out of the 900,000 fully accredited institutions of higher learning were in flames and surrounded by hitherto lethargic students, chiefly Female, but including a handful of Male fellow travelers, who barred access to local fire departments with a wall of living flesh. *"No more pencils, no more books,"* they sang, recalling a mindless ditty of their grade-school days. And *"No more teachers' crazy looks,"* they finished off, quite forgetting that their frenzy had been stirred by the example of precisely such crazy teachers.

At the earlier stages, it had still seemed possible that the fires could be controlled by low-altitude Meteorological Satellites. Such "Cloud Herders" were ordinarily used to bring rainstorms from remote mountain areas to arid tree plantations ravaged by fire, since they can move cloud masses by Vidar Impulses hundreds of miles per microsecond. But the rapid spread of arson from the University of the Peloponnesus to the Technological Colleges at both Poles paralyzed the rainmakers, who had to content themselves with watching the spread of desolation as they floated gravityless above the universities. It was they alone who saw the total configuration of flame and smoke. Yet only one of the nearly two hundred men and women involved has left a recorded version of the events, and he under the cloak of anonymity. Most of the others either applied for sick leaves, in the course of which they died, or retired early and disappeared from public view, or requested immediate transfer to the remoter planets, assignments ordinarily accepted only under protest.

I have myself listened to the last remaining copy of the Permatape made by that one Cloud Herder and kept in the Archives of the Crimean Demo-Socialist Republic. And I can recall it still, almost word for word. "You kept forgetting it was real," that

Meteorologist said, "it was so much like a fireworks display. Not just a random series of fires, you understand, like I expected, but a coherent pattern—elegant and, I don't know exactly how to say it, urgent, that's it, *urgent*. As if someone, I don't mean the arsonist Professors, but somebody to whom they were just—just instruments, tools, was writing with them, through them, a kind of message. No, not a message, really. As if someone was writing a name, or signing a manifesto, or a painting he was just starting to do, or maybe just finished, I don't know. I just don't *know* is what I mean.

"But it wasn't a signature either," he concluded, "because that means letters, don't it, what the communications people call a phonetic code. But this was more like an ideogram. Or do I mean a pictogram? An emblem, a seal, like those old-fashioned family coats of arms, sealing something once and for all, to say I did it, *me*—or was it, we did it? Anyhow, I thought—I thought while I was watching it that I knew who, whose name. But a minute later, I couldn't remember. Can't remember. *Can't.*"

It is hard to know how seriously to take this testimony, since immediately after making it, the unidentified speaker was committed at his own request for Total Psycho-Chemical Reconstruction, including a readjustment of his hormone balance from Male to Female. So, at least, some brief introductory remarks on the tape tell us, and I see no reason to doubt them; but I am puzzled about what they finally mean. The sex-shifting has always seemed to me the essential clue, suggesting that the Cloud Herder was deliberately making a switch of allegiance: a changeover from one side to another, as if in the face of an impending victory (was this the news he read in the fires?) by a former enemy. But this is idle speculation, born, I suppose, of my exposure to the Meta-Technician's paranoiac fear of women, and the Old Priest's maunderings about the eternal warfare of Yin and Yang.

Let me stick to the "facts," i.e., what the record tells us about the aftermath of the Holocaust—remembering always that it was kept by those who brutally subdued the rebels. According to these sources, when the last fires had burned down, the surviving students, all women it would appear, inscribed on their foreheads, with the ashes of their dead Professors, a Sign nowhere precisely described, then began a campaign of indiscriminate looting, rape and murder. Penned off in the gutted Sports Stadiums of the last "unpacified" Universities, they turned to killing each other, and, if the record is to be believed, to eating each other's bodies.

In any event, the Paramilitary Forces of the World Council, whose casualties by then exceeded the precalculated maximum for such an operation, applied for permission to use Anti-Predator Toxin. Previously APT had been employed only against creatures lower on the evolutionary scale than Man; but "mad dogs" was the term used for the prospective victims. And whether persuaded by such rhetoric, or merely weary to death of the violence, the Legislative Assembly gave the go-ahead. At first, no dissenting voice was raised; nor, indeed, could one have been heard over the constant blare of martial music broadcast during the official Month of Thanksgiving.

Later, however, the Moderates of all parties began to protest, particularly after the Month of Thanksgiving was followed by a Three-Day Mass Funeral, held at the request of certain guilt-ridden parents for the nearly half-million students killed in the final assault. It was a symbolic Rite, to be sure, since those bodies not consumed by fire had been totally disintegrated to prevent plague. Nonetheless, the Obsequies provoked a general outcry, to allay which the World Council passed an Eternal Decree forever banning the use of APT on human beings, no matter what the provocation. To this a Rider was attached (in what purported to be a surprise countermove by the Opposition, but had clearly been approved in advance by the Party in power) forbidding *"in perpetuo"* the expenditures of money public or private "for the construction, rebuilding or maintenance of any college, university, center for advanced studies or other institution, however denominated, dedicated primarily to 'Higher Education,' as defined in the relevant Statutes under subheading II or III of Section . . ."

I do not know how long the new sounds had been assailing my ears before I let them register, or how long the slight trembling of the earth beneath my feet had continued before I noticed it. I know only that I was reluctant to leave my musing. But I had reached the end of my scholarly dream. So that even before I was quite aware of it, I had begun to hear the unfamiliar rhythm of hiss, suck and plop, hiss, suck and plop, which evoked beneath my continuing reverie the image of some great saurian mired in the primeval slime, from which he struggled in vain to free himself, rising and falling, rising and falling, as if forever. *It is a bad dream,* I told myself, *another bad dream. You have fallen asleep again without realizing it.* And then, *You are awake and a fool. It is something that has fallen into the pond. A small animal. Or a bird.*

But when I rose stiffly and posted myself just outside the entrance to the cave, leaning back against the solid rock to stop my trembling, I could see nothing new or strange. Only the heaving waters themselves, agitated by some invisible force which bulged the whole surface again and again, so that at the very center it rose almost as high as the natural doorway beside which I stood. Like a distended bubble, I thought, or the hump of a wave that crests over and over but does not, cannot break—deflating instead with a sullen hiss. And I felt an ache in the pit of my own stomach each time the eruption failed. The color of the water had changed, too, becoming a pale, iridescent green, streaked by darker splotches of algae that quivered and writhed on the slopes of each rising crest; then lay inertly in the hollows of the concentric ripples which spread, after each collapse, slowly, slowly to the rim of the pool—as if the medium they wrinkled were mercury or molten lead.

In the intervals between each falling of the waters and the next rise—intervals which seemed to grow longer as I watched—the unruffled surface would reflect nothing. Not the sky, or the white-hot sun just then at its zenith, or me who had moved until I stood between it and the pond. But there would be a hissing like a deep suspiration. Then, as the waters began once more almost imperceptibly to heave upward, a hoarse sucking that grew more anguished each time, reaching a crescendo just before the dull plop of another failed consummation. And this in turn would fade in diminishing echoes toward a moment of silence, more intolerable than any of the sounds which it had succeeded.

Moved by an impulse I did not understand but could not resist, I knelt on the rocky rim and dipped my left hand into the temporarily quiet waters, which I found had become appreciably colder. Not yet cold to the touch, by any means, but nonwarm—like the flesh of a creature at the moment just after death. Even as I crouched there and dabbled, however, the slightly convex surface of the pool began, more quickly than before, it seemed to me, to bulge at the center, lifting higher and higher two objects as big, perhaps, as the eggs of a thrush or a wren. They did not float partly immersed, but rested on the skin of the water, scarcely denting it, as if they were nearly weightless. And silhouetted against the pale sky, they revealed what struck me even then as a peculiar kind of opacity. For one moment, I had the illusion that a voice was crying, "Now, now, *now!*" at a pitch of intensity that nearly split my skull. Then, before I quite knew what I was doing, I found myself in the water, with one of the "eggs" clutched in each hand.

At that precise instant, however, a gush of what felt like live steam rose from the bottom of the pond, scalding my flesh and roiling the waters about me like a sudden squall. Wave after wave, seeming as huge in that tiny basin as midocean breakers, crashed into my face. They succeeded each other so quickly, leaving the air so full of spray in the brief intervals between, that I could not breathe at all, though I managed somehow to stay afloat. They subsided quickly, however, but even as I drew my first breath, I could feel the gush of a second subterranean current, this time as cold as the spring runoff of a glacier. Then the waters began to swirl about me faster and faster, creating a whirlpool which drew me to the central point of suction. And before I could think of anything except filling my lungs with one more gulp of air, they pulled me down into depths too profound for any hint of sunlight. In that absolute darkness, I had, with bursting lungs and splitting head, already resigned myself to certain death, when a new upward surge of hot water bore me momentarily to the surface. But this time, before I had even managed to fill my lungs, an immediately succeeding icy spout flung me half out of the water, which turned hot again before I was again submerged. Then cold, then hot, then cold, then hot, in a sequence so rapid I could scarcely register the changes of temperature.

And now the pool no longer circled round and round within its own perimeter. But it heaved over and over, bottom becoming top and top bottom, in almost instantaneous reversal, as I revolved with the revolving waters like one lashed to a wheel. I had, and indeed still have, no way of telling how long I was whirled about, turning head over heels within the large cycling of the pool. I dreamed first that I had fallen once more into the hands which had tormented my flesh and racked my bones on the crest of the ridge;

then that I drowned and was revived, drowned and was revived endlessly. I did not, however, see, as drowning men are reputed to do, the events of my life flash in rapid succession before me. Only—it seems to me in retrospect—a vision, momentary but dazzling, of what that life had meant, or might have meant, or could come to mean. For one instant it was all there, lucid, integral, even beautiful, as, I suppose, all men's lives thus seen are beautiful. And then it was gone—forever irrecoverable, forgotten.

I could have been in the water for no more than a couple of minutes all told, or I would not have survived to tell this story. But it seemed to me right afterward, as I lay, panting, battered and covered with blisters (yet somehow still clutching the "eggs"), that my immersion must have lasted for years: the whole lifetime of a pond, which ordinarily heaves over in such a fashion only once annually, as summer merges into autumn. And, indeed, the pond from which I had so astonishingly escaped was dying before my eyes. The air was still full of steamy droplets from the great geyser which I could dimly remember had cast me out, alive but barely conscious. When I dragged myself, however, to the nearest verge, washed only moments before by turbulent waters, I could see no water as deep as I looked; only hear the withdrawing gurgle of the underground springs that had fed the pool and, retreating, had left nothing but a jagged, bottomless hole. In the crevices of its broken sides, there were stranded fish, bloated, blanched and eyeless, and shell-less mollusks with multiple trailing antennae, which, even as I watched, shriveled into dust. *And so I am a hero, after all,* I said to myself aloud, forcing my hands open and looking down at the "eggs," which I knew then beyond doubt were the Urim and Tumim of the Arch-Priest of Israel. *I who was willing to settle for being a Scholar.*

But I had scarcely spoken those boastful words before both they and the gurgle of receding waters were drowned out by an underground rumble and roar. Then the earth bucked under me, like those unbroken horses I used to watch rejecting the Bedouin boys who leaped onto their backs. And a rattle of small stones from the slopes on either side of my cave announced the beginning of a landslide, which for a moment I feared would bury me. First sand, gravel and small rocks, then boulders as big as my head poured past, around, over me into the gaping hole that had once been a pond. But none struck or even grazed my almost lifeless body. Closing my fingers tightly once more around the Urim and Tumim, I tried to raise myself up on my extended arms, though I was too weary to stand, much less to run. And where could I have run to in any case?

Braced as I was on my fists, I could see, by lifting my wobbly head just a little, the ridge I had been able to cross only in sleep; and the line of "haze," which, even as I watched, seemed to funnel in on itself like a tornado, or a drill biting into the rock of the cliff. But I had not remembered that slope being so high or so steep, I thought, even as it was being cleft from top to base by a widening rift that extended itself, as I cried out in fear, across the valley which separated it from my cave. The gap, which opened at a speed too great for any man to outrun, was also, I could see at a glance, too wide for any man to leap, too steep for any man to climb. And it was pointed directly at the ledge where I lay, like a sword or a spear in the hands of an enemy.

I must have fainted then, or fallen into one of my sudden sleeps. When I woke, I discovered just a few inches from my head the façade of an irregular pyramid of stone, piled up in layers of diminishing size to a tiny peak, barely higher, I judged, than I could have reached with extended fingertips, had I been able to stand. Prone, I could not see over that mound the cleft I had been certain would engulf me. But two trenches, somewhat narrower than the original, ran on either side of it deep into the granite cliff to the right and left of the Arch-Priest's cave. It was as if the force which had rent the earth had met at that point some counterthrust or immovable obstacle stronger than itself; and like a river similarly checked, had branched out around it.

I had no way of being sure that the earthquake (if, indeed, that was what I had survived, and I dared give it no other name) was entirely over, since the ground beneath me continued to throb irregularly like a winded horse. And an occasional stone still rattled and bounced harmlessly down the hillside behind me. But I was, for the moment, safe; though caught, as it were, in a forked stick, cut off from any possibility of escape, except perhaps through the opening I had noticed earlier at the back of the cave. Surely it was a way out: an escape hatch contrived ages before by those who had first hacked that refuge out of some shallow recess in the rock. Why could I not, then, by the light of the PSSS, the Stone from M-M's poison ring, thread the dark mazes behind it? And fording its subterranean streams, if that proved necessary, make my way back to the world of order and sanity?

But I had not yet checked to see whether the Stone had survived, along with me and the Urim and Tumim, my recent perils. My heart, therefore, almost halted as, releasing for the first time the Old Priest's amulets, I flipped open the lid of the ring—to discover that the Stone was still there, even glowing a little in the dusk of the ending day, as if doubly to reassure me. Holding it in the palm of my left hand, I could feel the gentle warmth it exuded flow up my arm and across my chest, then into my still throbbing heart and queasy stomach, finally down into my wobbly legs. My courage enough restored to let me try, I found that gradually, gradually I was able to rise to my knees, my feet—and even to take my first faltering steps.

Nearly an hour had passed, however, before I managed to negotiate the short distance which separated me from the cave, where I found the Scrolls and my own translation intact. I had carried the PSSS in my left hand, the Priest's two "eggs" in my right, feeling in both an oddly syncopated throbbing clearly distinguishable from the regular pumping of my own heart. I had not before, however, detected the slightest hint of such a pulse in M-M's Stone, which I presumed, therefore, must have been activated by the Urim and Tumim. Certainly, as I moved my hands closer together, its pulsing grew stronger, then diminished again as I moved them apart. Even at its most intense, however, it remained palpable only—imperceptible to the eye or ear. I understood then, and my heart leaped up once more, that the "sacred jewels" which had once graced the Arch-Priest's breastplate must be precisely such solid-state power sources as the one I had stolen from Melissa-Melinda. Both were natural focusing devices for zeta rays, which moving at a speed greater than that of light become infinitely small rather than infinitely large, as Classical Physics had hypothesized. Consequently, both were no more, and no less, mysterious than burning-glasses, which men have used for millennia to make the rays of the sun work on their behalf.

When I chafed the Urim and Tumim between my palms, however, they neither grew warm nor glowed, only pulsed a little faster and more erratically, like signals in some unknown code. And yet they were the same uncanny texture and the same uncolor as the PSSS: a dull quasi-black, which was somehow not quite opaque, like the dark center of the human iris, into which one cannot see, but out of which something seems to look. Obviously, they had been keyed to communication rather than the production of light and heat; and their size, also dissimilar, must be a function of that differing purpose. But when I placed my own Stone side by side with them for comparison, it appeared to have grown perceptibly larger, too large, in fact, to be put back into the tiny compartment of the poison ring. And why not? I thought, since such solid-state devices are crystalline in structure, and crystals notoriously grow, like men or trees or lies. The Stone, however, seemed to be not merely waxing in bulk, but waning in brilliance as well: lighting up a considerably smaller circle than usual, even after I had touched it to my groin. Or was it merely that my eyes were dimming, as sleep assailed me once more, blurring from focus as the lids grew heavier and heavier until . . .

When I awoke at the first light of the following day, the PSSS was fully as large as the Urim and Tumim; and, indeed, I could distinguish it from them only by the luminescence which surrounded it still, although it was pearled with the morning dew. Clutching it to me, I sensed what I could not help thinking of as the pulsing of its life's blood: slow and dreamy, like my own at the moment between sleeping and waking. But it flared into full brilliance at my touch, lighting up the gloomy interior of the cave, so that the shadow cast by each rocky protuberance was defined on the sandy floor as sharply as under the noonday sun. *I was wrong*, I thought then. *It has not faded at all.* Hope leaped up in me, therefore, along with a kind of desperate joy. I felt suddenly restored, refreshed, redeemed; knowing that all things were possible for me once more, or rather that they had always been—though I had doubted for a while.

Never mind the fallen rocks and the Y-cleft that cut me off from returning by the way I had come. The earth was stable under my feet again, solid as on the day of creation. And the man-sized fissure was still there in the back of the cave, I could see, ready to serve me, as it had doubtlessly served innumerable trapped beasts and men over the millennia. Like all good burrows, my burrow had two exits; so what matter if one was blocked? Besides, I had the Stone to light me on my way, a beacon that would not fail in the darkness beyond. But would I be able to slip through that narrow slit laden with a double Scroll, my own manuscript, enough supplies to sustain me on the journey—plus, of course, the Urim and Tumim? I rushed to the back wall to check; and discovered that though I could thrust my arm into it still, the fissure had closed up under the stresses of the earthquake—not quite tight, to be sure, but tight enough so that my shoulders could no longer enter it, or my head.

For a moment I was tempted to bang that too-large head in despair against the solid rock, as I have seen mourning Bedouin women do, pitting physical pain against inner anguish until they black out and fall to the ground. But before I could begin the bloody work, I was pushed past hysteria into paralysis by a new calamity. At first, I was aware only that all had grown dark around me; then, looking down, I realized that the rosy gleam of the Stone in my hand had dimmed to an ashen gray. In another instant it was glowing brightly again, though somehow not quite as steadily as before. *It is phasing out,* I told myself, not really knowing the proper term, *or perhaps only rephasing itself as a communications device. But it is light and heat that I need, not an unreadable message from a distant star.* How long it would be between blackouts, or how many blackouts before the onset of total darkness, I had no way of telling. And so I stood there unmoving, incapable of motion: a man with nowhere to go, and no way to get there if there were. Even my shadow, cast onto the cavern roof by the PSSS, which had fallen from my unclenched fingers, seemed frozen, fixed forever like the stones across which it was cast. "You move first," I found myself shouting at it, like an imbecile, "and I'll follow."

Then, all at once, I was at peace; knowing that for the first time in my life (even in Upper Columbia, I could have run away), I had no options, and therefore no grounds for anguish before action, or regret afterward. There at my feet lay the Scrolls, paper, pens—a task to be done, the paraphernalia to do it, and no one except me to undertake it. I was, in short, whether by gods or fate or sheer chance, "chosen," i.e., left without choice. And so I settled down into the scribe's position: quite sure of what must be accomplished in whatever time I had, totally unsure of how long that time would be. I had first to complete the translation of Scroll Two, add footnotes and glossary, then set it in the context of my own story, of which it had now become a part: my calling, my ordeal, my triumph and my defeat.

It was not so much vanity that moved me as the sense that I might well die with my task only half-done; and that I must, therefore, leave a record for my successor, as the Arch-Priest had left his for me. Yet at some level I must still have believed that finishing the task would constitute a spell, a charm potent enough to bring the Meta-Technicians down out of the skies to deliver me. After all, no cleft or fissure or barrier of rock barred the pathway of the heavens. If only I could finish, working day and night. Fighting sleep. Substituting work for food. If only the light would last.

It was six, perhaps seven hours before the PSSS blinked off again, then on; and if its glow had grown dimmer and less steady this time, it would have taken a more sensitive instrument than my eye to register the change. But I had begun to suspect that there was no hope really, that it would continue to fade. And therefore it did not surprise me to hear my own voice crying aloud an apposite verse from the Holy Book of the Arch-Priest's people, "Work for the night cometh." Or was it a tag from those rival Scriptures, the so-called Book of the New Covenant, revered by the followers of the false Messiah whom he had so loved and distrusted? But what difference could it have made to me in any event, to whom nothing mattered any longer except to write? And so I wrote, though the phrase continued to ring in my head, echoing and reechoing without speech until it had become a kind of silent thunder: "Work for the night cometh. *Work for the night cometh.* WORK FOR THE NIGHT COMETH."

THE SECOND SCROLL

OF

ELIEZAR ben YAAKOV ha-KOHEN

(with a glossary of

unfamiliar names

and terms

by

Jacob Mindyson)

I was not aware at first of how long I had slept, as I had not been aware of how long I had gone without sleeping in the days before the crucifixion. Nearly a week of waking, nearly forty-eight hours of sleeping, when my eldest son roused me where I sat slumped in my chair, my head cradled in my arms, this scroll my only pillow. G-d knows how long I might have slumbered on if he had not come to bring me the news. Perhaps until death overtook me.

"Excuse me, father. I did not believe them when they told me you were sleeping. At a moment like *this!*" He stood before me with his customary air of bewilderment and indignation, this white-headed, white-whiskered oldster (only his eyebrows still red): the firstborn of my first wife, he—as they say—who openeth the womb.

"Next time believe them, my son," I responded, rising to stretch, since I felt myself sore in every muscle, sore to the marrow of my brittle bones. "It is a sin to wake the sleeping at any moment. Especially one like this."

"But you are needed, father. Everywhere men cry, 'Where is the Arch-Priest? Who will help us in the hour of our distress?' And you sleep through it all. Unbelievable! The Blasphemer has been taken down from the cross, placed in a sealed tomb under guard. There are soldiers in the streets with swords drawn, and the followers of the false Messiah are in hiding or flight. Yehudah, accursed be his name forever, has hanged himself in despair."

Or has been hanged by you and your brothers, I found myself thinking, *lest he talk under torture, or turn to blackmail.* Yet I had no cause for suspicion, except long distrust of the aging man before me, who lived only for espionage and deceit. But *murder?* His seasoned liar's face betrayed nothing, so I said nothing except, "May he rest in peace."

"May he rot in Gehenna with other hirelings and traitors. And may Maryam, your kinswoman, rot in Gehenna with him. Do you know what she is doing at this very moment?"

Why does he always question me thus? As if he were a lawyer or my father, and I some shabby criminal or mischievous child. In my annoyance, I answered to him as discretion dictated I should not. "She is waiting outside the tomb with two other women also called Maryam,[34] with a whore and a layer-out of the dead. A mother, a whore and a layer-out of the dead, all called by the same name. To signify *what?* Riddle me that, you who will be the Arch-Priest after me."

Blessed in his ignorance, he could not answer. And so I continued, "In the morning, which is to say, even now—for I see the first light at the eastern windows—they will wake, the three of them, not knowing they have slept, to find the rocks which seal the tomb removed and the crypt empty. Later, they will speak of a Messenger having appeared to them, but it will be a lie. The body they thought to have carried off for their abominable rites will be gone, is already gone, praised be the Eternal."

"But how can you know this which the waking do not yet know, you who have slept?" His jaw with its scraggle of hair had dropped down, leaving his mouth agape, and the stupidity, usually concealed by a mask of cunning, nakedly displayed.

"You are not the only one," I answered, "who has informers and spies." Perhaps I should have confessed to him then that the Elim had appeared to me in the sleep from which he had waked me, to tell me all that had occurred on the cross and at the tomb. For the first time (and, my foreboding heart suggested, the last), I had seen them as well as heard them, the Old Ones, the Masters. It is by such names as these, rooted in the awe small children feel for grandfathers and teachers, that I am moved to call them. Yet no image remained of what I saw, or thought I saw, dreaming; for I had perceived the Elim not as I perceived my son before me or myself in the mirror which made up the whole wall behind him;

---

[34] It is, indeed, odd that the three women at the tomb of the crucified Jesus are all called Mary. And odd, too, that the footnote in which by sheer chance, I record the fact be 34, i.e., a combination of the matriarchal 3 and patriarchal 4, but with the mother number coming first.

but on another plane, in another dimension, and therefore as simultaneously strange and familiar.

My very first experience of myself in that mirror, however, is the analogy which occurs to me when I seek now to describe how I perceived them. And perhaps that is appropriate, since that "looking glass," as they call it, is another gift from the Elim. More wonderful, I sometimes think, than the Scanner, in which I watch the making and unmaking of worlds; or the Urim and Tumim, with which I call up their voices. If you have never looked at yourself in a mirror, I do not know how to tell you what it is like. The distorted image of our faces glimpsed in still waters resembles it a little, but only a little; for in glass backed with silver, we behold clearly a self otherwise secret to us, the visible self we present to others: incredibly vivid, but finally unreal.

If only, I think sometimes standing before my reflected image, I possessed other "reflectors" capable of revealing how we sound, smell, feel and taste to others, perhaps then I would know myself fully. But all such reproductions added together would add up only to a beautiful lie; since we are not the sum total of the selves available to the senses—even our own, much less those of our neighbors. This is the lesson I learn and relearn at my mirror.

To be sure, it provides me amusement as well as such somber wisdom; showing me, then, for instance, the back of my son, his braced shoulders and trembling hams, which he did not realize were being observed; and which betrayed him, therefore, as his carefully composed face did not. How vanity-ridden he is, poor fellow, how brazen in his uncertainty.

And what could he have been saying to me anyhow, his mouth moving and moving, his eyes seeking mine. I must have responded with nods and grunts from time to time, as I am accustomed to do at such junctures; but I am not sure, for I was lost and bemused. Odd how little difference it makes whether one really listens or not at such presumably important moments.

Why had the Elim come to me this time, I kept asking myself, without the mediation of the Urim and Tumim; appearing while I slept, so that I could tell no one of my experience, least of all the son waiting to supplant me. "Why do you tell me your dreams, old man?" he would say, laughing his false laugh. "Surely you have not begun to confuse reality and dreams."

Even if I had tried to put it all in context, recounting the history of the connection between our people and the Elim, it would not have helped. What bond of faith could there be between an aging son and a ninety-year-old father, who, by simply living so long, has cheated him of a meaningful life? He would not even have pretended to hear me out; his eyes glazing over, as his thoughts turned to what was for him the real world: the whispered conferences and public debates, for which he is eternally preparing false promises and meaningless smiles. It would have been offensive to have spoken to him of a realm beyond the stars, or the Cosmic War, in which he would doubtless have chosen the wrong side, anyhow, mama's boy that he is.

So I played the role expected of me. "Go," I said, interrupting his monologue, "go find out what has happened at the tomb. Find out once more that your father is right. I am asking you to admit nothing, only to learn, and to leave me in peace. But first, for your soul's sake, let me tell you once more what I have told you so often. You are a fool, like your mother before you."

He has always thought himself her special darling; though she had merely used him in a battle with me whose bitterness I had not suspected, until on her deathbed she had spoken to me candidly for the first time.

My remark therefore rankled, as I had hoped it would. "This is no way to talk to a dutiful son, dear father," he said, trying to control his anger. "After all, it is I who will pray for you after you are dead, I in whom you will live on when your body has crumbled to dust."

"A good reason for living forever," I answered, waving him to the door. "But be assured I shall not do it. That I would not, even if I could." I was tired, tired—as if my long sleep had exhausted rather than refreshed me. And perhaps, I could not help suspecting, the immortal Elim had troubled my sleep for that end, hating us all, because, though the prisoners of our senses, we can at least die.

It would have been simpler, would it not, to have briefed me ten days earlier, when, waking, I had activated the Urim and Tumim to ask their advice. The Son of the Messenger, I had told them then, must by law of Caesar and the will of the Unnameable die. Indeed, he should never have been born, and would not have, if they had lived up to their word as we have.

"A regrettable error," they murmured. "A foible of immaturity."

"A breach of contract," I insisted. "But no matter. Looking backward, we turn, as it is written, into pillars of salt. What is at stake is not the irreversible past but the still open future. The question is what to do now."

"Why, let him die," one of them answered. "For you humans, that is always the easiest solution, is it not?"

"So be it," I responded. "But the body must not remain in the hands of the three women, who, scenting his death, follow him like vultures, or rather like priestesses in quest of a cult. Once he is a corpse, they will embalm him in the manner of Mitzraim, as they have been taught by the fourth Maryam, who came from that land.[35] And when they have thus made him 'immortal,' they will erect in his honor a Temple to rival our own. Converting him, who calls himself the Son of the Father, into another Son of the Mother: a dying and reborn son-husband, like Osiris or Attis or Adonis."

"What do you want then, old thunderer, you who desire to play God to your gods? What would you have us to?" There was a rumble as of thunder behind these un-words of the El, who seem never to tire of impressing us with signs and wonders.

"I want just one thing," I answered, ignoring the fireworks. "That there be no body. That is all. There must be no body left."

"So be it," the Elim answered in parody of my own sacerdotal style, being, it would seem, able to communicate only in the language of their interlocutors; so that talking to them is like talking to oneself.

"Amen," I said, before they could change their minds. "But to know what to do next, I must know their next move. Or else I will be stymied."

[35] Here the Arch-Priest seems to have gone out of his way to drag in the fourth Mary, known historically as "Mary the Egyptian"; though he may only have been motivated by a desire to make a case against the embalming of the dead, which the Ancient Jews found another matriarchal "abomination."

They would tell me nothing, however, though the future strategy of the Ashtorites must have been already present to them; like my request, which they had merely pretended to elicit.

No, they preferred to reveal what lay ahead ambiguously and in their own good time, waiting for sleep to overtake me. Only then did they say that they would, in due course, send Messengers; or had sent them, or were sending them. It was hard to be sure of the tenses, because in dreams time does not exist for us, as it does not ever for them. Those Messengers, they continued, would descend on the Great Square, just as he who thought himself the Messiah hung close to death on the cross. They would come in a spaceship and hover just above his bloody head, their jets blasting at full. The flesh of those closest to the cross would be seared: spectators hungry for blood, as well as the two common criminals who had been crucified beside him as a final degradation. And everyone to the furthest rim of the crowd would be deafened by the roar of the great engines which had powered their flight.[36]

"A spaceship," I remember protesting, contentious even in my sleep. "In full sight of everyone. But will this not give away everything we have for so long concealed?"

"*You* would have seen a spaceship," the El interrupted. "The bystanders saw only a stroke of lightning, darkness at noon, the trembling of the great facades which rim the Square as if in an earthquake."

"But *was* it a spaceship?" I asked foolishly.

"Is what you are experiencing a dream?" Like good Jews, the Elim love to answer a question with a counterquestion. "Is it not everything finally a way of speaking, a choice of metaphors?"

"Please," I cried, raising a dream hand to stop them; while they rocked back and forth with amusement. "Please, not the usual metaphysics, or I shall fall asleep in my sleep. So, your spaceship will descend. Well and good. But what will be done with the Son of the Messenger?"

"The Messengers will take their brother into the ship, and

[36] The official accounts of the Christians speak of wonderful portents at the moment of the Crucifixion, all of which Eliezar here explains away, as if bent on demythologizing the event—by replacing the "magic" of his own age with a "technology" that in the end seems, as he renders it, quite as mysterious. An odd passage.

168

transport him to the world of Shamaim. Even as he foretold."

They intended, I take it, a kind of theological joke; but I, refusing to laugh, continued to press them. "How can he survive, live—be viably reconstructed, as you have taught me to say, in Shamaim? After all, he is only human, the son of an earthly mother, and a father who—"

Their renewed laughter drowned out my final words, which I may not even have said. "Did we not take Moshe in similar fashion from the top of the mountain where he stood looking out at the land he could never enter? And was not Enoch, too, transported in the flesh to our far-off home? [37] Why not one, then, who is in some sense the Son of a Messenger, one of us?"

But what do we really know, I found myself thinking, about the fate of Moshe after, what the ancients called "the Kiss"? Or of Enoch beyond the moment of his translation? There is no record of their reappearance on earth, even in dreams; so maybe there is only one-way traffic between Eretz and Shamaim. Or perhaps Moshe and Enoch have been scattered to the multiple corners of space as a blur of fractured possibilities: evidence of a failed experiment, which, of course, the Elim would never confess.

Absurdly, my mind drifted back to my childhood, recalling the riddle with which we used to amuse ourselves at school, scholars even in our jesting: "Methusaleh lived longer than any other human, but he died before his father, Enoch. Explain." And at this point, my son woke me.

By then, however, I knew that the tomb would be empty when the stones were rolled away. What would be laid in it would be a simulacrum, a mirror image, as it were, without a mirror: visible only as long as there were eyes to see it, minds to insist that it was there. For such minds, I supposed, it would exist in terms of all the senses: not merely sight, but touch and hearing and, especially, smell. I imagined, therefore, the mother bending over the corpse, which, though not really there, reeked of feces and urine, since a crucified man cannot contain himself any more than a child; the physicians, whose profession depends on assuming the

[37] The Ancient Hebrews did not believe originally in personal immortality. But their Scriptures speak of three men who were "translated" after death to the abode of the Immortals; and two of them are mentioned here.

reality of all bodies, declaring him dead; finally, Yussef,[38] the rich man who appeared so aptly at the foot of the cross, bringing linens for a shroud and fragrant spices to mitigate the stench of the nonexistent flesh. In a sense, there would be nothing strange about the event. The dead are always simulacra: reminders, like our reflections in the glass, that we live in a realm of illusion from our first breath to our last. Perhaps even beyond.

It is a pity, nonetheless, tnat we were not able to continue our conversation just a little longer, the Elim and I. But my son could not have entered when he did without the connivance of those Powers; and I did not, in any case, need them to tell me what the three Maryams and the Stranger from Arimithaea were going to do next. I have other sources to fill in what the Elim have left blank: certain informants, for instance, who claim that the Stranger is a Eunuch-Priest from the Temple of the Black Diana of Ephesus, the Seven-Breasted One.

And whatever the truth of this (informants have to say something, lest they seem useless, dispensable), they go on to confirm what I have also learned elsewhere: that he has in his possession the Golden Goblet [39] from which the Son of the Messenger drank the required four cups of Passover wine; the Silver Dish on which he displayed, as we are accustomed to say, "the poor bread which our forebears ate in the Land of Mitzraim"; the Lance with which a merciful Centurion pierced his side to shorten his

---

[38] There are two Yussefs or Josephs in the story of Jesus, as well as three Marys (four, if we count the Egyptian); for the Israelites of those days used relatively few names, mostly those of their distinguished dead. This Yussef or Joseph of Arimathaea is the very opposite of the impotent old man who fostered the child. He comes out of nowhere, but takes charge once Jesus is dead and he has mysteriously appeared. Certain skeptical antireligionists of the nineteenth and twentieth centuries, in fact, actually accused him of faking the death of the "false Messiah," and spiriting him away alive.

[39] This is the "Holy Grail," famous in legend and story (as the Arch-Priest himself prophesies), especially from the thirteenth century until just a couple of hundred years ago. According to some, and Eliezar's account seems to verify this, the Holy Vessel was transported to Glastonbury in western England, where a rival Christian Church was started, finally suppressed by the official Cult at Canterbury. It survived, however, in poetry, and perhaps also in the tarot pack: fortune-telling cards whose suits are derived from the Cup, Dish, Lance and Sword.

suffering; the Sword with which one of the rabble of fisher-folk [40] who surround him sought to protect him from the soldiers sent to arrest him.

It was from the Procurator himself that I learned all this; and what better source than one whose career depends on listening to rumor and sifting the true from the false. "I have put no obstacle in the way," a letter from the Palace "hastens to inform" me, after listing the four objects. *"Sacra,"* the Procurator calls them in his own tongue, which is to say, "Hallows." "Yussef of Arimathaea is, it would appear," his missive continues, "a collector of ritual objects, a student of Comparative Religion, and I could not gracefully say no to his request. I am sure that you yourself would not have wanted to stand in the way of the pursuit of knowledge, even on so secular a plane."

Idiot! Know-nothing! I am no "student of Comparative Religion." But I have lived long enough in a world of competing sects to know the significance of the *combination* of Cup and Lance, Dish and Sword to Mother-worshiping *goyim,* who confuse the sacred and the sexual; bowing down before graven images of their own genitals, male and female. "Pursuit of knowledge," indeed. Say, rather, abomination of abominations! Yet we have been ever since the transgression, in the Garden the abject slaves of our flesh, so what need to apotheosize it? To bow down before symbols of phallus and vulva?

And now, another courier. This one bearded and careful to remain covered in the House of the Eternal; in short, a Jew who grovels before me, holding up a parchment scroll, but turning his eyes away from my face, as I reach out to take it. He has been sent, I assume, by my second son, a mere youngster of sixty-two, who hopes to outlive his older brother as well as me. But the courier does not say so, says nothing in fact, only breathes hard and lets the anonymous message speak for itself.

"It is possible," the scroll runs, "that the Blasphemer may have repented at the end. Those who stood closest to him report

---

[40] This is the famous Simon the Rock, called St. Peter and reported to have been the founder of the immensely influential Christian Sect, now finally destroyed, which called itself the Roman Catholic Church.

that just before the thunderclap and the earthquake, he apparently quoted from the Psalms the verse beginning *'Eli, eli, lama sabachtani.'*[41] Would it not be well to publicize his last-minute recantation against the heretics who begin to speak of him as the incarnation of G-d?" Another idiot! And this time, to make it worse, an idiot afraid to sign his name or come in person to confront his own father.

And yet there is comfort for me in the news that my other son, the bastard I can never acknowledge, had reproached by name in his last agony (though only in a form which would seem to the unenlightened a quotation) the El who has tormented and abandoned us both. Perhaps he might have been spared that agony had he been willing to do so earlier. It was not that I had kept him in ignorance. Indeed, on several occasions I had met with him secretly to explain in what sense we Jews, in general, and he, in particular, had been "Chosen." And by whom. And how they had forsaken us.

On one of those occasions, I even tried to tell him in all its confusing detail the story of his birth. But he would not hear me out, having been persuaded by that madman, Yohannan,[42] his mother's sister's son, that he was the *Mashiach*, the Anointed One, whose coming had been foretold by all the prophets. There is, indeed, a strange tale, often repeated and widely believed, that when Yohannan was pouring over him the waters of the Jordan, according to the practice of the Essenes, a voice was heard from the clouds, declaring, *"This is my only begotten son."* Had the Messenger who sired him really manifested himself in that voice, or, as others would have it, as a bird: a dove or a pigeon descending from the Heavens? It is possible, I suppose, that he may have mounted the charade, moved by improbable guilt, or perhaps only the desire to

---

[41] This means literally—in Aramaic—"My God, my God, why hast thou forsaken me," and is one of the seven last words attributed to Jesus in the garbled and contradictory accounts of the Crucifixion which survive. The Arch-Priest's efforts to make "Eli" apply to his "Elim," or "Masters," I find unconvincing, a piece of palpable self-deceit.

[42] This is that John the Baptist, famous in story and painting, for two episodes: his Baptism of Jesus (described here), and his beheading at the behest of Salome, a concubine of the Jewish puppet-king in Antioch—which was even more celebrated on a popular level.

play one more prank. And that the Elim, for their own reasons, permitted it. Most likely, however, the whole thing is a fabrication of Maryam—more mythology prompted by her secret sponsors, or her own ambitious heart.

In any case, her son had certainly not understood that voice (if it existed to all outside his own head, and the heads of the by-standers who had stood in expectation of baptism, hour after hour under the intolerable desert sun) as declaring him the offspring of an Incubus, a Malaach lusting after the daughter of men. To him, what spoke was nothing less than the *Ruach Elohim*, the Spirit [43] of the Lord G-d without Name or Shape or Habitation, which in the Beginning had hovered on the face of the waters. And I could not dissuade him.

"You are the victim of your mother," I told him, "who desires nothing but your death, who has all your life long sought only to exploit you."

"Dear master," he rejoined, "old foster father, godfather, soul of my soul, all mothers seek only to exploit their sons. As all fathers the mothers of those sons. Do not be deceived. I know what you have never hinted to me: that you longed once to become my father in the flesh. And that except for my mother's holy vow of virginity, she might have—"

But I could not let him finish, an old man remembering passions long cooled, a woman who, passing me on the street, turns her head away and spits! "Never mind your mother," I said. "It is not she who victimizes you, but the language you share. You will never know your true father." How I longed to embrace him, to tell him, "*I* am your true father. I and a Messenger." But I could not.

"Of all who walk the earth, sweet teacher whom I must in the

---

[43] The word *ruach,* meaning "spirit," is in Hebrew of indeterminate gender, either feminine or masculine. And the whole phrase *Ruach Elohim* was translated, via Greek, by the early Christians as "Holy Spirit" or "Holy Ghost." They used this as the name of the third person in their "divine trinity"; thus making out of the matriarchal triad, Father, Son, Mother—a patriarchal one, Father, Son and (sexless) Holy Ghost. But alas for Eliezar, the "Mother" returned in the form of a deified Maryam; on a popular level, at least, once Christianity had moved to Europe, where the real—rather than official—trinity became Joseph, Jesus and Mary: Cuckold, Son and Blessed Virgin.

end deny even as you deny me, I alone know my Father who is in Shamaim."

"Exactly," I responded, "your father *is* in Shamaim. It is what I have been trying to tell you."

But we were both of us aware that the words we spoke in common did not join but separate us. Even so, they would continue to separate, I foresaw, those who would remain Jews like me, and those who would slay them for not becoming what would be called, after a while, Christians: meaning those who believed the Son of the Messenger to be the Anointed One, or, in the language of Yavan, which they prefer to our own, the *Christos*.[44] It is all perhaps, as the Elim delight in saying and I am sometimes tempted to echo, only a choice of metaphors, a manner of speaking. But we who die, die for such choices, such manners of speaking.

Would that the son bred of my loins and a mother I never possessed had listened to me. I must be grateful, I suppose, that when it was too late to save his followers from their error or my people from them—he at last recognized the Elim for what they were. But what do they say to each other, I wonder, he and the Power he berated from the cross? If, indeed, he has been successfully translated to Shamaim. If it is not all a hoax and a delusion from beginning to end.

It is odd how little I remember of the words he spoke in our several encounters, carried on always under cover of night and in whispers, lest either, both of us be compromised. Beyond the few sentences I have written down above, I recall chiefly the terms of endearment which were always on his lips, plus certain traditional phrases which we would repeat antiphonally. Like a thousand fathers and sons, priests and celebrants before us; and, I suppose, after us, for as long as time lasts.

I have not forgotten my own reproaches eternally delivered for something he had done wrong or failed to do right. Did I never congratulate him on anything, praise him for anything? If so, I do not remember. "Get married," I would urge him, "you are thirty years old, and people are talking." Or I would cry in protest that

---

[44] The Hebrew *Mashiach*, sometimes transliterated simply as "Messiah," means literally the "Anointed One," which is in Greek *Christos,* transliterated "Christ"—a word used by simple anti-Jewish Christians for centuries with no sense of its Jewish roots.

he must not allow his message to be obscured by wonder-working, the multiplication of loaves and fishes, the casting out of demons, the raising of the dead; or that he must not offend the deepest pieties of simple believers by teaching men to turn their backs on their parents, whether living or dead; or that he must not speak arrogantly, as if the wisdom he preached was from himself rather than G-d.

"Always before you," I would explain, "prophets have been careful to preface new doctrine with reassuring phrases like 'It is written' or 'Thus sayeth the Lord.' Why then do you keep repeating 'Verily, *I* say unto you'? This is *chutzpah* and deserves to be punished." But chiefly I bombarded him, as is, I fear, the habit of old men, with quotations that seemed to me apropos. "The World is a Wedding," I would say, or "Even the Magicians of Pharaoh can perform miracles," or "Honor thy father and thy mother that thy days may be prolonged upon the face of the earth," or "A false prophet shall be put to death."

In some sense, however—as I can now confess—he was a true prophet; though he had fallen, alas, into the hands of, been born out of the womb of one who would use his truth in the interests of confusion. Yet it was he rather than she, his own misreading of his role, which led to our most bitter debate: over whether he was in fact the Son of David, the Son of Man, the Son of (G-d forgive me for writing it down) G-d. The climax came when he dared to ride into the Holy City on the foal of an ass, as had been foretold of the Messiah; the carefully coached crowds about him waving palm leaves and crying, "Blessed be he who comes in the Name of the Lord": the messianic blessing.

"The worst sin of all," I remember screaming at him the following day, "is to hasten the End, to try to take the Kingdom of Heaven by storm."

But he only smiled at me, calling me "Dearest godfather," "Beloved master," "Old friend"; then giving me, right cheek to left, the kiss of peace. Perhaps it was at that point (it is hard to sort these things out) that he reassured me, as I have already recorded, that not one *yod* or tittle of the Law should pass away in the New Era he fondly believed himself to be ushering in.

And maybe it is only proper that I remember so few of his words; since what chiefly bound us together were other men's words, which is to say, the rituals and ceremonies of our people; from the *Pinyan-ha-ben* at the beginning to the Hearing in Council [45] at the end of his life. In my dreams, which he haunts, like his mother before him, he is invariably dumb. Yet I feel him at ease and at home there, in a way he never was in the world of the waking; as if dreams and Shamaim were one, and he truly transported, repatriated, as the Elim have promised.

I do not mean it has not occurred to me before that the Heavens and Dreamland are one. Often bending over the smoking sacrifice on the altar, or leaning forward to follow the pointer of the Levite, tracing on the Holy Scroll the passage I read, the censer swinging behind me, I have sensed that even the Scrolls and the sacrifice are delusions from which we must somehow learn to awake. But afterward, the swish of fans and the slapping of the mops of the cleaners, the rush of air through the Sanctuary as they open the Great Doors to let in the light, let out the smoke, have driven it all from my head. This time, however, I will not forget, since I have grown too old for forgetting.

But remembering, I will find it hard to believe that it matters who wins or who loses, I or Maryam, Yang or Yin, the Seed or the Egg. What if the rich Yussef manages to reach those remote islands in the Northern Sea to which (I am informed by a certain ship's purser, my creature, yet clearly tempted by the Arimathaean) he is planning to sail. To find a place of safekeeping for the Four Hallows, the awestruck seaman goes on to tell me: a place known, I gather, as "The Castle of Women." There the Cup and the Lance, the Dish and the Sword will be guarded with spells of great power until the coming of a pure warrior, the virgin offspring of a Jewish Priest and a Princess also virgin, though pagan by birth. Only such a warrior—the ship's purser continues—will be able to heal the Wounded King, the Castrated Father, who, until his coming, must be tended by maidens and grandmothers: women not yet inducted into the mystery of sex, or

[45] This is the famous Sanhedrin, which haunted the dark undermind of Christian Europe for two thousand years, lending credence to the slanderous "Protector of Zion" and other documents of that anti-Semitism which was one of the blackest aspects of Christianity— grounds enough (though apparently the Jews answered in kind) for its final dissolution. How fortunate we are to live in a time which has abolished both persecuting Sects!

already beyond it.[46] It is another parable, I realize, not prophecy but history disguised as prophecy—like all myths of the Goddess, who can only look backward, frozen in the salt of her own tears; since her Empire is always the Past.

"Go," I say to my agent, "go in peace." I know he is already converted, suborned; but I am convinced it makes no difference. "Take the money of the Arimathaean. All will be well."

Nothing will come of the mad venture to the Ultima Thule, of this much I am sure; certainly not the Universal Church of which the rich Yussef dreams. Only perhaps a song, and a tale told by the fire: what the *goyim* came to call a little later "literature."

No, if there is a real threat at all, it will develop closer to home; through that merchant from Tarshish, so proud that—unlike most other Jews—he is a citizen of the Empire, a "real Roman," he likes to say. But the really real Romans treat him with contempt, calling him not Saul, which is his given name, but Paulus, which is to say, the "Little One," the "Shrimp." [47] Like the ship's purser, he, too, began as my agent, recruited from among, as he also sometimes boasts, those who "sat at my feet." Not a serious student, you understand, dedicated entirely to the study of the Law, but one of those pious businessmen willing to devote his spare time to learning what his kind call "the tradition of our people." It was in the name of that tradition that I persuaded him to spy on certain adherents of the Son of the Messenger. And he is still, he has just sent word to assure me, faithful; ready even to persecute the followers of the crucified one, if they persist in their folly.

He has been primarily concerned with the role played in the

[46] This represents in capsule form the whole legend of the Holy Grail; and once again my suspicions are aroused. How did Eliezar, I ask myself, come to know so well a tale which the best evidence suggests was not invented in this form until the High Middle Ages? True, its presumable author was a crypto-Jew called Christian (it was a name taken by many converts) of Troyes. But it is hard to believe in its oral transmission over twelve hundred years or more.

[47] This is, of course, the once-famous Apostle to the Gentiles, St. Paul, who did in fact remake the Christian religion, becoming its earliest spokesman to the world—though he had never actually known Jesus or heard him preach. It took nearly a thousand years, in fact, for the Female element in the new faith to reassert itself against the misogynistic cast of his thought.

movement on which he spies by the three Maryams, especially her of Magdala, the reformed whore; for he is a passionate hater of women and sexuality. Indeed, it is for this that I chose him in the beginning; though like all such fanatics he is at the mercy of an unsuspected ambivalence, easily turned into duplicity. To make a fetish of virginity is like making a fetish of fucking, a form of idolatry: the conversion of an indifferent means to an End. Good or Bad. Besides it has been reported to me by many, including Jacob,[48] the bastard foster brother of the bastard son of the Messenger, that the Merchant of Tarshish has sometimes spoken against the practice of circumcision. Imagine it!

It is a barbaric survival, he argues, a symbol which, however useful once, has ended by replacing that for which it stands, "the circumcision of the heart." What he would substitute for the cutting of the foreskin (since he knows that men always and everywhere stand in need of symbols) is the sprinkling of water on the head—in the style of Yohannan the Baptizer, that rabid denier of life, whom even the self-righteous Essenes finally disavowed. In any case, it is the penis which the Shrimp fears, preferring to make the ritual center of his revised faith man's actual head or metaphorical heart. Yet the rejection of circumcision implies, whatever the "real Roman" may intend, the reinstitution of child sacrifice, which it was invented to replace; and this in turn means a return to the Dark Reign of the Goddess, female prostitution, the castration of priests.

Still he is a fascinating fellow, our Paulus; and, on balance, I do not regret enlisting him in our cause. Totally bald and almost a dwarf, with a limp and a cast in one eye, he can—as they say in the marketplace—charm the birds down out of the trees: sell anything to anyone, shoddy merchandise, equivocal ideas, his unseemly self. It is not so much his command of language (he speaks a dozen tongues elegantly) as his mysterious charm, the aura which, phy-

[48] James, he is called by most Christians, who, of course, insist he was only a foster brother of Jesus, since Mary remained "virgin" not only through his birth, but forever after. And the Priest's account jibes with this. But some debunkers in the twentieth and twenty-first centuries insisted that he was Mary's child, this defender of the Circumcision, who was finally outargued and outsmarted by Paul.

sicians have told me, is associated with the Falling Sickness to which he is prey. I have seen him in one of his fits: writhing on the ground like a woman in childbirth or sexual ecstasy—his tongue thrust out between his teeth, his eyes rolled up in his head, his thighs spread painfully wide and his knees pulled back against his stomach. It is like a visitation of the Great Mother, and I do not wish to behold it again.

Still, he has insisted to me that it is well worth the terror and the pain; for at such moments he has revelations, visions of a New Heaven and a New Earth, of man redeemed from sin and glorified for all eternity. Such talk, however, leaves me uncomfortable; since what comes to a mind thus out of control is likely to appear with its original affect and value reversed. Why, for instance, should he not someday see and adore in such a fit the Son of the Messenger, on whom he never laid eyes, but who for that reason has especially haunted him? It is, in any case, precisely such figures who appear—or should I say, appear to appear—to visionaries, whether they be epileptics, madmen or the chosen of G-d. Nonetheless, if there is to be a new sect centered around the Son of the Messenger, far better that it be molded from the start by a misogynist with his eye always on Rome (which compromises everything, betrays all), than by a well-heeled mystic carrying from East to West the Insignia of the Great Goddess in the name of *Christos.*

Have I forgotten so soon what I swore only a moment ago that I would always remember: that it does not matter, that nothing matters? I have not forgotten, only realized that my great revelation was a half-truth, which is to say, a half-lie. Even if nothing else matters, it matters that we behave as if everything mattered. Does that make sense, or am I indeed dithering, as my sons have long suspected? Never mind, I shall let the sentence stand, blot nothing out.

I find myself, however, at a loss. And so I have decided to go one last time into the Sanctuary, where I shall begin by activating the Scanner, turning up the power to full, as I have never dared do before. There will be revealed to me then not only all of space, the whole universe I inhabit, but all of time, the sum total of possible universes. Thus, I will learn simultaneously the Future, which I fear, and the Past that has created in me that fear. The present, however, will remain invisible to me, as it is necessarily invisible (thanks be to G-d) to those who are in it.

I realize that it is probability only which the Scanner computes: the probability of an instant which an instant can change. And I shall, therefore, not write down in these pages what it reveals, lest inscribing the Future convert it into even more dire calamity than I surmise. Moreover, I have learned from the career of the Son of the Messenger how prophecy can enslave; and I desire those who come after me to be free.

When I prepare to leave the Scanner this time, I shall, therefore, switch on signals of maximum dissonance, creating a pattern of interference, static, white noise, which will turn the once-transparent east wall into a substance opaque, impenetrable, impacted—almost indestructible. It alone will remain when the House of the Eternal is burned to the ground by ravaging *goyim:* immune to vandalism and decay, until pilgrim Jews from lands as alien as the remotest star shall melt it away with the slow dripping of tears over millennia of exile and pain.[49] Only when its last stone will have crumbled to dust will it be possible to construct a new Temple; and gathering the scattered seed of the *Kohanim,* to rekindle the sacrificial fires, so that smoke can ascend once more to Him without Shape or Form or Beginning or End.

Next I shall enter the concealed room behind the western wall, where I will follow for the final time the prescribed forms for communicating with the Eliın: lighting the Golden Menorah, which bears in its seven branches forged of a metal not mined by men, seven candles made of the tallow from beasts not butchered by any human hand. This time I shall light them, however, not as is customary with a cedar spill, but with the flame of the Everlasting Light we burn before the Ark in honor of the wonders wrought by YHVH for Yehudah the Hammer, who delivered us

---

[49] At this point, I begin to regret the earlier skepticism registered in those notes about the veracity of the Arch-Priest's account; for I have seen the Wall, his Wall as it has survived into my own time; and have felt, despite a lifetime of antireligious conditioning, its authentic power. Small credit to me, however, that it takes a pile of stones to convince me: a *goy* after all, as the hunchbacked Yitt so aptly called me.

from an earlier oppressor. And when the candles are all rekindled, I will blow out that Light.

I shall take my position, then, as we have always done—I and my father and my father's fathers back to the time of Aaron: stationing myself at the spot where an axis drawn along the slant of light that falls from the south window at the dawn of midsummer meets one which follows the last beam of the setting sun at midwinter. An ignorant observer would take all this, I suppose, for what is called in our world "magic." But the Elim, who have taught us these forms, prefer to say "science."

Finally, I shall turn the dials on my breastplate, the Urim and Tumim [50]—or rather, I shall *think* turning those dials: *right, left, left, left, right;* and before the voices can respond: *left, left, right.* Then the connection so long and perilously maintained will be broken at last; the Elim dead to us forever, the Messengers able to come no more. Not until the end of all time. If the Elim have spoken the truth, however, we may before that end learn to go to them. But that is the concern of those not yet born, perhaps of you who will read this record when I am long dead and the very names of all gods but the Nameless forgotten. For me, it will be enough to have done what no man before me ever dared do—to choose to be free.

I shall depart in peace, therefore, when the last candle has guttered out; jamming the locks of the doors and leaving the place of communication to darkness and gathering dust, until, for one instant, it is lighted brighter than day by the fire to come.

I have done it; destroyed the Scanner, sealed the Sanctuary, killed the gods. Afterward, I slept once more, though for a little time only, rising with the first light. My mind is made up. I will finish this record and take it with me into the *Midbar,* the Desert whose sands preserve papyrus and parchment forever—but not men.

---

[50] It is here, where the Arch-Priest approaches his end, that a reader interested in *using* this record—the Meta-Technicians, if they come, or their successors in whatever unforeseen future—must begin. For here, if anywhere, except perhaps the earlier passages dealing with the Urim and Tumim, lies the clue to establishing communications with Alien Intelligences: a clue I do not myself understand.

There is no use dissembling. I am going to the Desert to die; for it is time, and I am beset by doubts which I cannot resolve. Not in this world anyhow. But for us Jews, there is no other world: no afterlife, no persistence of the soul or resurrection of the body, as the sages of Yavan and our own heretics (including, I fear, the Son of the Messenger) falsely teach. I have always believed it to be the final mercy of YHVH that we do not live forever. If, that is to say, YHVH exists at all. If I have not killed him in killing the Elim.

Let me abandon metaphor for once and confess that I fear the Nameless One may always have been, may be now and forever only another "parable" of the Elim, another lie intended to enlist us in their Cosmic War against the forces of the Dark Mother. Certainly the world I have lived in for more than ninety years seems more a shambles, a battleground, the contested plaything of immoral and conflicting Powers than the creation of a single just and omnipotent G-d. The only wonder to me is that in such a world, creatures like us have been able to create the illusion, the promise, the hope of such a Being. We could not, I suspect, without the intervention of Intelligences greater than our own. And yet in a very few minutes, I shall repeat the Three Benedictions I have spoken every morning of my life since my thirteenth year—blessing the G-d who did not make me for having created me a free man, a Jew and a one who, as we say, pisses against the wall.

If he existed in fact, he would, I suspect, find these Three Benedictions an offense, being above all distinction of class, race or sex. If, on the other hand, he is the invention of those who happen to have been free and Jewish and male, what could be more fitting and proper. Therefore—

BLESSED ART THOU, O LORD, OUR G-D, KING OF THE UNIVERSE,
WHO HAST NOT MADE ME A HEATHEN
BLESSED ART THOU, O LORD, OUR G-D, KING OF THE UNIVERSE,
WHO HAST NOT MADE ME A SLAVE
BLESSED ART THOU, O LORD, OUR G-D, KING OF THE UNIVERSE,
WHO HAST NOT MADE ME A WOMAN.

And now there remains only to say Kaddish for my dead son. And then . . . to the Desert . . .

After a while, I suppose, not the sun alone but hunger and thirst will addle my head; for I shall take with me only a single water bag, one small wallet of food—and I shall ask no alms, even if I should improbably encounter pious travelers on the way. G-d knows what jinns and demons will beset me, what horrors emerge from the chasms and caverns of the wilderness, or from the dark places of my own mind. Perhaps I shall die screaming. One thing I do know, however. The Messengers will not come to me. The Messengers will come no more.

A GLOSSARY OF UNFAMILIAR NAMES AND TERMS

ADONIS: One of the several names given to the dying and reborn Son-Husband of the Mother Goddess in the Eastern Mediterranean Fertility Cults. A compromise perhaps with Patriarchal Mythologies—or at least a later stage of development in the Mother mythos than those implicit in Mysteries celebrating the renewal of the earth in terms of a Mother and a Daughter. (See also ATTIS, OSIRIS, CERES.)

APHRODITE: Greek name for the Goddess of Love and Beauty, called by the Romans "Venus." One of the innumerable avatars of the Great Mother or Triple Goddess in her more benign aspect. (See also ASHTORETH, ASTARTE, DEMETER, DIANA, HECATE, ISHTAR, ISIS, LILITH, RHEA, SHEKHINAH.)

ARIMATHAEA: The place of origin of that Yussef (q.v.), or Joseph, who comes to claim the body of the crucified Jesus; and who, according to legend, carried to Glastonbury in England the Cup out of which that false Messiah (q.v.) drank at the Last Supper (q.v.). (See also HALLOWS, PASSOVER SEDER, SACRA.)

ARK: An ambiguous word signifying, on the one hand, the vessel in which Noah escaped the Flood sent to destroy the rest of mankind. But here used to mean the Chest or Container in which the Ancient Jews were accustomed to keep the Scrolls of the Torah (q.v.).

ASHTORETH: One of the names of the Great Goddess, whence the term "Ashtorites" for followers of the Mother Religion, or, as Eliezar uses it, for Witches (q.v.). (See also APHRODITE.)

ASTARTE: See APHRODITE.

ATTIS: See ADONIS.

BAR MITZVAH: An essential *rite de passage* of the Jewish faith, by which, at age thirteen, Males were inducted into full membership in the religious community. Replaced during the Age of Gynocracy and before the abolition of the Three Persecuting Faiths, by a corresponding rite for thirteen-year-old girls, called *Bath Mitzvah.*

BIBLE: "The Book" or "The Books": an arrogant term ascribing to the Old Testament and the New (qq.v.) special authority denied to the mythologies of people other than adherents of Judaism and the two other intolerant Sects derived from that "Faith," i.e., Christianity and Islam.

BRITH: See CIRCUMCISION.

CENTURIONS: Soldiers of Caesar, secular head of the Roman State, which was occupying Jerusalem at the moment of the Crucifixion. One of these soldiers, on guard during the Crucifixion, presumably gave Jesus the *coup de grâce* with a spear or lance; thus providing an appropriately phallic symbol to go with the female symbols of Cup and Dish, associated with the Last Supper (q.v.). (See also HALLOWS, PASSOVER SEDER, SACRA.)

CHANNAH: Otherwise Anna or Anne, the Mother of Mary, Mother of Jesus. She assumed more and more mythological importance during the years when European Christianity went in search of mothers to fill in the symbolic vacuum at the heart of Patriarchal Judaism, and its offshoot, the primitive Nazarene Cult.

CHESS: A board game of Egyptian or Indian origin, which enjoyed immense popularity from medieval times up to the twenty-third century, in which it was transformed into a three-dimensional equivalent of much greater complexity, called "Chest." Earlier, perhaps as early as the twelfth century, it had been partly converted from a patriarchal war game into a symbol of matriarchal protest, when its most powerful figure was renamed the "Queen."

CHRIST: Otherwise, *Christos:* a translation into Greek, and then a transliteration into English (and still later American) of the

Hebrew *Mashiach* (q.v.) meaning literally the "Anointed One." This term, originally a kenning for a King, became attached to the King Messiah. (See also SON OF DAVID, SON OF THE FATHER, SON OF GOD, SON OF MAN.)

CHUTZPAH: Originally a Hebrew word, which passed into the folk language, Yiddish (from which the present-day Palestinian dialect Yitsch directly descends) after the Diaspora. It means a special kind of supreme arrogance; an aesthetically pleasing or comically disarming insolence. A quality prized by many Jews, as well as not a few North Americans, on whom the Jews appear to have had an immense cultural influence, down nearly to our own time.

CIRCUMCISION: A therapeutic operation detaching the prepuce from the penis of an eight-day-old child—given mythic significance by the superstitious Israelites, but later restored to its true meaning by the Cult of Old Science. To the Hebrews it represented the Promise (q.v.) inscribed in the flesh. (See BRITH.)

COW GODDESS: See GOLDEN HEIFER, ISIS.

DEBORAH: A female Judge in Ancient Israel; and consequently a heroine of the gynocratic forces, before scholarship had disappeared completely from their ranks, and the reading of Judeo-Christian texts was banned for all time.

DEMETER: Called also "Ceres"; center of an exclusively Female Fertility Cult, along with her daughter, Kore, or Persephone. (See also APHRODITE.)

DIANA: The Black Diana of Ephesus referred to in Eliezar's text, and also by Saul or Paul, the misogynist publicist for the Christian faith, is not to be confused with the chaste Moon Goddess of the Ancient Romans; though in fact ritual virginity and sacred promiscuity seem mythologically interchangeable. The former is portrayed as flagrantly sexual and fertile, being endowed with seven breasts. She has been, moreover, identified from remote antiquity with the Cult of Witchcraft. (See also APHRODITE, WITCH.)

ELIM: Literally, "gods" or "divine beings." In the corrupt form, *Elohim*, a name used by the Ancient Hebrews for a Creator God, otherwise thought of as nameless—or referred to only by the unpronounceable un-name, JHVH (q.v.). For Eliezar, they are the masters of a technology capable of travel through space and

186

time; and the founders of Patriarchal Faiths in China, Greece and Israel. They come, according to that same source, from a remote region known as Shamaim (q.v.) and control all of the Cosmos not in the hands of the forces of Yin (q.v.).

ENOCH: The father of Methuselah, allegedly transported directly to the abode of the Elim and Malaachim (q.v.). One of the three men, therefore, the two others also transported like him, to have survived death according to the Old Testament. It should be remembered that the Hebrew Faith did not include a belief in personal immortality—at least not until decadence had set in, just before the time of Jesus.

ERETZ: Literally, "land" or "earth." The proper name, according to Eliezar once more, of the domain of the mortals. Certainly, *Eretz Yisroel,* or the "Land of Israel," was, through a good deal of the twentieth and twenty-first centuries, the official name of the central territory of the Second Jewish Empire.

ESTHER: Name of the Jewish Queen who, in the shortest "book" in the Bible, is purported to have married an historical Persian King, Ahasuerus; and to have saved her people, with the help of her uncle, Mordecai, from the King's evil Prime Minister, Haman. Her name, however, is suspiciously like Ishtar, Ashtoreth, Astarte (qq.v.), and that of her uncle closely resembles Marduk, another fertility demon. Besides, she enters her story dancing naked; so there seems real reason to believe that she represents an incursion of the Mother Goddess into the most patriarchal of all "holy books."

FIRST COMMANDMENT: The injunction attributed to JHVH or the Elim (q.v.) in Genesis, urging mankind to go forth and multiply as a primary religious duty. Perhaps even more than the Circumcision, this constitutes the center of Patriarchal Faith. It has, therefore, been a Commandment especially despised by later advocates of Contraception, Abortion, Coitus Interruptus, Polymorphous Perverse Sexuality, and Infanticide: all the variants, in fact, of the "sin" known mythologically as "spilling seed upon the ground."

GALIL (THE): More customarily known in English as Galilee: the home of Jesus; but also a remote and backward province, which the Jews of Jerusalem found inherently comic. The notion of a Savior or Messiah (q.v.) coming out of such a place struck them as absurd, quite like the notion in our time of a New Cult promulgated by some Squatter or Deportee on the Gamma Satellite of Uranus.

GEHENNA: A term of vague if sinister application; at first associated with darkness and death, but transformed, as heathen notions of immortality took over in Ancient Israel, as an even more repulsive variety of Hades: a place of suffering for dead "sinners."

GOLDEN HEIFER: To translate this, as is usually done, merely as "Golden Calf" destroys the significance, by suppressing the gender of the idol. What the backsliding Jewish rabble were worshiping at the foot of Sinai (q.v.), while Moses was conferring with YHVH on its summit, was an image of the Cow Goddess (q.v.) Isis, chief avatar of the Mother in Egypt, from which they had just escaped—in body only, it would seem.

GOY: The plural, in which at first it customarily appeared, is *goyim*, meaning precisely what the Latin *gentilis* mean; i.e., the peoples as opposed to the People, the Chosen Race, Israel. Its primary signification then is "pagan" or "heathen"; though it later becomes in the mouths of persecuted and desperate Jews a term of supreme opprobrium and contempt, directed at their oppressors. Implicit in the epithet *goy* at that point are notions of lubricity, drunkenness and stupidity. (See also SHIKSE.)

HALLOWS (THE FOUR): Originally mementos, or perhaps objects in which some manna was thought to reside, of the life and death of Jesus: the Dish from which he ate at his last Passover Seder (q.v.); the Cup from which he drank; the Lance with which the Centurion (q.v.) pierced his side; the Sword with which one of his followers resisted the Roman soldiers. Eliezar believes the sexual significance of this double pair of phalluses and yoni to have been obvious even to Joseph (q.v.); and therefore associates Joseph with the Fertility Cults of the Goddess he so detests. (See also HOLY GRAIL.)

HECATE: A Greek avatar of the Goddess in her malign aspect. (See also APHRODITE.)

HEROD: See Footnote 30.

HIGH PLACES (THE): The hilltop shrines of the gods and goddesses to whom the Israelites and their neighbors had both sacrificed children before the invention of the Circumcision. They were objects of anathema always to the Priests, the Kohanim (q.v.), and of fear as well; since the heathen neighbors of the Jews never ceased such practices, and the Jews had a demonstrated talent for backsliding.

HOLY GHOST: Otherwise, Holy Spirit; or more literally, the Spirit of the Lord, originally celebrated for having "hovered on the face of the waters" during the Creation. A direct translation from the Hebrew used in that passage, *Ruach Elohim,* it soon lost, however, such connotations; being employed chiefly as a name for the Third Person in the Christian Trinity, i.e., as a substitute for the Mother in the Pagan Trinity of Father, Son, Mother. The word *ruach* can be of both or either gender in Hebrew, and is therefore an equivocal substitution at first. But it seemed to play into the hands of the patriarchal party in the Early Christian Church. And it was therefore subverted by the matriarchal wing of the Cult, who seem to have encouraged a popular tendency to replace the official Trinity with the grouping, so loved by painters, of Joseph, Mary and Jesus, which is to say, Cuckold, Mother and Son. That triad in turn seems clearly modeled on the Classical group of Vulcan, Aphrodite (q.v.) and Cupid. And, indeed, many of the attributes of Aphrodite came, among unlettered people especially, to be associated with the so-called Blessed Virgin.

INCUBUS: An "evil spirit" in Male form, popularly believed to enter into sexual relations with sleeping Females; even, according to Eliezar, to impregnate such Females with seed, presumably extracted from Males to whom they have appeared in Female form, called succubi (q.v.). Such fanciful creatures seem clearly embodiments or projections of the impulses which cause erotic or "wet" dreams, in societies where sexual taboos are especially repressive. But Eliezar would have us believe that such legends are born of an imperfect apprehension of the Messengers or Malaachim (q.v.) in their sexual relations with humans.

ISAIAH: The name of an apparently historical figure, who, though born into the Priesthood, became a Prophet, setting himself in opposition to his own kinsmen. The single name was, however, attached to a rather disparate group of "prophetic" writings by various hands. In the Arch-Priest's text, the particular Isaiah referred to is the author of the fifty-third chapter of the Book that bears his name. In this chapter, there is developed at some length the theory of vicarious atonement: the notion that the sins of one individual or group can be atoned for by the suffering of another individual or group. A dubious theory of great historical importance, for both Christians and Jews, perhaps precisely because of the moral flabbiness at its core.

ISHTAR: See Aphrodite.

ISIS: See Aphrodite, Cow Goddess, Golden Heifer.

JOHN THE BAPTIST: See Essene.

JOSEPH: See Arimathaea, Yussef.

KADDISH: The Ancient Hebrew prayer for the dead, still used, it is believed, among the unreconstructed Yitts of Palestine; though vigorous police action has been taken to stamp all such prayers out of existence. The prayer itself is not particularly dangerous in content, being merely a string of extravagant praises of YHVH, without any mention of death. But the sentimental associations which have accrued to it over the ages have made it a threat to all who would separate the present from the past, in the interests of the future. For Jews, the Kaddish has come to symbolize exactly the opposite, the link joining sons to fathers, for instance, whatever be their differences. In Yiddish, as a matter of fact, most sentimental of tongues, the term was used as a name of endearment by parents speaking to their Male children.

KATHAI: More commonly written Cathay: an old name for China, with which Eliezar seems disconcertingly well acquainted. To be sure, he attributes his improbable knowledge of that remote land to the intervention of the Elim or their Messengers. But it seems finally an odd subject to have been discussed between them.

KISS (THE): A term applied in the mystic, or "unwritten," tradition of the Jews to the way in which Moses died: his breath, soul, being allegedly sucked away by his God. For hundreds of years, misguided devotees of that God sought by fasting and prayer to create in themselves states of consciousness, in which they might "attain the Kiss," i.e., expire in ecstasy. The fear of genital sexuality and the emphasis on the oral is to be found everywhere in Judaism; but most notably here, and in their extreme concern with food taboos.

KOHEN, Plural, KOHANIM: This is the Hebrew word for Priest. But it should not be confused with that term as used, for instance, in the late Roman Catholic Church. To the Ancient

Jews, *Kohen* described not just a position or a function, but also denominated a Caste or Class from which all who performed the sacerdotal function were to be drawn. To add confusion, the word has long survived in the Western world as a proper name, which varies a good deal in form and is sometimes attached, for reasons they themselves do not remember, to some Jews who are not members of that Caste at all, though called Cohen, Cohn, Kahn, Kahan, Kaplan (which is a Slavic equivalent) or even Katz, an acronym for *Kohen-ha-Tzaddik,* the Just Priest. Each Priest also has, of course, a given name; and these are recorded not only for the reigning Arch-Priest but for his Chief Associates, at the time of the Crucifixion of Jesus. According to the Book of Acts, one of the canonical works of Christian Scripture, those names are Annas, Caiaphas, John and Alexander. It is hard to be sure how reliable a source this is; Alexander, for instance, being an improbable name for a religious Jew. But it is certainly worth noting that the name Eliezar is *not* among those listed. It is true, however, that Eleazar (a name often confused with the former) is a legitimate priestly name, being that of the son and successor of Aaron, first of the Arch-Priests.

KYBELE, also CYBELE: See APHRODITE.

LAST SUPPER (THE): See PASSOVER SEDER.

LAW (THE): See TORAH.

LEVITE: A Temple Servant, drawn exclusively from the Tribe of Levi; and consequently the name of a Caste intermediate between the Kohanim (q.v.) and the common people, called simply Israel. For the reading of the Law or Torah (q.v.), it remained necessary until the Time of Dissolution to have present in the congregation representatives of each of the three Castes. The Levites must not be thought of as higher domestics, but as a group chosen to take upon themselves the obligation (originally incumbent on all Jews) to dedicate their firstborn to service in the Temple. This obligation stems, mythologically, from the fact that God, who took from the Egyptians in the last of the Ten Plagues their firstborn sons, left those sons to the Jews, who thereafter felt they owed them to the Power that had spared them. (See also PINYAN-HA-BEN.)

LILITH: In popular Jewish legend, the demon first wife of Adam, who offended both him and his patriarchal God by insisting on assuming the superior position during the sex act. Actually, one more avatar of the Great Mother in her more threatening form. (See APHRODITE, but especially DIANA, HECATE.)

MALAACH, plural MALAACHIM: The Hebrew word represented in Greek by the term *angeloi*, transliterated into English as "angels." Both words mean literally "Messenger," which Eliezar calls them. To him they are the intermediaries between the Priests and the Elim (q.v.), though the latter two can also communicate by means of the Urim and Tumim (q.v.) alone.

MANNA: See Footnote 20.

MASHIACH: Ordinarily rendered in English as Messiah. (See CHRIST.)

MATZAH, plural MATZOS: The unleavened bread eaten by all believing Jews on the Festival of the Passover, to memorialize the escape from Egypt, or Mitzraim (q.v.). On the eve of their departure, they presumably did not have time to let their bread rise; and therefore have continued to eat it unleavened for eight days each year in the early springtime. The connection of the Festival with the natural turn of the year, and the lack of any documentation outside of the sacred texts of the Jews themselves which attests to its historicity, tempts a reader to more universal symbolic interpretations of everything related to it. Actually, the ritual consumption of bread prepared without yeast seems to depend on an identification of leavening with the "Evil Impulse" or the Devil. And apparently some sense of this remained either in Jesus himself, or among his followers, who came to identify him, as the embodiment of Unspotted Good, with unleavened bread; thus leading to the institution of the Mass.

MENORAH: The seven-branched candlestick used in ordinary Temple service, or for the weekly observance of the Sabbath. But also the nine-branched one used on the festival of Chanukah, which celebrates the victories of Yehudah the Hammer (q.v.) over the forces of the Syrian Greeks; and the temporary end of the Hellenization of the Jews.

METHUSALEH: A depressing figure in legend, really, who did nothing notable except live longer than anyone else; but is remembered simply for that, while men of real achievement are forgotten.

MITZRAIM: The Hebrew name for Egypt: meaning literally, the "Swampland" or "Muddy Place." Whatever the historical basis for the legend of their enslavement in that land, it has remained for Jews (who during their Second Empire three and four hundred years ago engaged in a war with that state) the symbol of oppression as opposed to freedom. (See LAST SUPPER, MANNA, PASSOVER SEDER.)

MOMSER: Hebrew for "bastard" or "illegitimate child." It must be remembered, however, that the term cuts a little differently than its equivalents in most European tongues, especially as these were used in the time of supreme antisexual hysteria from, say, A.D. 300 to 2300. For the Hebrews, the child begotten of a rape was considered the legitimate child of his mother's husband; but a baby conceived by intercourse during the taboo period of menstruation was classified as a *momser*. Later, like the corresponding terms in other languages, merely an insult, like *goy*.

MOSES: According to Hebrew Scriptures, the brother of Aaron and Maryam, or Miriam. His name, however, appears to be a truncated suffix found in many royal Egyptian names connected to a god prefix (Ramses, or Ra-Moses, would be an example); suggesting that he may have been born an Egyptian, and have become a Jew by conversion or adoption. All his life long, he remained, even according to the Jewish sources, reluctant to perform orthodox Jewish rites: the Circumcision, for example, of his own sons. To be sure, such laxity on his part may have come from pressure on the part of his *shikse* (q.v.) wife; or, as Eliezar suggests, his early training at the hands of an Egyptian Princess, who must have been also a Priestess of Isis. Yet in the end he came to be called *Moshe Rabbenu,* "Moses our Master."

MOSHE: See MOSES.

NEW TESTAMENT: The portion of the Bible (q.v.) added by the dissident Jewish Sect from which the Christian Faith eventually developed.

OLD TESTAMENT: The portion of the Bible (q.v.) to which Jews, Christians and Muslims, who agree on so little else, agree on ascribing divine authority.

OSIRIS: See ADONIS.

PASSOVER SEDER: The ritualized eating of unleavened bread and drinking of wine with which Jews, gathered in family groups, have ever since their exodus from Egypt remembered that blessed deliverance. An observant Jew at the end as at the beginning of his life, Jesus attended such a Seder just before his arrest by Roman authorities. Aware of what was to come, he seems deliberately to have altered the symbolism of that occasion so that it pointed toward the future rather than memorialized the past. By making a ceremonial meal symbolic of his coming sacrifice, however, he succeeded only in reawakening in his disciples memories of pagan rites in which the Son of the Mother is eaten by his communicants. Called the Love Feast or Communion or Mass, such symbolic anthropophagy remained central to the ritual of the Christian Churches up to the moment of their Final Dissolution.

PHYLACTERIES: Tiny leather-covered boxes, containing phrases from the Torah (q.v.), which Orthodox Jews have continued to tie to their arms and foreheads for nearly two and a half millennia; following the orders of their tribal deity with a literal-mindedness which had always infuriated their enemies and embarrassed their friends. To protests against such literalness, they have always answered that the letter of the Law (q.v.) is all God has given us; the spirit depending on (often contradictory) human interpretations.

PINYAN-HA-BEN: Literally, the "ransoming of the son." A ceremony involving the payment of money to a representative of the Priesthood, by which a Jewish father delivers his firstborn son, shortly after birth, from the obligation to devote his entire life to the service of God. (See LEVITE.)

PROCURATOR OF JUDEA: See Footnotes 22 and 29.

RHEA: See APHRODITE.

RUACH ELOHIM: See HOLY GHOST.

RUTH: Heroine of a Book almost as antithetical to the rest of Hebrew Scripture as the Book of Esther. Esther at least is Jewish. Ruth is not merely a woman but a Gentile, a *shikse* (q.v.) in short, who becomes the spiritual, as well as physical, founder of the royal line that culminates in King David. In response to the ethnocentric and Male sexist prejudices of the Editors who gave final form to the Old Testament, however, the emphasis is placed in her story on her willingness to surrender not only the values by which she has been brought up, but her very sense of self, to the requirements of her (dead) Jewish husband's God, as interpreted by her mother-in-law.

SACRA: See HALLOWS.

SANCTUARY: The inner shrine of the Jewish Temple, around which, from the first, rumors have proliferated; perhaps only because its nature has been kept secret from the profane. Some, who thought of Jews as atheists, have claimed that it contained simply nothing. Others, who resented the food taboos of the Jews and especially their avoidance of pork, claimed that a pig or a boar (symbol of Set, enemy of Osiris [q.v.]) was stabled there. Eliezar makes it the place of communication with the Alien Intelligences, whom he thinks of as the pioneers of a supermagic called "Science."

SHAMAIM: The sky, the heavens, the Kingdom of Heaven. An ambiguous word at best, which Eliezar tries to make even more ambiguous by using it as the proper name of the extragalactic world from which the Messengers come.

SHEKHINAH: A ritual name for the Glory or Indwelling Presence or Immanence of YHVH, who, in transcendental form, is referred to as the "Ancient of Days" or the "Limitless," or the "Place" or "Nothing." Medieval Jewish mystics, the so-called Cabalists, thought bf the whole process of Creation as depending upon the copulation of the Ancient of Days with his Shekhinah. But such a belief is not really, as Eliezar seems to intend us to believe, a part of an ancient tradition in Judaism; only a later addition by feminizing Neoplatonists, unable to endure the rigor of totally aniconic paternalism.

SHIKSE: The ordinary word among the Jewish descendants of the Ancient Hebrews for a Gentile woman. It means literally "abomination"; and expresses the fear and loathing of trans-ethnic sexuality, contradicted to be sure by the Books of Esther and Ruth (qq.v.), but central to the traditions of Israel at their most authentic—and terrifying.

SHOLOMO BEN DAVID: Commonly called Solomon, he is the second King of Israel and the founder of the Temple.

SINAI: The Holy Mountain in the Desert, where, in the midst of their wandering, the Israelites received the Law (q.v.) of God. While Moses (q.v.) was on the Mountain, however, the people, with the consent (or connivance) of Aaron and Miriam, had set up the Golden Heifer (q.v.). In his rage at their apostasy, Moses smashed the First Tablets of the Law. YHVH, who shared his rage, gave him a second set of Commandments much stricter than the first.

SISERA: See Deborah, Yael.

SODOM AND GOMORRAH: The so-called Cities of the Plain, destroyed by the Jewish God for their evil-doing and refusal to repent. They have been remembered particularly as centers for homosexual brutality. Eliezar, as a matter of fact, refers in his text to the attempted homosexual rape of a Malaach, or Messenger; which, from the point of view of the naively pious Jew, must have seemed to verge on blasphemy, and to deserve, therefore, the rain of fire and brimstone in which the cities perished. In the light of what Eliezar himself tells us of the sexual tastes and proclivities of the Messengers, the whole episode seems much more equivocal.

SON OF DAVID, SON OF THE FATHER, SON OF GOD, SON OF MAN: Ambiguous names, in the usage of Eliezar's time, when they seem sometimes to have been used specifically as Messianic titles; sometimes more generally as honorifics for good Jews or, indeed, any Jews. Eventually, they were all applied to Jesus, either by himself or his followers. (See also CHRIST, MASHIACH.)

SUCCUBUS: A Female "evil spirit" able to extract seed from her human Male victim, to whom she allegedly came at night, perhaps in the form of a dream. For Eliezar, another form assumed by the lustful Messengers, who could put on, as the whim moved them or strategy dictated, the outward form of either human sex. (See also INCUBUS.)

TORAH: The Law (q.v.) of God, from which, as Eliezar keeps reminding us, Jesus promised that nothing would pass away. Sometimes by the Law or Torah, the Jews seem to have meant quite specifically the Ten Commandments, given on Sinai (q.v.)—with or without the minor injunctions in which they are embedded in Scripture. Sometimes, more usually, in fact, they seem to have meant all five of the first books of the Bible, Genesis, Exodus, Leviticus, Numbers and Deuteronomy, which were believed to have been written by Moses (q.v.). For the Jews, these books seemed of utmost importance; for they considered salvation to be by and through the Law rather than Love, or, as later theologians would have expressed it, through Works not Grace. Many disputations have occurred over the relative merits of the two ways, though it is doubtful whether anyone ever understood very clearly what was at stake. In the end, at any rate, the whole argument grew tedious and vain—pointless, I am tempted to say. Yet many died on both sides, as Christians fought first the Jews, then each other.

ULTIMA THULE: A mythological name for a remote region in Northwestern Europe, or beyond. Eliezar, having picked it up who knows where, uses it to refer to England, of which one also does not expect him to have heard.

URIM AND TUMIM: Even to the learned among the Jews, the exact reference of these two words remained always a puzzle. And whether Eliezar has cleared it up or not, the reader will have to decide for himself. He has in his text, to be sure, several passages explaining their function in "scientific" terms. For me, at this moment, though I possess the objects themselves, the Arch-Priest's words remain nearly as mysterious as the original scriptural passage enjoining the Kohanim (q.v.) to wear them: "And thou shalt put in the breastplate of judgment the Urim and Tumim; and they shall be upon Aaron's heart, when he goeth in before the LORD. . . ."

WITCH: One who uses "magic" outside, sometimes against the Established Cult, and always for antilife ends: to induce sterility or abortion, to break up marriages or to hasten death (poisons, before their naturalization by chemistry, were considered in the witch's province). According to Jewish Law (lapsed, we are told, in Eliezar's time), witches were subject to capital punishment or, rather, stoning. The word slowly changed in meaning after Christianity, being used more specifically as a label for the underground Communicants of the Great Mother, whose secret cultus was destroyed in a wave of persecutions coming to a climax between the thirteenth and seventeenth centuries. Since a good many, though by no means all, of the members of the witch covens were women, the term then became an abusive epithet directed against all women who resisted, or seemed to resist, Male authority. During the feminist revolutions of the late twentieth and early twenty-first centuries, the term was proudly adopted by more militant and *enragé* members of the Movement.

YAEL: Sometimes rendered Jael; one of the female destroyers of men, in her case of the evil Sisera, toward whom the Ancient Jews seem to have taken so ambivalent an attitude. They are, in effect,

nightmares promoted to official heroic status. (See also YEHU-
DITH.)

YANG AND YIN: Chinese terms for the two great principles out of
whose conflict the universe is eternally created, destroyed and
renewed. Identified primarily with Male and Female by humans, among whom there are only two viable sexes, and who
have been traditionally much obsessed by this bipolar split in
their species. They can, however, also be interpreted as meaning Right and Left, Light and Dark, Day and Night, Rigor and
Mercy, Law (q.v.) and Love, etc., etc. In the late twentieth
century, the notion was rather cavalierly readapted to the uses
of a youth cult which applied the terms to various natural foods
and regulated their diets thereby. Their Cult survives as the
Reformed Church of Macrobiotics.

YAVAN: See Footnote 21.

YEHUDAH: More commonly referred to in English as Judah or Judas,
this name is shared by three Biblical figures; the first two
important in the Old Testament, the second central to the New.
The first Judah is the founder of one of the twelve original
Tribes of Israel: the one from which (since the others were
"lost," destroyed by wars, dispersed irrecoverably in exile) most
historical Jews, along with the present-day Yitts, descended. Of
him, his father Jacob, who is also called Israel, says in a
deathbed blessing: "Judah, thou art he whom thy brethren
shall praise: thy hand shall be in the neck of thine enemies; thy
father's children shall bow down before thee. . . ." The second
Yehudah is called Judah the Hammer, or Judas Maccabeus.
His festival is held during Chanukah, the Feast of Lights, celebrated to memorialize not just his military victories over the
Syrian Greeks, but his restoration of their Jewishness to the
Jewish People. The third is that Judas who betrays Jesus to the
Priests, after having pledged his fealty with a kiss, then hangs
himself in remorse. Quite clearly, wherever the name appears,
we are dealing with an attempt, more or less conscious, to
represent all of Jewry allegorically: its beginnings; its resistance
to the Gentile world; and in the basically anti-Judaic if not
downright anti-Semitic New Testament, its rejection of the
New Dispensation, which turns out to mean its own suicide.

YEHUDITH: A feminine form of the same name, attached only to a single character of note in the official Hebrew mythology. Another of those destroyers of Male enemies of the Jews, not only (however equivocally) prized by the Jews themselves, but a special favorite as well of Christian painters in the ever more matriarchal and feminizing Middle Ages and Renaissance.

YUSSEF: Otherwise, Joseph: a name attributed to three central figures in Judeo-Christian myth, twice in the Old Testament, and once in the New. The first Yussef is the Son of Jacob, possessor of the Coat of Many Colors, whose story ends in success; but whose success means the beginnings of the exile and enslavement of the Jews in Egypt, or Mitzraim (q.v.). The second is the impotent carpenter who becomes the foster father of Yehoshuah, or Jesus, thus initiating the events, at the grim close of which he has disappeared; leaving the stage to the third of the name, the Merchant from Arimathaea (q.v.).

A FINAL NOTE ON NAMES

An attentive reader will have noticed that "Yehoshuah," or "Jesus," has been omitted from my list, since it does not appear in the Scrolls of the Arch-Priest. Yet it, too, links the New Testament to the Old, being used not only for the false Messiah, the Son of the Messenger, but also for the successor to Moses, who led the Israelites into their Promised Land, as Moses, for his sins, could not. Moreover, I have also omitted Yaakov or Jacob, since that name belongs not to Eliezar's story but to mine: the story of the *finding* of the Scrolls, rather than their writing. And the Arch-Priest does not reveal, except on his title page, that he, like me, is the Son of Jacob.

My name, I am moved to remind my readers at this point, is Jacob son of Jacob son of Jacob son of Jacob . . . back to the beginnings of it all. But "the beginnings of it all," for the Jews at least, is the Patriarch Yaakov, whose name was changed to Israel after he had wrestled the Angel of the Lord; and whose sons are the founders of the Twelve Tribes. In some sense, then, it occurs to me as I near the completion of my task, I am also a Jew, the end of a line and the beginning of a new one, if the Jacob who is my son still lives: the inheritor of the Promise (q.v.). (See also Circumcision.)

NINE

So, I am done, finished: the last words of the Arch-Priest's manuscript englished, the last entry in my Glossary completed. There remains only to describe my own ending, which threatens also to end a twenty-five-hundred-year-old story which once seemed as if it would be coterminous with the history of mankind. But my spell is wound up, and the Meta-Technicians have not come, while the light by which I work fades fast. The rain, which I took at first for the kind of quick cloudburst rare but not untypical of Desert weather, I know now will continue indefinitely. At first, there were clearing spells between downpours; but I have not seen the sun for three days, and Melissa-Melinda's Stone seems at the point of blacking out forever.

It has continued to grow, however, until it is bigger than my head, as large as an ostrich or a dinosaur egg. I sit on it as I write, like some gaunt, brooding bird, knowing it will hatch nothing—no fledgling to fly to the Stars, not even a monster to mock that hope. But it warms my bottom a little; and though it cannot stop the trembling of my fingers, enables me to control them enough so that I can hold a pen. There is no time to ask myself where the clouds have come from and the cold. No time for wonder. Besides, I have grown as incapable of wonder as a character in a fairy tale or a dream. And as heedless of time. My only clock is the Stone, which continues to grow dim, as it blinks off and on faster and faster; the rhythm of alternating light and dark synchronized now with its scarcely perceptible pulse. I have the sense that its pulse has meaning—even a specific meaning for *me*. But what is it saying, faithful still to its Makers, who coded into it aeons ago a message in search of a listener?

No matter. I could not answer, even if I understood; and I find myself reaching down to pat its throbbing sides, as if to say: *Thank you, thanks anyhow.* Clearly, I could not have survived without it. Indeed, I might well have died long since of pneumonia, or have been shaken apart by chills and fever; for as the rains have persisted, the rocks around me have grown furred over with frosty mold, and the roof is hung with great pseudo stalactites, half icicle and half bearded moss. Nor is there anything left now for me to burn. Only the gift of Melissa-Melinda to warm my bones.

At first I would go outside whenever the sun shone through the gaps in the scudding clouds, though I would regret every minute stolen from my work, and stretching myself out on the rock I would lap up the water in its hollows like a dog. Then, stripping off my sodden clothes, I would stretch myself out on the sun-warmed ledge between the two chasms cut by the earthquake. There, barely awake enough to roll from back to belly, belly to back, I would toast myself—trying to store up heat and energy for the sunless days to follow and the restless nights. The storm never let up at night, so that though I would rise sometimes to peer out through the entryway, I never saw the Stars, of which the Meta-Technicians had set me dreaming. Perhaps they, too, have gone out, I would think. And I would shiver helplessly, clutching the PSSS to me for warmth.

For a long time I have been close to starvation, and for the last few days I have been entirely without water; though I have tended to eat and drink less and less as I have become more deeply involved with the text before me, more and more convinced of the veracity of the Old Priest's account. Maybe it was only the prolonged fast, which weakened me until I would find myself laughing aloud at his momentary triumphs, or crying out in anguish at his inevitable defeats. And reaching up to touch my face, I would discover it wet with tears.

Sometimes I was tempted to collect those tears and drink them; though my father, I dimly recalled, used to tell me as a boy the story of a space castaway who had been driven mad doing precisely that. Or was it alien seawater he had drunk? And all the while I could hear the water pounding down outside the cave's entrance—tantalizing, unattainable. I dared not venture out in the marvelous downpour lest I be crushed flat; but I would kneel sometimes just inside the doorway, my mouth open and my swollen tongue extended in an effort to catch the occasional drop that splashed upward off the stone.

I even swallowed my sperm at one point, since a week or two into Scroll Two, I found myself masturbating regularly, and it seemed a shame to waste the seed. But why did I keep waking, each time as urgently erect as I had been under the full moon in the Negev? Was the moon full again behind the unbreaking night clouds? I had lost track of its phases. Once, in my madness, I hacked open a vein in my left wrist with a small stone and sucked at the blood as long as it flowed. Only now, when it is too late for hope, can I smile at the absurdity of trying to stay alive by consuming myself. Like a snake gnawing on its own tail.

At first, in sheer desperation I was willing to try anything, drinking the stagnant dew that condensed in the hollows of the cave floor, and gnawing at the algae which had dried on the rocks, the icy mold and the frozen moss stalactites. But the dew was foul-tasting—savoring of something between rust and rot, so that I could keep down no more than a swallow at a time. Yet even that little helped keep me alive. The algae and moss, however, impregnated with the same moisture grown stagnant, I could not manage at all: puking and retching after each mouthful. I had better luck with the small vermin which would come out and rustle about me in the dark, spiders, dung beetles and cockroaches, plus other archaic forms of insect life I could not recognize. Occasionally they would crawl across my body or face while I slept, having lived, I supposed, in some ecological chain which my intrusion had disrupted. I could not help suspecting that sooner or later they would discover me as a new source of nourishment, but I never detected any trace of a sting or bite. Even when I cut my wrist, they did not gather to snuffle or sip at the dripping blood. No, it was only *I* who ate *them*.

First, however, I had to catch them. I would, therefore, secretly chafe the PSSS against my upper thigh, then whip it out from under the last rags of my clothing, which I no longer wore but beneath which I slept. For an instant, they would be transfixed, paralyzed by its sudden glare; and I would grab them up by the handful, at first stuffing them raw into my mouth. But after my initial panic had worn off, I would cook them, using the heat of that same blessed Stone, while it was still strong enough to work. I got rather fond of that unaccustomed fare after a while, particularly of the cockroaches, which, properly toasted, are crisp in the mouth, like goosefat cracklings. They never made me ill, these tiny creatures, even when the PSSS had grown so weak that it could scarcely warm them. But in the quantities I could manage to gather, they never satisfied me, leaving me with a cumulative hunger that became an unending ache in the pit of my stomach.

Once, in the flare-up of Melissa-Melinda's Stone, I caught a bat, and once a great, fat snake, both doubtless visitors from beyond the cleft in the rear wall. The bat I found particularly revolting, even when I shut my eyes against the stupid malice of its little rat's face. But the snake turned out to be delicious, and exercising great self-control, I succeeded in making it last for three days. Neither, however, had any noticeable effect on my inexorable wasting away. I grew thinner and thinner, until I could no longer stand to look at the frail, fleshless tubes of my arms. Yet no matter how I shrunk, I could not get through the crack in the back of the cave, into which I would hurl myself over and over until I was bruised and bleeding. Actually, my belly bloated grotesquely in the last stages of my gradual starvation.

It was a long time before it even occurred to me to use my Auto-Digger in an attempt to widen the opening. But by then I had scarcely strength enough to hold it against the rocky sides. And in any case, its point, intended only to pierce sand and clay and gravel, sparked ineffectively on the stubborn stone. Even if I had succeeded, however, I would have been too weak to negotiate more than a few miles in the passages beyond. Yet weak as I got, I could not stop masturbating, though it weakened me still further. Finally, I could not even come, only jerking in dry spasms at the moment of climax, like a fisherman hooked on his own line.

But my senses grew more acute as my strength failed, particularly my sense of smell. And this turned out to be a further torment; for by this time the cave was full of my own excrement, in which I would sometimes slip and fall, particularly after dark. At first, I would force myself, when I had to move my bowels, to go out onto the ledge of rock in front of the cave. Finally, however, I could scarcely crawl to the entrance; or once outside, abide the rain, which would beat me to the ground in seconds, pinning me down so that I could barely slither on my belly back to safety—and my own stinking shit. During the last two days, in which I have eaten almost nothing (the light of the PSSS grown too dim to attract more than a few vermin, and I too enervated to pounce quickly), my feces have grown black and odorless. But the cumulative stench seems stronger than ever in the heavy, moisture-laden air, making it impossible to draw breath without wanting to vomit.

I can escape my nausea only in sleep, or when, deep into my writing, I am transported out of the body I inhabit and the moment of time through which I move toward death. But when I sleep, or rather half-sleep, I fall into half-dreams, whose details I cannot recall though I wake trembling with the terror they have stirred. And, looking down, I find myself tugging once more on my aching cock. I have, therefore, forced myself to work at my manuscript longer and longer each day; fighting sleep by propping my eyes open with my fingers, slapping my own face or banging my head against the rocks behind me. Once I even dared to stick it out for an instant into the rain, which now threatens to split my skull, yet revives me for a little while. For nearly seventy-two hours before last night, I had succeeded—except for momentary noddings-off too brief for nightmares—in keeping myself awake.

But I completed my translation just before sunset, of whose coming I was somehow aware, despite the thick cloud cover through which the light scarcely changed as the sun went below the horizon. And I relaxed, my chin jerking forward and down before I knew it, and my pen hitting the floor. My first deep suspiration in that foul air, however, shocked me out of sleep; and I awoke tasting my own bile. "Let them come," I prayed then. Yes, shamelessly and openly prayed, like some simple communicant of long ago, to whose naiveté even Eliezar would have condescended.

Yet as I prayed, I was assailed by fresh doubts. If, as they claimed, the Meta-Technicians were really natives of New New-York, why had they addressed me (I thought to ask for the first time) in English? Spanish is the official language of that city-state, and Hispano-Pidgin the tongue its inhabitants customarily speak abroad. True, two Ameranglophone ghettos remain in New New-York despite efforts to wipe them out; and from one of these, the Meta-Technicians may indeed have come.

But the larger was inhabited exclusively by members of the Garveyite-Leninist Tabernacle, crypto-Muslims who refused to emigrate with the city's other Blacks to the slave state of New Alabama, because its Established Cult is Non-Animist Voodoo. Since the Meta-Technicians were patently not Negroes, this leaves only the Reformed Ethical Culturists as a possibility. But this even tinier minority of English-speaking Manhattanites consists of crypto-Jews. But if this is the case, I have fallen into the hands of underground Yitts: fanatic reactionaries, who have mounted this charade not for the sake of achieving the Stars, but to recover a Cult Object valuable only to them. The Meta-Technicians, then, have failed to return not because they have been cut off by Cosmic Powers too vast to comprehend, but out of fear of the Palestinian Police. And I will therefore die, not like the Homeric hero I have been foolish enough to fancy myself, caught between contending Immortals; but as the unwitting tool of the losing side in a petty religious war.

Where such doubts came from, I do not know even now, though I suspect they were suggested to me by the forces that had split the earth and opened the heavens. Or perhaps this is just another form of self-deceit. I am sure of only one thing: that my doubts—whatever their origin—failed to shake me at the level where I still prayed, "Let them come, let them come, let them come, Oh God, let them *come.*"

"God," I said, and I confess it freely, no more ashamed of that than of the doubts themselves. Or any prouder, either. Given the choice, I who have never had any choice, I would have preferred like the Arch-Priest to will that no Messenger ever come, so that our human freedom remain forever uncurtailed. We men may not be a "Unique Accident" in the Universe, as our politicos have tried to persuade us. But it is probably good for us to act as if we were: cutting ourselves off from whatever Alien Intelligences may be pursuing through us ends of their own. Why then did I call for help not even on the Masters of Space, but on their ridiculous go-betweens?

I had braced myself against the Stone that had once been small enough to fit into a poison ring, determined to await their coming awake; but I fell almost immediately into a sleep deeper than any I had slept since setting forth on my journey. And in that sleep I dreamed in a way I had never dreamed before. I do not know quite how to explain it, except to say that this dream did not flicker or change like ordinary dreams, but seemed fixed once and for all in focus and tint—even in time: a single figure in a frame beyond which there was nothing. Perfectly bisymmetrical, it could be seen only from in front. And the light which illuminated it came from behind the viewer, behind me, leaving it without shadow or any hint of depth. It seemed in fact more like a Byzantine Mosaic than any dream dreamed since the invention of film. Except that it talked. And I answered.

I never thought for an instant, however, that I shared its world, much less that I was its dreamer. Rather, I felt myself a waking observer, aware of my body, the pressure of the Stone against my back, my waking past, recent and remote. But somehow I also felt out of my body, truly at rest. I wanted, therefore, to express my gratitude, to bow or kneel as if in the presence of a Master to that featureless, scarcely iconic, clearly nonhuman thing, which seemed all the same Male and worthy of reverence. I wanting to call it by some honorific name I had never spoken. "Sage," perhaps, though I had no clear notion of what a Sage might be. Or "Saint," though for me that was a term of derision. Or "Angel," though the pictures of Angels in the Museums of Atheism were Female—all icons representing them in masculine form having been destroyed by militant feminists ages ago.

"Are you an Angel?" I thought I asked finally. But if I spoke, it gave no sign, no quiver of response breaking its repose.

"Are you one of the Meta-Technicians?" I tried next, hearing in answer a sound perhaps intended for laughter.

"Why do you mock me?" I asked then.

"I do not know what 'mock' means," the figure said, not in words, though I can render what I understood only in words. "I come because you call, though you do not know whom you call. To tell you that the Meta-Technicians will not come. Because they cannot. And it does not matter."

"But why?" I cried. "Why *not?*" I had known for a long time really, but I had not known that I knew. And I was near tears, like a child denied what he has realized all along that he cannot have.

I had forgotten my tears, however, before the explanation was over, not fully understanding, but somehow soothed. The forces of

Yin, I thought I was told, had descended to the tiny strip of land where I dreamed, to keep the Arch-Priest's Scrolls from being recovered and their Ancient Truce with Yang broken. By that Truce, the Female Principle had been given dominion over nighttime fantasy, the Male Principle over daylight rationality. To be sure, each side had encroached on the territory of the other: Yang, for example, trying to recapture the night for reason through a line of Jewish Explainers of Dreams which culminated in Sigmund Freud; and Yin inducing certain Male scientists to create intoxicants able to destroy the perceptual grid by which "sense" is made of phenomena.

Perhaps, he suggested, the forces of the Mother had only endured Science itself for three hundred years because they had foreseen that the Age of Hallucinogens was to be followed by the Age of Gynocracy. But even in that era, reason had survived underground, working toward the communications breakthrough described to me by the Meta-Technicians. Once this was completed by the recovery of the Urim, the Tumim and the Scrolls, however, the terran forces of Yang might link up with their Brothers in Space, upsetting the balance of power forever. For this reason, the cosmic hosts of Yin had tried to destroy the place in which the Scrolls were buried, and incidentally—me.

"And so they have won, those Others?" I interrupted him then.

"No, not won. You are alive, the Scrolls undamaged, the Urim and Tumim intact. Moreover, there is the new Message Stone, against which your head rests, and by virtue of which I can visit you thus. It is a stalemate, another impasse we will end by calling, like the first, a Truce."

But though still in possession of his "Side," he went on, the part of the world which held these treasures and me had been "tilted askew," made discontinuous with the time and space viable to men.

"Yet you are here," I protested. "How have you come?"

"By the grace of the Message Stone, as I have already told you. Which is to say, not by way of your world at all. By another way, a way barred forever to Them."

"Then you must be—" I began, so sure now I dealt with a Malaach or an El that I forgot to remember I was dreaming.

He, however, did not, interrupting me before I could finish.

"Don't say it. Because saying it, you will hear it. And hearing it, you will not believe it. And not believing it, you will wake. But you must not wake. Not yet, for there is still much I must tell. Much you must do."

"But I *am* awake," I protested. "How else could I feel, even as you talk, my living flesh, the Stone on which I lie, the chill that shakes me?"

"You only dream that you are awake. As, really waking, you will know."

"Let me dream then that I say your name. You are—"

"I am what you see. What do you see?"

"I see nothing," I said, telling myself foolishly that if I was not awake, I must be asleep. And all at once everything began to change around him, in me. "You are right. I am only having a dream."

"Not 'having,'" he answered, "'seeing.' You are seeing a dream. And I am what you see."

It was as if, word by word and step by step, he were ceasing to be other, becoming a part of me. *I must really be waking now,* I thought, *not just dreaming I wake.* But it was not the wall of the cave I saw as he apparently faded. Only another face that winked and grimaced and stuck out its tongue behind him, through him: the face of Melissa-Melinda. And it was not my own voice I heard behind his, through his. Not my own morning voice screaming myself awake under the echoing vault. Only Melissa-Melinda's voice crying, "Psychedelic!" and "Far fuckin' out!": the voice of an ordinary dream saying, "Hey, man, it's me, whaddaya know. Me like always."

But it was not "like always," and I fought neither to wake nor to sleep, though "like always" I was tempted to yell back, "Go away. Get lost."

She seemed to be straddling the Stone behind my head. But I could see her without turning my head, see myself seeing her, naked as an egg, a worm, a peeled twig, a jaybird, the ball of any eye. And I could hear her yelling now loud enough almost to drown out the great resonance of the Male voice whose words I could no longer comprehend. "Hey, man, there's a lot more where this came from," she said, pointing first to the Stone egg on which she sat, then to her own hole, slit, slot, snatch, twat, cunt, box, knish, quim, cooze, poontang, pussy, quiff. And it seemed as if I could hear all the names I ever knew for the mystery of her sex ringing simultaneously in my head.

Then I yelled in turn what was for me the most potent Name of all, not knowing why really, but thinking, *It's not a dream, not only a dream. I don't want it to be only a dream.* "Holy Quiff," I hollered. And this time it must have been really aloud, for the echoes rebounded from the stone vault above me, doubling and redoubling until the exhausted blasphemy seemed living and terrible. It was as if I were four years old again and speaking the forbidden words in the presence of my mother, repeating them over and over until she struck me across the mouth.

"Holy Quiff," I repeated, "Holy Quiff, Holy Quiff, Holy Quiff! Don't let it be only a dream." And this time, too, the blow came, out of the darkness, out of nowhere, smashing my head so hard against the Stone that I felt the roots of my teeth loosened, and tasted my blood as it mingled with the tears that ran down into my open mouth.

Melissa-Melinda was gone, but I knew I neither wakened nor slept, as I heard again the Male voice saying, "Ask while there is still time. Ask!"

But before I could ask, I had to say into the darkness, the nothing beyond that imperious head, say to the place where Melissa-Melinda no longer was, "I love you." It was, I suppose, the final blasphemy to both sides; for not only did my head jerk once more and thud backward against the Stone, but the image before me—I do not quite know how to say it—shrank and withdrew. Yet only after saying that last obscenity was I able to ask, "What must I do?"

"You must hide the Scrolls as I tell you, against the final catastrophe which I am forbidden to reveal." He gave me explicit instructions, not just about the tasks which lay ahead, but about the order in which they must be performed. First, I was to dig a hole with my Auto-Digger, as close as possible to the Priest's original hiding place. Then I must wrap the Urim and Tumim in the Scrolls, the Scrolls in my Perdurium sack, placing the sealed packet at the bottom of the excavation. Next I must drop the

Message Stone into the hole, filling up the remaining space with earth and rocks. Last of all, I must lie down on top of it, and wait.

"Wait?" I asked.

"Wait."

"But for what?" I persisted.

"Do you know a prayer for the dead? Any prayer for the dead?"

I did not, of course. "Are you trying to tell me that I shall die?"

"All men die."

"But not before I have—"

"Have no fear. You will not die before your task is done."

"Because *you* will not allow it, I suppose," I asked scornfully.

"No," he, it answered—fading fast now, fading from me and leaving me with a sense of loss I had not foreseen. *But what is it I have lost?* I asked myself. *What was it I had?*

Meanwhile, his, its voice continued, still clear, though the speaking image flickered for the first time—flickered and was gone. "Because *you* will not allow it. Being your dream, I will cease to exist, immortal that I am, once you have ceased to dream me." And now the voice was fading, too. "But have no fear. You will do it and die . . . do it and die . . . do it and die . . . do it . . . and . . . die . . . die . . . die. . . ."

The last words seemed not to be repeated by anyone but to repeat themselves; reverberating inside my head as in an echo chamber, finally overlapping and blurring to an intolerable noise. So that waking, I found myself with both hands clapped over my ears and my own voice yelling, "I won't. I won't. I won't. I will never die."

Even that desperate lie was lost almost immediately in the whoosh and splash of the increasing storm; the rain coming down, I could see from where I lay, not in drops or spurts or freshets or sheets, but in an immense colonnade. There was no wind, so it seemed to fall straight down from the invisible sky, or to rise straight out of the invisible earth; sometimes just to stand like shimmering pillars, joining earth and sky together. It did not appear quite solid, however, only on the point of solidifying, and trapping whatever moved through it in a translucent prison. But, of course, nothing moved through it, and nothing could, as I discovered when I rose and stuck my right hand out through the cave mouth to test the force of the downpour. In an instant it was smashed and battered: the skin bleeding from a hundred tiny lacerations and puffing up over the fractured bones until I could not close my fingers.

Holding my hand out before me in an unmeditated gesture of supplication proved so painful that I nearly fainted; but dropping it again to my side did not really help, since the mere weight of it caused me intolerable anguish. "Let me die," I cried then. "I want to die." But the plea for extinction was as meaningless as my boast of immortality. And now the rain was being whipped by gale-force winds that dashed it into my face and soaked the last rags of my clothing; running down my goose-pimpled flesh until I stood ankle-deep in a puddle just behind the lintel of the cave. When I backed off out of range of the storm, however, retreating step by step to the rear wall, I found the stench of my own excrement still too strong to bear.

"What the hell can I do now?" I cried to no one in particular. I crouched down onto my hams, leaning forward until my head rested on my knees. I could hear my stomach churn with nausea and hunger, feel the continuing throb of my wounded hand harder than the beating of my heart. "What the hell can I *do?*" Only the rain answered, and my increasing pain. The two together seemed to fill the whole world around me, so that earth, stone, air and water appeared to move with a pulse indistinguishable from my own—and the rhythm of the Stone, which grew audible and visible now that its heat and light had departed. *Wait, for there will be time,* that rhythm seemed to be saying. *Wait, for there will be time.* But it was one more lie in a world of lies; since there was no time. Only a task to be done and no time to do it. None. And yet the Scrolls at least had to be saved. And the Stone. And my own manuscript as well, even though the El, or my dream, had not instructed me so.

No matter. I alone would be directing my own course of action from here to the end. My dream and I were fused at least; and in any case, I would sleep no more until I died. This much I knew. Yet I did not know whether anyone would ever be able to find what I had to conceal. Or finding it—in an era as remote from the Age of Print as it from the time of the first paintings on stone— whether they would be able to decipher what Eliezar had written in his tongue, or I in mine. But that did not matter either. What mattered was that the gesture be made: that whatever I succeeded in salvaging be confided to earth. I did not even trouble to ask myself whether I would be planting a seed in expectation of harvest or burying a corpse without hope of resurrection. This, too, seemed beside the point.

What Eliezar had dreamed, and I redreamed for a world incredibly different from his, someone would dream for a third time. Someone not yet born, who would not even have to set out in quest of a place tilted out of time to recover what we two had saved and lost. It would be enough for him to dream us again with no help at all from the past. So, perhaps, he was already dreaming me dreaming Eliezar dreaming the El; and none of the rest of us existed outside of his unborn head. *But this makes no sense at all,* I told myself even then. And writing it down, I know that I must have been, for that moment at least, mad out of my head; though maybe the maddest thing I have ever done is to go on writing, now that I know my last excuse for delay is gone. Even as I set down these words, I am aware that the rain has stopped: not slowly decreased, or dribbled to a halt, but stopped all at once. And outside my cavern the whole world is blazing with light.

Simply to have escaped from the dark and the damp and the pervasive stink of the cave seemed to me for the first moment or two a sufficient blessing. Once out, I felt as if I had been confined for all of those days inside myself: imprisoned in my own intestines, or marooned on the sunless side of my mind. No wonder I had been on the verge of insanity, or just over it. The light, however, proved as unremitting an assault as the rain. Owl-blind, bat-blind, I was forced to fall onto my knees and pat the earth before me with my good hand to be sure I did not tumble into one of the chasms to the right or the left. In a little while my eyes grew accustomed to the white blaze of the shadowless world, in whi h the sun appeared to stand, fixed and unmoving, at midsum er zenith, absolute noon. But it proved impossible to get used to the heat that sucked up the last few remaining pools, even as I scrabbled across the burning rock to lap them down.

I would have thought that my leathery flesh could never sweat again. But the perspiration began almost immediately to stream down my face, my belly, my flanks; aggravating my thirst as it trickled into my mouth, increasing the pain in my lacerated hand as it poured down my arm, and making me half-blind once more as it ran into my eyes. Yet I managed somehow to set up my Auto-Digger, which I had carried in my Perdurium sack from the cave to the ledge—along with the Scrolls, my manuscript, the Urim and Tumim, and the PSSS. I had wondered whether I would be able to handle the last, but despite its extraordinary growth, it had remained nearly weightless. Still, I was glad that it was no larger, since even its present bulk proved almost too much for me in my debilitated state. But where to begin?

The excavation I had originally dug had disappeared without a trace, filled in no doubt during the earthquake. And its exact coordinates, I discovered, had gone from my muddled head, along with most of the other details of the Meta-Technicians' laser projection. My disorientation seemed finally fitting enough, however; since if my dream vision was to be trusted (and why not, after all?), I was truly "nowhere." Yet I was determined, for reasons I had no time to examine, to locate my cache at the exact spot where the Arch-Priest had buried his. And in the end, I satisfied myself that I had found it, though how I knew this I could not have said. The actual digging proved to be the easiest part, almost an anticlimax, for once I had activated the Auto-Digger, it needed no guidance or supervision. I lowered myself, therefore, slowly and stiffly to the ground, and stretched myself out to rest for a while; bracing my head, as I had grown accustomed to do, on the friendly bulge of the PSSS, and watching the dirt pile up beside the deepening hole.

My ear close to the ground, I noticed for the first time the sound of rushing water, which I should have missed earlier, I suppose. All the rain that had fallen during the days before could not have disappeared so completely in so short a time—no matter how dry the air, how parched and porous the ground. Every crack and crevasse should have been flooded to the brim. But I could barely see at the bottom of the ditch next to me, so far down that the light barely touched its surface, a tiny runnel of green water. I had turned onto my stomach and edged myself forward until my head hung over the side of the chasm. And as I watched, the level of the water seemed ever so slowly to mount upward toward me, and the noise of its motion to grow louder.

But I was too weary to worry long about such matters. Moreover, what seemed really important at a moment so close to my death was not what might happen next or why, but what had been happening to me all along. It was not, you understand, the metaphysics of the larger situation which concerned me: Eliezar's so-called War of the Seed and the Egg, which I had resigned myself to accepting as another "mystery," i.e., one more incomprehensible given in the great world. No, it was only my own small part in that great world that I wanted to comprehend. I was no longer willing, as I had been tempted to do at one stage, to see myself as Achilles, or, better, Hector, caught in a senseless conflict between irresponsible though all-powerful deities; and therefore destined to die a death at once comic and tragic, the stuff of poetry.

I am convinced finally that there is nothing special in my prosaic case. Every man must die, like me, deserted by all, yet ground down between the hammer and anvil of Male and Female, by which we were forged in the beginning. Not just heroes, as the Greeks believed, but all mortals, as the Jews knew, are destroyed in the War of Egg against Seed: mother against father, before we are even ourselves; then mother against son, girl against boy, wife against husband, daughter against father. And when we are dead, our daughters continue it against our sons; until with the first grandchild, the cycle is ready to begin all over again. Yet at the heart of the division and strife, we remain forever *alone*. There is no other way.

At least I die knowing what has killed me, as most men, I suspect, do not. But I deserve no credit, since in my case the universal conflict has been, I do not know quite how to say it without falling again into vanity, heightened, exaggerated. Or maybe it has rather been projected from the inner world to the outer: from the dinner table and the conjugal bed to the Desert, where even as the patriarchal god was made manifest, the people he chose were bowing their knee to a metal image of the Cow Goddess. It is small wisdom to have attained at the end of so grueling a quest. But reaching back into my sack, I draw out these last sheets to write it down, along with the events which bring my story to its close.

I write against time, scribbling now at the risk of incoherence, for the sound of the water in the clefts beside me grows louder and louder. So far below the surface when I first looked that I was not sure I really saw them, those tiny runnels have swelled to a pair of rivers which threaten to overflow their banks. But the noise they make is drowned out by a new sound: a vast rumbling which makes the earth and air seem to tremble as I tremble in redoubled fear. Looking out across the great valley, which seemed on my first descent a small hollow in the hills, I perceive hanging over the ridge I passed with such pain something I cannot at first identify. It is a wave, I see finally, heaved upward higher than the towering cliff which that ridge has become: a mile-high wall of glaucous green that threatens to bury in water what I have just buried in earth.

Even as I watch its progress, I am wrapping the Urim and Tumim in the Arch-Priest's Scrolls, which I then place at the bottom of my Perdurium sack, topping them with the Stone of Melissa-Melinda, and all of my manuscript except for this sheet. And now I rise to drop the sack, which at one point I tried to eat, at one point to burn—both times, thank God, in vain—into the completed excavation. Into that hole, I shall throw this page, too, when I have finished; and last of all, myself.

There is no time to fill it with the piled-up dirt and rocks beside me. And I could not, broken as I am, do it even if I had still before me all the years I have already lived. I will, therefore, lie face down forever over the treasures, which I have, after all, preserved: my back hunched against the impact of the returning sea; and my eyes hidden, lest I cry out in terror as it smashes down to engulf me. I do not want to end on a scream, but a prayer. If I knew a prayer for the dead, I would say it, being my own sole mourner. But I do not.

And in any case, I sense that it would be more appropriate to end, like Eliezar, with not a valedictory but a formula for beginning the day. Yet I cannot repeat the free man's benediction with which he greeted his death, as if it were just another dawn. Being everything he meant by a *goy*, a slave, a woman, I shall therefore say, as is proper, the other benediction reserved for those like me, and be done:

BLESSED ART THOU, OUR LORD G-D, KING OF THE UNIVERSE,
WHO HAS MADE ME WHAT THOU WILLST.

Leslie A. Fiedler
Buffalo, New York
Rosh ha Shanah,
Chanukah, 1973;
Pesach, 1974

216